Green

The Awakening

S.M. Huggins

Green
The Awakening

ISBN 978-1-61364-547-5

For Erno

Contents

Chapter One

And I fall... But this journey I do not make alone. I hold him in my arms. I hold him close as gravity draws us downward. The fall seems endless, but it is not. I can see what I believe to be the imminent-appearing surface. I never thought that my destiny would commence with his ending. With profound regret, I bring him home.

While rolling onto my back, I open my eyes. The obscurity of the hour appears to mirror the gloom and ambiguity this recurring dream has cast. Shivering, I burrow beneath my comforter. It seems that even my body wishes to shake off the lingering emotional anguish. But, heavy and dense, it hangs in the air around me creating an ache in the pit in my stomach.

Underneath my covers, I close my eyes again. My breath, halted by my comforter, journeys downward where it settles on the skin of my face. Blanketed by warmth, I'm hopeful that this peaceful moment will usher me back to sleep. I ignore my mind as it attempts to make sense of that horrible dream. My plan works for about three breaths but sure enough, the persistent creeping... no, skulking of that nightmare, accumulating in increments over the last few nights, becomes unavoidable.

It has taken root while it sucked hours of much-needed sleep from me. Hasn't it done enough? Apparently not, because here it comes! It is a swift-moving train without brakes. With a sigh, I face the inevitable—the inescapable, hoping to resolve it. I allow my mind to run full steam ahead.

In half a breath's time, I recall the vivid sense of falling. It is the gap between light and dark, good and evil. This space is indifferent and not bound by reason. Woven into my reeling and unsettled thoughts is every detail—each daunting element. I remember the clamorous background sounds of car horns. I even smelled the ensuing fragrance of a city—the combination of smog, oil from cars and low tide. Although I seem to retain everything, I still struggle to make out who it is in my arms. Bringing my mind to the second before I tilted forward and gravity drew me downward, all I can make out in my arms is an obscure face that is blurred in the shadows. But somehow I know that I care deeply for him. He's my friend... my only friend, and I didn't want to let him go, leaving me utterly heartbroken. The sense was so real. Reliving it now, that sense is quite real and sad, as I experience it anew. Unwanted tears well up behind the lids of my eyes. I fight them with all my might. But a few escape this determination. Tenacious, their warmth kisses both sides of my face as they trail downward. Since my first night in this apartment, the nightmare has plagued me.

While drying my eyes, I hear the faint scream of sirens from outside my apartment building and they lure me from beneath my covers and, for a moment, away from that vision. The constant soft coo of New York City traffic reminds me that I am no longer trapped in a dreadful dream. The sounds of sirens and horns twenty-four hours a day is as foreign to me as the city that I now call home. My father's job has brought us here. He works for a cutting-edge company promoting environment-friendly living. We've lived all over the world. He's even been published and written about. As proud as I am of him, his passion relocates us every one to two years, forcing me to begin anew each time. Nearing the midpoint of my senior year in high school, I am starting again at a new school. Tomorrow or perhaps even in a few hours I'll begin my first day at Religards Academy, "a private school striving for excellence." With the thought of Religards comes a reminder of my need for sleep! A steamy cup of chamomile tea should do the job.

Sitting up, I feel around the bottom of my bed with my hand and locate my robe. I swathe myself in its cozy, soft fabric then tie the belt nice and tight. My father must have turned down the heat, I am freezing! I bet I can see my breath. A hot cup of tea never sounded better. With every step, I put distance between me and that dream. As I open my bedroom door, I'm greeted by the soft radiance emitted from the kitchen. It draws me to it as a moth is drawn to light.

"Awake again, Meelah?" I hear my father ask in a soft tone.

Following the trail of his soothing voice, I see him taking down two mugs from a kitchen shelf. The kettle is already on the stove. The burner is heated red and within seconds it whines a high-pitched whistle. The steady column of steam escaping the spout becomes lost in the surrounding cool air. I watch its journey as it diffuses then vanishes. For a moment, I stand silent and still. Tucking my hair behind my ears I observe the most important person in my life.

How does he always know when I need him? I wonder. Still gazing at my father as he pours the near-boiling water into the two prepared cups, I say to him, "We must stop meeting like this. Neither of us is nocturnal."

"Indeed," he replies with his little grin. "Can't sleep again? Perhaps you are nervous about tomorrow?"

"I'm not looking forward to school but I'm not anxious about it." I stop there. I didn't wish to discuss the nauseating dream. At present, I have put adequate distance between it and my waking thoughts, though I sense it lurking in the shadows of my mind. Thankfully, it remains at bay.

While I try not to focus on the reason I'm awake, I hear my father say, "I purchased fresh-dried chamomile earlier today. This should calm the both of us."

As my father hands me a cup, I reply with a soft, "Thank you." Inhaling the pleasing scent of chamomile, I ask him, "But why are you awake—again?"

"Just doing some last minute modifications to my presentation for tomorrow. And I'm still unpacking. I seem to have misplaced a few boxes. Tomorrow I'll locate them, I'm sure."

"But tomorrow is already upon us."

"Twenty-four hours in one day is insufficient for the demands of my life," he explains, while blowing into his tea.

The steam infused with the calming herb wafting in my face, I take my first gulp. I watch my father as he does the same. Comfortable with our silence, neither of us says another word. Instead, I gaze at the man before me. My father, Samuel Neegry, is as fair-complexioned as the ceiling in this kitchen and freckled from head to toe. His wavy dark red hair and pale complexion are the polar opposite of me; but his authentic kind-hearted nature pairs us well. My father is all I have, other than a few boxes of books and sentimental keepsakes, and I would have it no other way. Moving as frequently as we do, I don't have the privilege of nesting. He is everything to me and if moving to New York in my senior year is necessary then I will make it work.

Since my father adopted me in East London, South Africa, my birthparents are something of a mystery. This is not to say that I was immaculately conceived or that I just appeared like Superman did. But I'm told I was found as a toddler. As I was meandering about the busy city, my father, who was there on business, happened upon me. After an extensive search for anyone connected to me, I became a daughter and my father became a dad. I am grateful for his presence in my life.

Breaking the silence I hear him say, "It is quite late, my Pocahontas."

"Really? That was cute when I was ten. But how old am I now?" He answers me with a smile. "Anyway, I look nothing like her."

"I beg to differ. Your hair is as black as hers, and as long. The tone of your skin is just as lovely. But your spirit, Meelah," he expressed with a pause. "You are more than even I can conceptualize."

His words leave his mouth in a manner that has me intrigued. He remains pensive all the while looking gently at me. His eyes appear sad somehow, forlorn, as if he has lost someone very close to his heart. Clearing his throat and righting his stance, he returns to his naturally blithe demeanor. Adorned in a white, button-down dress shirt with a loosened yellow tie, black slacks and matching black shoes, his clothes the same as the previous day, he stands before me as if yesterday never ended.

Gently I take his cup, still warm but empty, from his hand and wash it out. No further words are exchanged nor are they needed. He waits for me and as our eyes meet, both of us smile at the other and in our unspoken manner we bid the other goodnight. Warmed by the soothing tea, I return to my room. Before I close my bedroom door, I see that the kitchen lights are doused. All is peaceful now, making our home conducive for sleeping.

Waiting for the chamomile to take effect, I walk over to the oversized windows stretching across my room. They are like eyes to this amazing city. Drawn to them, I fumble around the bottom of these magnificent windows and finally manage to unclip the magnetic tab holding the blackout curtains in place. As I raise them in unison, soft luminosity from the city that never sleeps filters into my room. Perching on the sill, I observe automobiles appearing as minuscule toys making their way down avenues and streets. At 3:23 a.m., taxis are still running and a few people are journeying on foot. As the puffs of breath released during my persistent yawning fog a portion of glass in front of me, I again feel fatigued.

After twisting my hair, I tie it into a bun atop my head. With a yawn, I toss my robe on the bottom of my bed then slip beneath my comforter. After plumping up my pillow, I nestle my head into it. This is my favorite down pillow. It has travelled the world with me and has always given me comfort. My room, now perfectly lit from the partially opened curtain, gives clarity to the white ceiling above me. After a few blinks, my eyelids grow heavy. In a breath, sleep finds me.

Ring, ring, ring. "No!" I moan. Ring, ring, ring. "Just few moments more."

Exhaustion hardly defines the level of fatigue that consumes me. Struggling to wake up, my hand moves about the nightstand. Searching little by little, I finally press the button atop my clock before it fires off its irritating alarm again. Lazing in bed, feeling warm and snug, I still don't want to get up. Opening my eyes, I see that dawn has indeed arrived. Gradually and with great reluctance I sit up and there it is. Hanging on my closet door is my clean and fresh-pressed Religards uniform. It mocks me all the way from the across the room. I turn again to my clock, pondering how much time I have before I must get up.

Enough stalling, it's time to drag my butt out of bed and dragging it is precisely what I do. With effort, I make it to the edge of my bed. That's a beginning, I suppose. But, since this is the first day at a new school, I must allot myself extra time for dressing so reluctantly, I do it—I stand up. Slowly but surely, I get myself into the bathroom. Every movement feels strenuous. My entire body is sore, but my arms especially ache. They throb like I have been working out or carried something quite heavy. Rubbing them seems to help, but the discomfort remains deep within my muscles.

Turning on the shower, I prepare to steam myself into a more awakened state. While awaiting the optimal searing water temperature, I gaze at my reflection in the mirror. Loosening my bun, I watch as my long black hair rests against my back. My hair is crimped and holds a slight wave from the sweat-fest of my deep power sleep. I run my fingers through the tangles. Like untying a shoelace, I pull at the bundled strands and free them. As steam begins to paint the surface of the mirror, I know the water temperature has reached my usual scorching hot.

Stepping into the shower, I commence my faithful awakening ritual. The hot water rejuvenates me as it rushes over my shoulders. Dipping my head back, I soak my hair then lather it up with patchouli-scented shampoo. Its heady fragrance fills the steamy air. I breathe in its unique aroma deeply to absorb it. After rinsing, I turn and face the sizzling stream of water. Tilted downward, my forehead meets the direct flow. The tickling sensation of the warm water over my closed eyelids is soothing.

Over the sound of the shower spray I heard it: "Open your eyes! It is time for you to see. You must remember."

Startled, I wipe my eyes and glance around the small cubicle. Reaching for the shower lever, I find it won't move. I can't turn the water off. Flustered, I place my hand on the shower door. It refuses to slide open. I'm trapped! And there is someone in the bathroom with me.

Am I hearing things? I wonder. *Did someone just speak to me? If so, who was it?* Questions pour into my mind as fast as the hot shower rains down on me. Not panicking, though I am quite close, I take a deep breath.

"Meelah, you must see. Use the water," the same voice says, but now in a softer tone.

The strange male voice appears to be coming from above me. I feel my heart pounding in my chest as if ready to burst! Gazing around, I cannot see through the misty air. Wiping a small area of the shower door, I look ahead of me. I cannot even see the sink, let alone a stranger here in the bathroom with me. Taking another deep breath, I again try to turn off the water. This time the handle moves easily to the off position. I open the shower door and snatch a towel. After wrapping myself up, then grabbing the first object I can—a bottle of shampoo—I step out. Intent on seeing through the airborne steam, I feel a little foolish and begin questioning what a bottle of shampoo could do in my defense, but I am prepared to protect myself. I continue forward and open the bathroom door. Now standing in my bedroom with my shampoo in one hand and the other hand clenching my towel, I hear, knock, knock, knock.

"Yes?" I answer apprehensively.

"Meelah, its 6:20, the car will be here in twenty minutes," my father says in his chipper morning manner.

Relieved to hear the blissful sound of my father's voice, I begin to question who or what just spoke to me when I was in the shower. Sensing my father in the hallway awaiting a response, I answer him.

"I'll be ready soon."

"Is anything the matter, Meelah?"

"No, I'm just getting dressed."

"All right. I'll see you in twenty minutes, then."

Sitting down on my bed, I begin to wonder what just happened. Taking one more look around the room, I am sure I am alone.

Perhaps I didn't get enough sleep.

"Fifteen minutes, Meelah."

My father's unsolicited updates get me moving. On with the new uniform, commencing with a white button-down collar shirt tapered at the waistline. Over it goes a burgundy-colored sweater vest with a yellow embroidered "R" then tan slacks. I partially blow dry my hair then tie it up into a bun.

"My boots, where are my boots?"

"Meelah, five minutes; the car is downstairs."

Quickly, I slip into my comfy and worn black leather riding boots. I've made a tradition of wearing them on every first day—or at least, every first day at a new school—since I have had them. On with the scarf and jacket, then over my shoulder goes the proverbial backpack filled with books. As I sling the backpack onto my shoulder, I see a black smudge of something over the back of my hand.

"We must be leaving. The driver already buzzed...twice," my father persists.

"I'm ready; just need to rinse my hand. I'll be right there."

I stride back into the bathroom and run my hands under water. I rub the obscure smudge with vengeance until finally, I prevail. Drying my hands, I see my reflection in the mirror. I am not alone. Glancing up, I oddly feel compelled to raise my hands. A translucent light emits from them, but as quickly as it appears, it is gone. The stranger remains.

"Meelah," he says in a calming voice.

At that moment I did not know what worried me the most; the bizarre light that emanated from my hands or the strange man who appeared to have wings, who knew my name and was here in my bathroom.

"Meelah, you needn't be afraid of me."

And inexplicably, I'm not. His energy—his essence—seems reminiscent of someone I know, or knew. I feel safe with him.

"Really, Meelah, we must go!" my father insists.

This unusual being, appearing not much older than me, follows the sound of my father's voice with his eyes. He is beautiful. I know him, but how? He has wings. This is something you don't see every day, especially in my bathroom. He doesn't look like an angel. Not that I have seen an angel, but he is different from what I would expect. While he continues to look in my father's direction, I observe his face. His chiseled facial features and light blond hair cause him to stand apart from anyone I have ever seen. This stranger, less the wings, looks like a gladiator; muscular and dressed for battle. He turns toward me and his soft blue eyes connect with mine. Intoxicated by his gaze, I feel something stir within me. My breath catches and again I wonder how I know him. Entranced, I honor my need to smile and as I do, I see his expression brighten.

As the corners of his mouth lift, bringing with them a grin, I hear, "Go! Listen to him. I will contact you again."

The smooth sound of his voice is like nothing I have ever heard before, yet somehow, I know it, too. This contradiction intrigues me. Looking toward the doorway, I realize I must leave, though every fiber of me wishes not to. As I turn back to the winged stranger, again, I stand alone.

Chapter Two

"**A**re you well, Meelah?" my father asks on our ride to Religards.

"Yes, Father, I just didn't get enough sleep."

I wanted to share everything with him; my dream, the light that radiated from the palms of my hands and the winged visitor. My mind wanders back to the stranger's face. His expression was caring yet filled with purpose—a purpose that I strangely sense has a connection to me.

"Meelah, are you sure that you are well?" he repeats.

My father's warm voice distracts me and as I look at him I see his genuine concern reflected on his face. Sometimes I feel as though we are so deeply connected that we read each other's thoughts. Leaning forward, he gazes deep into my eyes. After studying them, he pulls back. Still observing him though my father is now lost in his own thoughts, I wonder if he saw everything I just experienced.

"I suppose you will talk when you are ready," my father says quietly while continuing to stare out the window.

The car stops and there it is—Religards. I can't help but sigh. Here I am at yet another school.

"Meelah, I can have a car pick you up after school if you wish."

I answer, "No, I'll be fine. I don't want to contribute to air pollution, now, do I?"

"Wisely stated, but unfortunately, I will be in the car for the majority of the morning. The train doesn't travel to where my conference is being held. Meelah, I am unsure when I'll be home," he adds.

"Are you seriously worried about me? I am almost eighteen and we have lived all over the world. I'll be fine, Dad."

Giving me a grand smile, he concludes, "I like when you call me Dad."

Smiling back at him briefly, I open the car door and step out. Proceeding forward, I don't look back, and I can hear that the car still has not moved. He's waiting for me to open the entry doors. He always waits. When I was younger, he would walk me in but I insisted he stop when I turned nine.

Reluctantly, I pull open the heavy glass door and step over its threshold. Glancing over my shoulder, I watch my father's car pulling out into traffic. I also see a peculiar man standing on the sidewalk. Dressed in tattered clothing, he looks like a vagrant. I must have walked right past him. This odd man's energy is anything but benevolent. His eyes are piercing as they remain fixed upon me. They fill me with a rather uncomfortable feeling. Once safe inside the doors, I turn and face him. When he opens his mouth, a black mist pours out from it. The mist remains suspended within the frigid morning air for a moment. Then it disperses as people walk into and through it as if they don't see it.

Looking again, I search for my father's car, but it has blended seamlessly into the ubiquitous slow-moving traffic. Taking a quick glance around, I wonder if anyone else notices this man. The sidewalk is filled with people, and no one acts as though they notice him or the mist that just emanated from his mouth. It's winter and the air is bitter, so it is reasonable that a mist could form from one's breath. But it is never black! He continues to stare fiercely at me and, fearlessly, I intently watch him. My heart begins to pound in my chest. I feel like a dog wishing to chase a cat.

After a silent interlude of studying him, I break the eye contact to determine if he, perhaps, is connected to another student. But everyone else seems unaffected by this anomalous man outside their school building.

"Who could possibly be connected to a person that emits black vapors?" I ask myself under my breath.

Though he continues to glare at me with his malevolent expression, inexplicably, something shifts within me and I begin to observe him almost as if in a detached manner. My heart is no longer racing and the impulsive desire to interact with him has also subsided. An inner strength that I didn't know I possessed washes over me. Grounded, I feel strong and fearless.

Who am I that I can be so unaffected by the sight before me? What is happening to me? First the dream last night, the pleasant winged stranger in my bathroom, the light that came out of my hands, then this, I silently question.

"Meelah Neegry, what a pleasure," I hear a kind voice from behind me say.

Turning around, I follow this sweet tone and see a slender older female. She exudes benevolence, beginning with the honesty in her eyes. Having always been able to see people for what their heart tells me is their truth I already like this new acquaintance.

"Dear, you seem lost. Did I pronounce your last name correctly?"

"Yes, you did, Ma'am."

"My name is Ms. Lucy and I am the headmistress of Religards. Again, what a pleasure it is to meet you. We rarely accept a new student mid-year, but your transcripts are quite impressive. You are fluent in twelve languages!"

Ms. Lucy continues praising my records, which she seems to have memorized, before directing me down the wide corridor. Students all dressed in the same uniform pass by. Glancing over my shoulder to learn if the strange man is still outside the building, I see that he is not. Bewildered by my unusual morning, I continue forward with Ms. Lucy.

"Do you have all your textbooks, dear? We shipped them out to your new address a few days ago to give you time to familiarize yourself with the subjects."

"Yes, Ms. Lucy, I have them."

"Here is your schedule and a map of our premises. Please excuse me; I have meetings this morning, but wished to meet you before my day became too hectic."

Looking into the eyes of this gentle, older woman, I see a bizarre glint of white light in her pupils. Intrigued by this, I lean forward and gaze more deeply.

"Are you well, dear?" Ms. Lucy asks with a raised brow.

Realizing how bizarre my behavior must seem, I stand upright and smile.

"Yes, yes, I am fine. Just taking everything in."

As awkward as the moment may be, I look into her eyes again to see if the light is still there. At this point I feel as though I might be losing it, but Ms. Lucy's eyes are simply a muted brown and nothing more. No glint, no shimmer of anything unusual resides within them now.

"Meelah," Ms. Lucy says as she waves at an approaching student. "Mr. Higgly will do," she mutters quietly and seemingly to herself. Then facing me again, she adds, "I must be going, but my door is always open to you."

"Thank you, Ms. Lucy. It was good to meet you."

"No, Meelah," she responds pensively. "It's an honor to finally meet you." After clearing her throat, she turns to Mr. Higgly and states, "Brandon, I would like you to meet Meelah Neegry. She's the newest addition to Religards. Meelah is also a senior, so please take her under your wing for today."

"Of course, Ms. Lucy," he answers in a complacent manner.

Again I smile at her as she leaves. Admittedly, not my best first impression, but the last twelve hours have been beyond atypical.

Mr. Higgly stands before me now. His light brown hair is feathered to the side, and his Religard vest appears to be too small against his brawny chest. I wonder how many hours he spends in the gym. Appearing quite confident, he seems to prefer the form-fitted look. I am grateful that his pants are not tight, as that would be an awkward sight. Abruptly, he looks past me and is beaming with a smile that positively brightens his face. Gazing over my shoulder, curious to what or who has Mr. Higgly nearly drooling, I see a blonde as she strolls toward us. She stands out from the other students that make their way down the hallway. Her long tresses bounce in cadence with her strut. With curves in all the right places, she fills out the Religard uniform, making it appealing, and that is not an easy feat. As uniforms go, this one is quite boring. These tan slacks are something my father would wear and this sweater vest? Can you even buy a sweater vest at a department store nowadays? I don't believe so. But here and now, the sweater vest in question looks great on this girl. About to pass me, casually she glances my way. I smile at this new acquaintance but as soon as our eyes meet she swiftly looks away, seeming unimpressed by my gesture. Mr. Higgly, now standing with his back toward me, continues to gawk at her. Looking at my watch, I see that my first class will soon begin. Flipping through the papers that Ms. Lucy just gave me I locate the map and open it up.

"My name is Brandon. Mr. Higgly is my father," the young man flatly states. The sound of me unfolding this well-plotted map must have disrupted his contemplation. About to introduce myself, I see him drop his gaze and blatantly look at my goods! Clearly he hasn't had his morning fill!

Clearing my throat loudly, I raise his focus back to my face and say, "Well, Brandon, I am most capable of seeing myself around campus, but thanks anyway."

Appearing shocked that I am unaffected by him, he stands awkwardly before me for a moment. Consulting the map again, I hear, "Ms. Lucy expects me to show you to your classes."

"Ms. Lucy gave me a map and I am sure you have better things to do. Thank you, though."

With map in hand, I see where my first class is located. I am grateful that the syllabus was included with my books. I spent some time familiarizing myself with it already. This is something that I have learned is a necessity when beginning a new school.

Brandon still stands before me unsure what to do with himself. Clearly, not too many people have said no to him. Again, I can sense him looking me over. Gross!

"I'm off. It was nice to meet you, Brandon," I monotone as I proceed down the corridor.

"Suit yourself, Meelee. What kind of name is Meelee anyway?" I hear him mumble behind me.

I could correct him but getting to my first class on time is where I choose to focus my attention. While continuing on, hopefully in the right direction, I refer to the map again.

This map is quite extensive and well plotted, even the ladies rooms are noted—all eight of them. A soft chime rings and I see that everyone has already disappeared into their classrooms. Uneventfully, I do, too.

The day moves forward as slowly as cold honey journeys down a half-empty container, but lunch finally arrives. This is a dreaded time of day for any new student. Usually the cafeteria is a place for social networking and interaction rather than eating, and I have never been the social type.

Following the map to the food symbol, I enter the rather posh cafeteria. It has three different eateries. One is for custom wraps or grinders; another is a salad bar. Then the recognizable: you-get-what-you-get line. So many go to sleep deprived of basic nutrition and here, there is such overindulgence. This is what living all over the world has instilled in me. I understand and appreciate the distinction between need and want.

Not hungry, I find a table out of the way and retrieve a book from my backpack. Lost in my own world, I sit surrounded by the clamor of voices, my mind moving from my book to focus on the earlier events of this morning. Specifically to the gorgeous winged man. Mulling over all that has transpired, I am still left feeling baffled.

"Hello there," I hear a kind voice say from beside me. Turning around, I see the sweetest of smiles. "My name is Joseph, and you are?"

"My name is Meelah."

"And you are not American," he replies. "Oh, that came out wrong. I am from Mars," the young man adds, speaking in an odd voice. "Wow, I'm still not making my introduction any better." As the bell sounds and I gather my things, I hear, "I would like to begin again. Hello, my name is Joseph and you have a beautiful accent. Where are you from?"

"It's nice to meet you, Joseph. But I really must be heading to my next class."

"Your accent will remain a mystery then."

Chuckling, I continue to smile as I pass the kind stranger named Joseph. With limited time to ponder this encounter, I grab my trusty map before making my way to my next class. In the hallway, amongst the other students finding their next classes, I pass the interesting Mr. Higgly. He smirks before winking at me. I give him a little smile to be polite. Pressing onward, I think of Joseph. Even though we barely spoke, I believe there is kindness at Religards.

My first day has swiftly come to a conclusion, and I am wrapping myself up in my jacket and scarf. Following the many students, grateful for dismissal, I am reminded of the daunting vagrant I saw earlier. Feeling a short-lived moment of unease, I pause before walking through the doors. But I proceed, clueless as to what or who I might encounter.

The sidewalks are filled with people walking swiftly. I join the swarm headed in the direction I intend to go. As I attempt to keep up with their rushed pace, I wonder if they're all running late. Though I'm now striding to keep up, no, nearly jogging, I'm still freezing. With every fleeting step, the wind strips me of what little warmth I have. Tomorrow a warmer coat is a must. With the dry, brisk air continuing to whip past me relentlessly, the sense of someone travelling closely behind becomes more apparent. Glancing over my shoulder trying to be inconspicuous, I see many people, but no one that is terribly close to me or even looking at me. Burrowing my head into my scarf, I push onward. About fifteen minutes later, I am home and the feeling of someone behind me has not let up. The doorman courteously greets me with a nod of his head then opens the door. Awaiting the elevator, I stand alone.

"I am here with you," a smooth voice states.

Startled, I turn around and see only the chilled doorman standing outside. He bounces from side to side in an effort to keep warm. Blowing into his gloves, he turns to me and kindly nods and I give him a polite nod and smile in return.

The door to the elevator opens and I step in. The golden reflective interior of the elevator glows around me. Pressing the button for the eighteenth floor, I begin to seriously question my sanity. But the presence I felt on my walk home surrounds me. It is obvious; there is no denying it. Oddly, it's reminiscent of the handsome winged gladiator in my bathroom.

"You find me to be handsome?" the cool voice asks.

On the defensive, I blurt out, "What? I did not say that!"

Again, I look around and see only my reflection in the elevator doors and walls.

"That's it, I am ill! I am hearing voices and hallucinating."

"No, Meelah. I am here and I am very real. It is time for you to wake up and remember."

I now feel him close behind me where I stand, his energy enveloping me. It is soothing, like a warm bath. Closing my eyes, I fall into his benevolent presence. Time seems to stop. I do not know who or even what this is, but it doesn't matter. I feel safe on a level that I never knew possible. The elevator doors open, lifting the spell, and I step out and move forward. On a whim, I stop and turn around, hoping to see him. Again, I see no one, but I know he is present.

"It is time for me to wake up and remember?" I ask as I unlock the door.

Pushing the door open, I see him there, standing inside, the winged man. Gently, he takes my hand and guides me in. I step forward as if in a trance. With his left hand, he closes the door behind me. He then gazes at me with his pale azure eyes. He's handsome and perfect in every way. Raising my hand, I caress his face.

"If you're a hallucination, I shouldn't be able to touch you, right?" I say softly.

Answering me without words, he leans into my hand as it meets his cheek, and then closes his eyes. I observe him silently. His breath deepens as he nestles his face against my hand. I watch his chest, which is covered in golden armor, rise and fall with each of his breaths. The tips of his wings lower as he seems to fully relax in the moment. He opens his eyes and sees me watching him then steps back in an effort to break the connection.

"Who and what are you?"

"I am Mikiel. I am a Light Warrior," he answers while lowering his head in respect.

"Mikiel?" I repeat.

"Do you know me?" he asks while nearing me again.

I gaze into his eyes whilst stepping forward. He looks down into mine. His energy and presence is like that of no one else. His warm breath caresses my face. He is not a hallucination. Of this, I am certain. I do know him, but I am uncertain how.

"There is so much I wish to say. You will understand all in time, Meelah," he states solemnly.

"And I want answers now. This, no, you appearing as you have to me, is bizarre. Who has a being like you materializing before them?" Furrowing his brow, he looks away. I see his welling frustration. There is much to say though he remains pensive and still. Hoping to bring his gaze back to mine I say, "Somehow, Mikiel, you are familiar to me. I struggle to comprehend this connection but, I do know you. Don't I?"

"I cannot answer you, Meelah. It is forbidden," he replies. As our eyes meet again he adds, "To honor your free will, I must allow you to awaken on your own. Only now have I been permitted to reveal myself to you, though I assure you, I have always been with you." Abruptly he raises his gaze to something behind me.

Expecting to see something, I glance over my shoulder as the door is thrown open. My father bursts in. Nearly breathless as if he has been running, I hear him ask, "Meelah, do you know where my statues are?" He slams the door closed and I watch as he oddly finagles the locks a few times. Continuing past me, flustered, he then pauses right where Mikiel was standing before vanishing into thin air. Rotating around, my father looks intently into my eyes. "Meelah, why are you just standing here still wearing your book bag?" For a brief and rather intense moment he continues to stare at me with suspicion. Then again he says, "The statues, Meelah, have you seen them? I must find them...now!"

"No, but I'm sure they are here. I'll help you look."

After I drop my backpack, we unpack several of the living room boxes.

"The statues are not here, Meelah," I hear Mikiel whispering in my ear. "They have been placed in your father's closet."

"Have you looked in your closet?" I ask.

"No. Please look; they must be found!"

My father's sense of urgency is disquieting. I power walk, nearing a sprint, into his room. Quickly I open his closet.

"Which box?" I whisper to Mikiel, so my father doesn't hear me. "Yes, I know. I'm engaging in dialogue with an invisible Light Warrior. I am certifiable, I'm sure of it."

"Give me your hand," he answers in his silky voice.

I feel a warm, yet invisible force on my hand, which is then guided to the second box from the bottom. I'm thinking that he could have just stated where it was rather than showing me.

After lifting off the top three boxes, I lower the heavier box to the floor. Opening the top flaps, I see the statues inside, securely concealed in shipping wrap.

"I have them!" I yell.

My father hastily comes in and begins to unpack these rather obtrusive ceramic statues. They are oval-shaped and come as a pair. Their worn, grey appearance is nothing special. Most wouldn't even look twice at them, but we have had them for as long as I can recall.

"Do you want me to help you?"

"No! You are never to touch these, Meelah! You know this!" he shouts.

He has never raised his voice to me before. I watch him pause for a moment. I can see that his abrupt and cold words have also pained him. Then, without making eye contact, he leaves with the two statues cradled in his arms. Following him, I observe my father mindfully place them at the front door, one on either side of it. Then he touches the tops of each of them. As a child, I remember asking him why he did this and he explained that he was turning them on. Still observing my father, I watch as he then picks up a small brown paper bag.

"More CFL bulbs; I didn't get to your bathroom," he says indifferently. After a moment of silence, he continues, "How was your first day at Religards?"

I figured that this day has been so extraordinary that it is only fitting for my father to be uncharacteristic in his manner, as well. A seemingly relieved and calmer father heads down the hallway then into my bedroom. Returning to my father's room to clean up the packing material, I accidently bump into the boxes that I precariously stacked. The top one falls, spilling its contents.

Wonderful, one step forward then five backward, I say in my mind.

"Meelah, everything occurs with purpose," Mikiel replies. His voice is now strangely muted.

"I am mindful of my word choice when speaking, but my thoughts, really! Is anything sacred?"

"As you wish, Meelah," he intones, as if speaking from a great distance.

Bending down, I begin to pick up the contents of my father's box. Miscellaneous pictures have spilled out and again, I sigh. One by one I take them, thinking that my father truly requires an album of some kind. My bun, loose from being twisted up all day, falls apart and my hair spills downward, obstructing my view. While tucking my hair behind my ears, I see a pile of pictures all neatly stacked.

What are the odds of this? I think to myself.

How is it possible that these pictures would spill out into a precisely stacked column? Picking up the top photo, I gaze at it. It is of me when I was about five. I remember this. We were living in Ireland, outside Killarney. Life there was simple. Everyone knew each other and, if they didn't, they made every effort to do so.

In the scene, my father is kneeling next to me glowing with a smile. My expression is quite different from his. I appear serious, but not angry or sad. My hair, even at this age, is long and, in this picture, slightly unkempt. The background is teeming with life. The trees are flourishing and the grass beneath our feet is brilliant in color, and lush.

I continue to glance through the stack of pictures and, again, they are all from Ireland and of my father and me. Subtly, my image in the pictures begins to look away from the camera. Flipping through the pictures at a quicker rate of speed, as if watching a slow film, I see that I am the only one moving while my father continues to kneel, wearing a smile upon his face.

In the last picture, I am pointing and looking to the left. Now tilting my head and squinting my eyes as if it will help me see myself more clearly, I follow my little pointing finger. Then I see it, or rather I see him! It is the vagrant from earlier today! His unmistakable eyes in the pictures are black and ominous in the same way as they were today. Even in a photograph, their darkness pierces through me. I was about five in this picture and the vagrant is the same age as he appeared this morning. His clothes are still tattered and his presence, even in a mere snapshot, is malevolent.

I see another neatly stacked pile of pictures. Again, there is no way they could have fallen out of the box and landed so precisely together. I flip through them and, reminiscent of the last stack, they are of my father and me. But this time, I was in second grade and we resided in England. I was dressed in a schoolgirl uniform—a navy blue skirt and a matching blazer. My knee socks didn't quite make it to my knees. My hair, still long, was neatly combed and pushed back by a red headband. Yet again, my father is wearing an ordinary smile and I, an un-remarkable expression. Once more I flip through the pictures sequentially and see only my image moving. In the final photograph, I am clearly pointing left. Following my finger, I see him again.

On to the next pile, then the next, each stack resulting in the same image of me pointing at the ubiquitous man who spouted black mist earlier in the day. Over the last twelve years, this *thing* has been in my life and only today I noticed him. These pictures are of me pointing to him, but I do not recall doing this. A feeling of rage consumes me. Others may be fearful in this circumstance, but I become furious.

Why and how has he been following me and my father? I ask myself.

I wait, hoping that Mikiel would chime in with a constructive response, but he doesn't. I don't sense him anymore. I am alone with my scattered thoughts.

"Meelah, where are you? I replaced all your light bulbs," I hear my father say.

Quickly, I pick up the pictures and return them to their box. I am unsure why my instinct is to keep this from my father. Perhaps I believe that I'm protecting him. Whatever it is, I know that for now I must conceal it. I need time to make sense of this and all the other events of today.

"What are you doing?" my father asks as he enters his bedroom. He gazes directly into my eyes. I know that I cannot lie to him so I don't.

"I knocked over a box when looking for the statues. I was just cleaning it up for you."

My father continues to search my eyes. I remain strong and resolute as I tuck my new findings away from him. Finally the silence is broken as he brings his attention to the contents of the top box.

"My sweaters, I needed one of these today. The forecast is for snow tomorrow. Looks like it will be a long winter, after all."

Happily, I observe my father as he rummages through his box of sweaters. Each one he pulls out is followed by a short anecdote of where he got it or who made it. Even though I remember all the stories, I'm quite content to listen anyway. This is the man I know to be my father. Not the stranger who barked at me mere minutes before. This familiar moment of comfort settles me.

"How was Religards, Meelah? I had Luther cover the last conference for today. I wanted to be home for you."

Luther Rutherford is a close friend of my father's. He is the closest thing I have to an uncle. He talks a mile a minute and continues speaking when on a roll regardless of one's interest. He is quite unique. Luther's passion is preserving the natural resources of Mother Earth. He always commences one of his garrulous, yet simply phrased speeches on this subject. And he is always half put together. His medium-length brown hair is rarely brushed and his clothes are a wardrobe nightmare. I have never been a trendsetter, but even I know more about style than he does. I plainly recognize that plaid pants and a striped shirt should never be paired together. Where did he even find plaid trousers? Most likely he found them in a secondhand shop; recycling in its truest form. My father is like his mature older brother. He has suits sent out to Luther by a carrier on a bike prior to any public appearance. The need for a suit should not increase one's carbon footprint.

My father stands before me amiably with a kind smile awaiting my answer regarding Religards. His love for me lights up his face. Again, silently, I question whether or not I should share the details of the day's supernatural happenings. My protective nature, especially for the only family that I possess, prevails. I choose to wait. Perhaps in time I will share when I better comprehend this turn of events.

"Religards was another day at school. There really isn't too much to say."

He waits patiently for a more detailed response.

"It was fine. It's so much fun hanging out with other kids all wearing the same uniform."

"A few of them might be nice," my father answers with a chuckle.

"Maybe," I say, while trying to hold back my smile.

"Tomorrow is a new day, Meelah."

My father's uncomplicated words ring in my mind. The shift back into his calm and loving demeanor is a perfect end to a rather unusual day.

Chapter Three

Tomorrow rapidly becomes the present. It has arrived far too soon for me. Exhaustion permeates my every cell. I feel as though I ran a marathon yesterday. My body rests heavy in my warm bed. Everything is conducive for more sleep—everything but the time.

Forcing myself to wake up, I roll onto my back and gaze at the ceiling. The peculiar events of yesterday replay in mind. At least last night was uneventful, as dreams go, but my sleep was hardly rejuvenating. I yearn for more.

Looking forward to a sizzling hot shower, I drag myself out of bed. For a moment I just stand in place but then I amble, reminiscent of a zombie, into the bathroom. Without thought, I turn the water onto the hottest setting possible and within seconds the air in the bathroom becomes foggy. A thin layer of mist quickly settles on the vanity mirror. I wipe it a few times with my free hand while brushing my teeth, but the mirror soon steams over again, obscuring my disheveled reflection.

Off with my pajamas then into the scorching water. I can't help but close my eyes. On most days, a searing shower rouses me, but today it returns me to my former drowsy state. I force myself not to succumb to the relaxing hot water by turning it to a more tepid setting. Still not effective, I turn the water to cold. It takes a while, but that does it. I'm wide awake! I suds up and then dance around as the cold water rinses me off. When it becomes unbearable, I adjust the water to a happy medium of warm. A tad more than tepid but not scorching, the water temperature satisfies my need to warm up. Standing beneath the stream of water, I allow it to massage my body. Lifting my face toward the spigot, I feel the water rush over my forehead, eyes and cheeks, warming my skin. The cold water rinses out of my long hair. I feel its cool sensation slither down my back like a snake.

I recall Mikiel's words, "Use the water." I wonder what he meant by this? Curious, I capture water in the palms of my hands and stare into it. After nothing seems to come of it, I chuckle to myself. "I'm looking into a pool of water for what? What am I supposed to see or do with water?" Again I laugh. Though at times I question my sanity, I certainly have retained my sense of humor.

Where is Mikiel, anyway? Yesterday he showed up when I showered to convey his vague suggestion of 'use the water.' It's rather convenient that he chose this moment when I just happened to be in my birthday suit. Why not communicate this epiphany when I am brushing my teeth or washing my hands. I use water at these times, as well.

Humored by the thought, I toss the puddle of water up into the air. To my astonishment, it remains suspended. And the shower water has stopped in its flow and is caught mid-flight all around me. I am astounded. The sound of my heart beating disrupts the quiet. Thump, thump...thump, thump...thump, thump. I have never been so aware of my heartbeat. But now its rhythmic sound consumes the strange space around me.

"What is this?" I ask in complete awe as I take in the miracle encircling me. I can't contain my smile. It beams from ear to ear as I stand amid hundreds of droplets of water immobilized and hovering mid-air. What an amazing sight.

Raising my hand, I tap one droplet. It bursts on contact then rains down on me. Again chuckling, I move my arm into, and then through the suspended beads of water, each rupturing, one after the next. The shattered droplets sprinkle down, sounding like a gentle spring rain.

"This is so amazing! I wonder if Mikiel is as amused as I am by this developmment. Is this what he meant by 'use the water'? I think he meant to infer something different. Nonetheless, this is incredible. It looks like I am surrounded by a clear hippy bead curtain, but each bead fractures and returns to its fluid state at my touch.

The pool of water that I held in my hand remains suspended above me. It looks like a small pane of glistening glass. Leaning forward to examine it, I burst the beads of water. For fun, I open my mouth and in go several droplets. They explode against the warm sides of my mouth. The cool fluid runs down my throat and I swallow it.

Cool water saturates the skin of my face then runs down my cheeks and drips off my chin. The surface of my face also cools, as does my body. But, more concerned about how long this bizarre reality will last, I look intently into the shimmering accumulation of droplets, and I see a glimmer of something.

With the tip of my finger, I touch the suspended mass. It is not cold like the droplets were. Improbably, it feels balmy—warmer than the air temperature within the shower stall. The heat is quite welcoming. My hand goes into, then through, this odd substance, disappearing from sight.

Curious, I continue to reach forward. My wrist and then my forearm disappear through the translucent window. The air on the other side of the mass is hot like a summer day. It feels wonderful against my chilled skin. Entranced, I continue to reach through this veil of water oblivious to what might lie beyond.

As my elbow begins to cross through, I feel something take hold of my hand and tug on me! Repeatedly, something yanks my hand, attempting to pull me in! Resolute that I am not taken in against my will, I wrench my arm back, biting my upper lip in the process. I can taste that I've drawn blood as I bite down harder, adamant that I can free myself.

"No!" I cry, freeing my upper lip.

An inner strength rises within me. I can feel my heart race and adrenaline surge through my bloodstream. Whatever has taken hold of my hand releases it.

I pull my arm back as fast as I can, but it moves only bit by bit. I thought things couldn't get any stranger, but they do. Everything shifts into slow motion. I continue to watch my arm as it returns to this world.

"Mee...lah, come home," a soothing female voice says, stretching out the words through the suspended mass of water. Everything has become sluggish. Even the audible words travelling from another place seem to be painstakingly slow in their utterance.

This unfamiliar voice seems gentle and quite benign. I can sense this truth. Honoring this instinct, I step closer to the window of suspended water and peer into it. I am unafraid, though I haven't a clue what I will see. Perhaps whatever grasped my hand will attempt to pull me in. But, I have to go forward. There is something waiting for me. Fearless, I continue.

The water moves on its own obscuring any clear view of what awaits beyond. Perhaps I jarred it when I yanked my arm back. Suddenly, I see what I believe to be a figure. Then little by little the water settles and the window into a new world comes into focus. A golden-robed being amidst a background of abundant greenery now stands on the other side of the suspended curtain of water. Its presence is both commanding and gentle. I know this sounds contradictory, but that is my impression. The being bows to me. Bowing back, I gaze downward and see my naked form.

With a gasp, I quickly cover my goods. Proceeding my worst greeting ever the suspension of water ends, as a gush of cold water rains down over me. The strange opening to another world is gone.

What a grand first impression. Why does all of this happen when I'm naked?

Shivering, I become aware of how cold I am. After adjusting the temperature of the now fluid water pouring over me, I enjoy the sensation of warmth as it rains down over my cold skin.

"What was that?"

I inspect my hand and forearm and see not even a red mark or a scratch.

"Who was that being and why is this happening to me?" I ask aloud.

As splendid as the hot water feels, I hastily turn it off and climb out of the shower. Drying myself off, I am consumed by questions; then I hear my father.

"Meelah, its 6:20, please be ready on time today. You have a fifteen-minute walk to school.

"Six-twenty? How is that possible? I got up at six-twenty. How did all of this occur with no lapse in time?" I say to myself.

"Is everything all right?" my father asks.

Having no idea what just happened, I remain silent. Again, I begin to shiver. I wrap myself in my robe then get back into bed. My bed is no longer warm. It feels as cold as I am.

"Meelah," my father says as he opens my door. "You haven't woken up yet? You're going to be late."

"I'm awake and I've showered," I answer from under my covers.

"Are you not well, then?"

What a relevant question, I say to myself. Perhaps I'm not well. I've been hearing voices and seeing things. None of this is indicative of sound mental health.

My father sits on the edge of my bed. Not saying a word, he reaches out to stroke my hair. His warm hand is soothing. I pull down the blanket covering my face and am greeted by my father's kind expression. He looks into my eyes and I into his.

My father's eyes are loving and reassuring. I feel as though I need not speak. He witnesses everything in my eyes and this silent communication I find quite satisfying. What I have seen, experienced and felt over the last twenty-four hours is a burden that, on one level, I wish to unload.

"All right then, all right then, Meelah," he murmurs.

"Thank you, Father," I reply, just as quiet.

"And what are you thanking me for?"

"For being you," I answer.

My father's eyes well up and he turns away from me. He seems to be sad, and wipes his face and sniffles.

"Are you all right, Dad?"

"I love when you call me Dad," he answers under his breath. "This has been a most enlightening talk, Meelah."

My curiosity is piqued. I gather the front of my robe and sit up. Finally, I am again warm. But my attention goes back to my father—"*Talk,* you just said *talk.* What was enlightening, Dad?"

"You're going to be late, Meelah," he says while standing up. "You better finish getting ready. I'll leave so you can get dressed."

I watch as he departs my room, closing the door behind him. I hear him continuing to walk away, avoiding the answer to my question. The hard soles of his dress shoes tap swiftly against the hardwood floor. The sound becomes fainter as he puts distance between us. Unintentionally, his actions have answered my query.

Chapter Four

Dressed and ready to go, I eagerly leave my room. I pop into the kitchen hoping to see my father, but he is nowhere in sight. I stand in our immaculate kitchen. As always, everything is in its rightful place—everything but a piece of yellow paper resting on the granite countertop. It sticks out like a pink dress would at a funeral.

The yellow paper is folded in half with my name written on it in script. My father's handwriting is beautiful. Even my name looks like a piece of artwork that should be displayed in a gallery on the West Side.

I pick it up with great anticipation. I am expecting a well-written answer to my earlier question.

When no words were exchanged between us why did he say that we had an enlightening talk? Can my father read my thoughts?

But hopeful I remain. His note is short, to say the least. Five words! These five words are phrased as a blunt statement devoid of all emotion.

I will be late tonight.

My father's avoidance to my question is quite odd. He has always been honest and open, but clearly something has shifted. Ironically, this shift has coincided with the occurance of my surreal events.

My infallible instinct has already provided me with my answer, but I would much rather hear it from him. Hear it in his voice—the voice that has afforded me comfort and ease as long as I can recall. I would like to know why he never told me that he could hear my unspoken words. I wonder how long he has been able to do this. I used to feel a sense of relief when he would silently sit by me, as if to console me. But now I feel unease.

The truth is, he can peer into my thoughts and somehow understand them. This reality gives me a sense of unrest. I trust and love my father, but my intimate thoughts are not his to know, certainly not without my consent.

Is this brief five-word note all the courage he has? This is all he can say to me, no, write to me? I have this epiphany and he runs?

I crumple the paper and toss it in the garbage. Disappointed, I head off to school. Down the elevator then out the door; properly bundled up with heavy winter wraps, I find the brisk morning air hardly affects me. My hurried gait coupled with my mind still steaming at my father, makes for a rapid walk. I now stand before the entryway to the school.

Students stream around me then through the doors. They look as though they are drawn through the opening into Religards, similar to the way ants are drawn back to their mound moments before dusk. They scuttle to get out of the winter air. They move past me as if I were invisible.

No part of me wishes to enter. No part of me feels as though this is where I belong. Nonetheless, this is where I stand. For the first time in my life, I am alone, although surrounded by other students.

"You are not alone," Mikiel whispers in my ear.

From behind, I feel him slide my bag full of books down my arm and rest it alongside my feet. He then wraps his arms around me. His presence and precise timing take my breath away.

I look down to see his arms around me, but he remains invisible. Only I can feel his embrace and only I can hear his smooth voice. I can't help but close my eyes, lost in the moment. The din from students, parents and professors all rushing into Religards falls silent.

I stand there enveloped by the arms of Mikiel. He holds me even tighter as a gust of frigid wind blows past us. Again, he feels so familiar to me but, frustrated, I just cannot place him.

After a few more breaths, I realize that my unsettled feelings from earlier are gone. I also stop processing my connection to this dreamlike being. It doesn't matter where he came from or what our bond is, I just want to savor this moment.

The sound of the morning bell reminds me where I stand. But, oddly, it is drawn out. I open my eyes and see that everything has slowed down. Students proceed past me, moving in slow motion; everyone but me.

I feel Mikiel turn me around to face him. There he is. His face is perfect in every way. But again, I cannot help but take notice of the bizarre movement around me.

"How is this happening?" I ask.

Not answering my question, Mikiel slides the hood of my jacket back. He then loosens my bun of hair as if he has been doing it my entire life. Gravity draws my tresses downward and the moving air tousles them. He gazes deep into my eyes. A strand of my hair floats across my face and I tuck it behind my ears in an effort to tame it. Mikiel takes hold of my hands, allowing my hair to travel across my face again. This is how he must remember me. I see this within his mesmerizing eyes.

"Mikiel, how is this happening? What has caused these people to move in this manner?"

"It is you, Meelah," he states.

"What do you mean?" I ask.

Sensing my earnestness, he turns to the people who are proceeding past us. This odd occurrence, reminiscent of the oddity of my shower scene, seems unsurprising to him. He appears unaffected by it. Instead, he focuses on me again. Unsure how to process his intensity, I turn around and observe the strange phenomenon around us.

"Mikiel, will you not answer me? Will no one answer me today?"

He stands in front of me as I become unyielding and resolute. His energy shifts, no doubt as a result of my response.

"It is you, Meelah. You are altering time, or the perception of time."

"And how am I doing this?"

"This is one of your many abilities."

"Abilities? Mikiel, what is happening to me? The day before last I was no different than any other seventeen-year-old."

"You have always been different, Meelah."

Frustrated, I begin to walk onward. He is not answering my questions and persists in being vague.

"Enough!" I shout, in an attempt to release my growing annoyance.

With that one word, or perhaps at the intensity of my reaction, everything comes to a halt; everything but me and Mikiel. The cars, pedestrians and all sound stops mid-action.

I turn to him and see that he is already sauntering toward me. We are surrounded by silence and living statues. My day has continued to become more and more unusual. He stands before me and suddenly, I see the vagrant from yesterday. He is moving within the encompassing stillness. There are wisps of darkness encircling him. The man that just twenty-four hours ago spewed out dark mist is clearly not human.

Mikiel sees the dark form in the reflection of my eyes. Instantly, he spreads his enormous white-and-grey wings and pushes me behind him. I cannot see anything from where I stand and hear only the sound of Mikiel's sword being drawn.

"Resume time and run into Religards, Meelah!"

"How do I do that?"

"Do it and do it now! And don't look back!"

"But what will happen to you?"

"You needn't worry for me. Now go!"

I use my instinct and with the force of my intention life resumes in present time. Cars move, people walk and the deafening sounds of morning in the city fill all space. I do as Mikiel says. I run into Religards, but I look back.

Despite the constant movement of unaware pedestrians, a battle has begun. Mikiel takes flight and pushes the dark energy, masked as a vagrant, up against the building across the street. Dust and debris fall onto the street. Bystanders, dumbfounded as to what has caused this, look upward. But still this fight is not for human eyes; they do not see the battle as I do.

Remaining within the safety of Religards as the battle ensues, I feel so helpless. I stand alone as school is in session. Everyone is in their rightful places, everyone but me.

Suddenly everything changes. Wisps of darkness stream past Mikiel as quickly as water moves from atop a waterfall.

Mikiel turns around and looks at me. The streams of darkness are headed my way.

"Don't look at it, Meelah!" he shouts.

But I am mesmerized by it and can't look away. It has some strange control over me. I am moving toward the door—toward the dark mass. It cannot come in, so it is drawing me out.

Mikiel struggles against it, but he appears to be defenseless to this vapor form. With his sword drawn he continues to strike at it, but to no avail. Something protrudes from the dark mist and cuts into Mikiel's arm. Though bleeding, he continues to hack and I continue to move forward. I put my hand on the door lever and push.

"He must not find it, Meelah! Look away!"

The door opens as I continue to push forward. I am inches away from the darkness as it draws me near. I feel no fear. I cannot even describe the overwhelming need to be immersed in it. It needs me or something from me and I want nothing more than to satisfy its desire.

The dark mist covers the glass doors of Religards. It waits for me. It calls to me. Mikiel continues to strike at and into it, but his efforts are futile. Then someone pulls on my left arm.

I am distracted by the warm and loving energy that holds my left hand. This gentle amorous energy guides me backward, away from the door. With every step I take, putting distance between me and the dark energy, I see the wicked form become increasingly agitated. The glass doors shake and the lights around me flicker.

"Meelah, my dear, look at me," a sweet voice says from behind me.

I feel as if I have been awakened from sleep. I look toward the sound of the kind voice and see Ms. Lucy. She smiles at me, exuding love.

"What's happened?" I ask.

Then I remember and look again outside. The dark energy has returned to its nasty physical host. Mikiel effortlessly overtakes it. I watch in awe as his winged body destroys the figure consumed by darkness. Mikiel tears into him, shredding him to pieces.

Breathless, he stands with his hands and clothing dripping blood. Lifting his head, he looks at me and I see the extent of his injuries. I see his blood covering the sidewalk where unaware humans walk at their hurried paces. They are oblivious.

I break away from Ms. Lucy and, exiting the doors of Religards, I run to him. It is my fault that he is now injured and bleeding. First he slips his sword back into its sleeve then he doubles over, winded. His energy or connection to me has altered as well. A wall he has just put up exists between us.

"I am sorry, Mikiel. I should not have looked. I did not do as you asked."

"No! I am the one who should be sorry," he states. "I am your protector and I nearly lost you."

Regardless of the injuries and his bleeding, he paces back and forth.

"I am so sorry."

"Do not apologize to me!"

He approaches me and announces, "Meelah, you have no idea who you are! You have no gauge of your power! You apologize for nothing! It is I who has shamed you!"

He moves his face closer to mine. I feel his warm breath against my mouth. He closes his eyes then, as if to negate our yearning for one another, and pulls away.

"Ms. Lucy, I am indebted to you," Mikiel says as he gazes over my shoulder.

Then he lowers his head, bows, and takes flight. I watch him ascend into the gloomy sky until I can no longer see him.

"Well, get your bag then, Meelah," I hear Ms. Lucy say from behind me.

A news van pulls up to the curb outside Religards and a crew pours out of it. They assemble lights and a camera team faster than I can pick up my bag. As I turn around, I am greeted by the kind face of Ms. Lucy.

"Come on, dear," she encourages me.

"Young lady, young lady, can you tell us what you saw here? There are reports of an isolated tornado, a tornado in New York City in the winter!"

"No, no, no! You will not interview any of my students without the permission of their parents or guardians! Please go to your class now, dear. I will take care of this," she says with a wink. She then continues ranting, "Perhaps it would serve you all well to wait for the police department. It seems that there has been an unfortunate casualty of this rather odd event. Imagine a tornado here during winter. Nonetheless, officials have been called and it's our civic duty to divert people away from this dreadful scene."

Her words are accurate; someone or something has died, and that leaves me with an unsettling feeling. I remain astonished that this battle appeared to be invisible to everyone but me. Furthermore, how has the vagrant's remains manifested physically yet no one saw the events that caused his demise?

"I will do my best to answer your questions soon," I hear Ms. Lucy say, though she stands at a distance with her back facing me. "Now go inside."

Perhaps her mysterious communication should surprise me, but somehow it doesn't. As I enter the building, I glance over my shoulder and see the news team descend upon the "awful scene," as vultures would to road kill. Police arrive and utter chaos surrounds the exterior of Religards. Students, professors and other staff fill the hallways, curious about what happened outside. I do my best to navigate through the mass.

"If they only knew," I say to myself.

"Only knew what, Meelah?" a meddlesome Brandon asks.

Where did he come from? I wonder to myself. Ignoring him, I continue through the sea of busybodies as fast as I can.

"Where are you going, Meelah? Aren't you curious about what happened?"

"Not particularly, Mr. Higgly."

"My name is Brandon," he intones, as if I'm stupid.

He moves with ease through the crowd. He's following me.

"Meelah, I heard that a gang came from the other side of town and killed one of their rivals to make a statement."

"Really? That sounds pretty unrealistic to me," I answer, while pushing my way against the flow of students. That was my mistake. I shouldn't have engaged in conversation with him. It seems to have given him hope, even if the exchange is regarding a death. I progress through the dense crowd as does Brandon, but he is gaining speed. The difficultly moving forward makes me feel like I am swimming upstream, like a wild salmon, perhaps. Brandon is like the bear, its natural predator. I usually see the good in everyone I meet, but Brandon is unique in that aspect.

"Meelah, I was just looking for you. I have the notes you asked me to take," Joseph voices. "Brandon, how's it going?"

Going with the flow, mainly because I hope it's in the direction that Brandon is not taking, I smile at Joseph. I add in a nod for plausibility. Interlocking arms with me, Joseph heads me away from the crowd and, most important, away from Brandon.

"I'm Joseph, remember from yesterday? I may have had the worst introduction ever."

"I've had far worse."

"Really? I would like to hear that story. I bet you didn't mention that you were from Mars. I am a special case."

Feeling overwhelmed I want nothing more than to get away from the mass of students that surrounds us. "Thank you for the diversion from Brandon but I should be going."

"And where might you be going?" he asks.

Truthfully, I have no idea.

My map is somewhere in my bag and my mind is still reeling over Mikiel and the scene outside the building. Awkwardly, I shrug my shoulders. Then, to my surprise, I begin to cry. Uncontrollable tears stream down my face.

"I have never had this effect on a girl before," he quips.

I laugh at his comment then start to cry all over again. I turn away from him and wipe my nose. It, too, is running like a faucet.

"Come with me. I know just where to take you," he says. "I take all the new female students there. Wow, that sounded kind of perverse, didn't it?"

I laugh again and fluid shoots out of my nose.

"You're like a party trick. Can you control that nose of yours or should I stand back? Just kidding, here's a handkerchief; yes, a handkerchief. I am a dying breed of gentlemen. It's even embroidered."

Joseph hands me a white linen handkerchief with the initials *J I H* on its corner. It seems far too good for my blubbering tears and dripping nose. Such a simple, kind act makes me smile.

"Thank you, but I can't ruin this. It's beautiful."

"It's only a handkerchief; I have others. Please, you have stuff on your face, chin and hands. Look at me. I'm not snotty. I don't need it."

Again he makes me chuckle and ordinarily that is no easy feat. Here stands a stranger who has managed to make me laugh more times than I have in the last six months, maybe even in a year.

"Thank you," I say, wholeheartedly. Then I wipe my face.

"It's only a handkerchief, really now," he answers. "Are you ready for our little adventure—you know, the place where I bring all the new students? I'm sure that they haven't resumed class yet and you still need to tell me about that accent of yours."

Not needing to be anywhere at this time, I nod yes. Joseph walks onward and I, for some inexplicable reason, follow. I continue to dry my face and attempt to gain control of my emotions. Up steps, four flights to be precise, then down a hallway we go. Surprisingly not winded by the four flights of stairs, I become curious as to where he is taking me. Soon, we stand before grey double doors. He reaches his hands over my shoulders, lifts my hood and secures it tight. Then he takes my bag and drops it to the floor.

"That's heavy. And to think that you have been carrying it all this way. Not very chivalrous of me, I suppose. Well, everyone has their faults."

"Joseph, where are we exactly?" I ask, interrupting his thought.

"At last, she speaks! Okay, okay, here we go, after you, madam."

I push open the double doors as I almost did about an hour ago. What a cathartic moment. Then I step forward into heaven.

"Ta-da! This is our conservatory. Ms. Lucy personally sees to it; Ms. Lucy and my father."

I take a moment to breathe in the glorious fragrances of the flowers. There is a heavy mist in the air. The humidity feels wonderful against my dry skin.

"Why did you raise my hood? It is so warm in here."

"I thought I'd keep you guessing. It's not as though you can read my mind."

"No, I suppose not," I answer, then chuckle again.

I unzip my jacket and place it on a nearby concrete bench. This place is exactly what I need; what I miss. This city, during its winter season, is devoid of green life. Gardens have a way of righting all wrongs. I follow the path and take in the sight of the enormous tropical plants and blossoming flowers. Joseph walks ahead of me.

Adorned in the same uniform, he stands a tad taller than me. His brown hair is wavy and rather long as it sits on his shoulders. His physique is athletic and his essence pure. He is genuine, unlike Mr. Brandon Higgly. He continues onward as if he is searching for something. He looks up, forward, and up again. Then I see it, a man sitting on scaffolding perfectly camouflaged among the hefty tropical greenery. He appears to be pruning the rather large plant.

"Hola Papa," Joseph says.

"Mi hijo," the slight-framed man says with a smile.

"That's my father. He takes care of this place."

"Yes, you mentioned that when we came in."

"We speak Spanish."

"Yes, you do."

"Mi hijo, que paso?" his father asks as he quickly scales down the scaffolding.

"He wants to know what happened outside."

"Mucho gusto, seňor Holmez," I say to his father.

Both father and son look at one another, pleasantly surprised. I have no idea why it would be so odd for me to speak Spanish. I step back and allow the two to talk.

Sitting upon another concrete bench, I mull over the events of the morning. Ms. Lucy can see Mikiel. She saved me from that creature this morning. What is happening? I'm exhausted and it's only 9:32 in the morning. I hold my head in my hands and stare at the floor.

"Hello, hello," I hear Ms. Lucy sing from somewhere behind me. "Ah, yes, Master and Mr. Holmez, it is always a pleasure. Would you please excuse me, fine sirs?"

"Oh, of course, Ms. Lucy," I hear Mr. Holmez respond.

"Meelah, I'll catch up with you later."

"Yes, Joseph, you needn't worry about Meelah. She is fine and in no trouble. Be on your way now. Classes have commenced."

The doors close behind them with a reverberating bam! Only the pitter-patter of Ms. Lucy's shoes remain. Then they stop. I lift my head, already sensing her presence. Tears stream wildly down my face again.

"Dear, dear," she says in a soft, comforting voice.

"No!" I yell back, surprising Ms. Lucy and myself.

I stand up in an attempt to regain my composure. I wipe my eyes and blow my nose then inhale. After I exhale, I look into Ms. Lucy's eyes. "No, No, No, NO," I repeat. "I need answers and need you to give them to me, NOW!"

"Wow, good for you, Meelah. It's about time!"

"What is?" I ask, confused by her response.

"You are awakening. In roughly six weeks you will have your eighteenth anniversary and not even Mikiel will be able to protect you."

"What! What is happening to me?" Then I begin to ramble, first in Spanish then French then German. I continue on, speaking in dialects that I didn't even know I could. "STOP!"

Then again, everything halts. I gaze up and see a little brown bird frozen midair. The moist vapors that mist the plants remain still; everything is suspended but me and Ms. Lucy.

"You must stop that, you know. It poses a problem with the world clock. Other parts of the world remain unaffected by this power of yours, at least unaffected for now. As your powers build, so will your abilities. That being said, Meelah...resume, please."

With my mind, I see the bird flying and mist moving and, as simple as that, they do. I close my eyes and feel the moist air caress my face. I wish for all of this to be an incredible dream from which, any minute, I'll wake.

"Do you really, now?" Ms. Lucy says with a strong hint of sarcasm.

"What, Ms. Lucy?"

Clearly, she, too, can hear my thoughts. First Mikiel, then my father and now Ms. Lucy. Is nothing sacred?

"When you are ready to stop feeling sorry for yourself, come and find me. Until then, I am a busy woman with a slaying right outside my building. Humans are clever. It is not easy masking the truth," she says, raising her hands in the air. While turning around and walking off she continues, "All that humans need knowledge of to really muck it all up is the reality of inter-dimensions. What chaos would ensue with that realization? They live on fear. They needn't know that life resides within the space between space. Well then, you know where to find me. Good day, Meelah."

"Please, Ms. Lucy. Please do not leave. I didn't mean to be rude. This, all of this, is a great deal to absorb."

"Yes, but greatness isn't born of ease. Greatness is earned. Though your essence is quite superior, you must earn the rest," she answers.

Then she sits on a bench across from me and signals me over to join her. I sit next to her, humbled by her words. She takes my hand and rests it in hers. Her palm is warm and her energy calming.

"I am grateful for what you did this morning. I apologize for not acknowledging your actions as soon as I saw you. You saved my life."

"Yes I did, but soon you will do the same for all life. Meelah, there is a war brewing and you, my dear, are the only one with the means to stop it. I mustn't say too much. It may influence your free will. I realize that you feel frustration regarding our vague references, but this is the way it must be for now. Only you can reveal your path, not me, not Mikiel or your father, or the hundreds of others who are sworn to protect you. Everything is destined to evolve on its own. What I may say is: You do not walk alone, though you feel as though you do."

After a gentle squeeze of my hand, she gets up and stands before a beautiful flowering orchid. Her face appears to soften in its presence. Her genuine smile is contagious. I watch her push a few stands of grey hair from her face as she commands absolute composure.

"Meelah, look at this white orchid. Can you see its beauty and smell its aroma? What did Mr. Holmez or I have to do to help it grow into its splendor?"

"You kept it warm, moist and fertilized?"

"Yes, just as your father has kept you safe and nourished. Now look again. Is this a tulip or daffodil?"

"No."

"Could it become a tulip or daffodil?"

"No," I answer again.

"Why not, Meelah?"

"There are specific varieties of flowers. One cannot be the other."

"But aren't they grown here in the same soil and moistened by the same mist and finally fertilized in the same manner?"

"I suppose they are."

"Then what makes them different from one another?"

"They simply are different."

"Yes, and you are different from all others even though you have been reared as a typical human child. You may appear to be a human, but you are not." A persistent tapping on the conservatory door pulls Ms. Lucy's attention away from our discussion.

"What! Can't this facility function on its own for twenty minutes?" she mumbles in frustration. "Meelah, I have to iron out the lingering issues from this morning. You are safe, for now anyway. We will meet again tomorrow morning. Say hello to your father and don't be too hard on him. You, my dear, are telepathic, too, and you have the ability to block all of us from your thoughts. But back to your father; he loves you. Though he was been asked not to become attached to you, he most certainly has. He has risked a great deal for you. But you seem to have an affect on males, don't you?" With a grin she proceeds through the heavy double doors. "Oh, one more thing, Meelah, take the rest of today off. Go home and soak in a nice warm bath. See where the water takes you."

Chapter Five

After she leaves, I begin to mull over Ms. Lucy's words. They resonate with me. Truthfully, I have always felt out of place. Even though I lived in over fifteen countries, I have never fit in anywhere. I've never had the sense of being home.

Kids have an instinctual wisdom like animals do. They sense someone's intentions. They can perceive that someone is different than they are. I have always felt that animals and young kids look at me as though they see in me what most adults don't. My heart has always had a soft spot for animals. They live in the now, the precious present moment. Their innocence touches me. I am unlike most other people I've met, though I never pondered the possibility that I am not human.

I feel an inexplicable shift coming, but a war? A war against whom or what is in my future? Though I may not be human, I wish no harm to come to anyone. Someone has already died. I am unsure what the vagrant was; perhaps he, too, was not human. I have never before seen a human being spew black mist or alter its form into pure malicious darkness.

The loud chime of the bell signaling a class change jars me back to reality. I inhale the moist, sweet-smelling air, gather my belongings and exit the healing garden.

I can't leave through the entry doors to Religards. I'm sure that it is still crawling with police and news crews. Closing my eyes, I see a rear exit in my mind. I allow instinct to guide me. First I go down what feels like endless flights of stairs then through corridors. Travelling through the bowels of the school, I follow this invisible lead. It's as though I have been journeying these halls for years. In a few minutes I'm rewarded by the success of my little experiment as I exit the rear door of the building.

Before I know it, I am nearing home. Though the sky is clearing and the sun is beginning to shine, winter has a firm grip on the season. It is cold. I am cold. I power walk the next two blocks. I notice I am walking faster than everyone else. This is a first. Usually I can hardly keep up with the masses.

I'm home and am greeted by a new doorman. He is stout and cheery. His smile extends from ear to ear.

"Meelah, it is my pleasure."

What? How does he know my name, I wonder? I pause, turn around and go back to him. He is still beaming and his cheeks are red from the cold winter air. I gaze into his eyes. Though my actions seem odd, they are also fruitful.

"Tonight you are safe. This is my honor."

His lips didn't move, yet I heard everything he said. Still unsure of my senses, I wait for another unspoken message. He could be a talented ventriloquist, after all.

"Are you well?" he asks in a polite and robust voice.

"Yes, I am well. Thank you."

I turn and proceed to the elevator. Quickly I press the arrow for "up" and wait. I am certain that I heard his thoughts. Then I recall Ms. Lucy's words, "You are not alone."

I consider at the doorman's reflection through the glass and, with my thoughts, I ask, "What is your name?"

"My name is Desitere."

I did it! I hear thoughts. I look back at Desitere and see that his back is to me. I watch him greet strangers who are travelling past him.

"I would like to thank you, Desitere. Thank you for your protection," I transmit telepathically.

"It is my honor," he says as he turns toward me. As he swivels my way, I can see that he still wears his kind smile.

The elevator opens and rather than step in, I choose to remain locked in this silent exchange with Desitere. The thought of someone I don't know wanting to keep me safe touches my heart. Today I have seen what is out there, or a piece of what is out there. I have felt its powerful energy and I have seen a warrior struggle to defeat it. Why would someone I don't know put themselves in this position?

Desitere doesn't answer with words or even a thought. Instead, I see a radiant white light around him. It follows the outline of his physical form. It is beautiful and pure. He, too, is not human. He lowers his head to me and I return the reverent gesture by lowering my head to him.

The elevator doors open again and this time I step in. On the ride up I recall how alone I felt earlier this morning and now realize how wrong I was.

When I reach our apartment, I open the door and remember how my day began; but now I only feel love for my father. He, too, has kept me safe. I feel so humbled by the events of the day. I look at the clock in my room; it is only eleven-fifty-two. What a morning. I'm exhausted by all that has happened and by the enlightening news I received.

A hot bath, as suggested by Ms. Lucy, does sound wonderful, then perhaps a nap. I run the water and add some of my favorite lavender-infused bath salts. Once the salts hit the water, they emit a soothing aroma that permeates the air. I make sure that the water is hot, and I mean hot.

I hurry to the front door to ensure that it's locked. Seriously, I have seen what is out there. I wonder what good would a little lock on my front door do? I'm sure that even a door wouldn't be a barrier of protection. But nonetheless, this action, even if it's futile, feels right. Checking the door lock three times, I am certain it is indeed secure.

Taking a handful of my father's homemade granola, I head back to my room. Perhaps tonight I should make dinner for us. Then I recall his brief note saying that he'll be home late. Tomorrow I'll make dinner, then.

While thinking of great recipes, I step into the scalding water and, man—it's pure perfection. My body sinks into the soothing water while my head rests on the tiled wall behind me. All is silent and peaceful. In this restful state, my mind returns to the events of yesterday, this morning, my father then Mikiel and Ms. Lucy. Even the remembrance of the encounter with my new friend, Joseph, floats through my rambling thoughts of all that has led up to where I now rest, and the entirety of it all begins to ruin my much-needed relaxing moment. However, with Desitere keeping watch, I assure myself that this is my moment—my time to recharge.

I follow my intuition. First, I clear my thoughts like a waitress would clear a table. I do not pick through any of them. I sweep them all away. Needing a little help with the process, I imagine my resistant lingering thoughts flying away like doves being released after a wedding. I watch as they leave. They are free and no longer attached to me. They do not weigh me down.

All that has occurred to me in the last twenty-four hours, I have freed from my mind. This knowledge has changed who I am and what I can do, but this moment is now dedicated to silence—to stillness.

All is at rest. I no longer feel alone. I no longer possess any thoughts in my mind. At last tranquil, I feel every muscle in my body loosen up. I am submerged in hot water, all but my head. There is no effort from my mind or my body; my arms are suspended within the water, as is my hair. The only movement is that of my chest as it rises then falls with my every breath. I slip into the water until I am completely underwater. Holding my breath, I fall deeper into a relaxing state. I can feel my hair tickle my face as it floats around me. But eventually, even my hair becomes still. I need air. Breaking this wonderful moment, I lift my head and take a breath of air then return to the relaxing state. This time, I slip further than I knew possible. With the need of another breath, I attempt to lift my head as I did only moments ago. But I can't. Raising my hands above me, I feel a translucent barrier that I cannot penetrate. Beginning to panic as my body's need for air becomes a necessity I kick and punch at the barrier, but to no avail. I cannot get through it. Beneath the barrier I remain.

I stop moving. All falls still again. Oddly, I'm no longer panicking. My final breath leaves me and I exhale. Tiny bubbles rise to rest against the barrier above me. Something within me tells me to close my eyes, and I do—I submit to whatever is to come.

A cold rush of water gushes in all around me and I'm somehow able to take a breath. I inhale before the need to cough brings tears to my eyes. As water ejects from my mouth, I look downward and see small stones beneath me. Again, I inhale—I'm still trying to catch my breath. But where am I, and how have I gotten here? Looking around, I see a foreign land.

Surrounded by abundant greenery, this place is like nothing I've ever experienced. It is breathtaking.

"Welcome home, Meelah," a gentle female voice says from behind me.

Following the voice, I gaze over my shoulder and see an older female with white hair twisted in a bun atop her head. Donning a golden robe that shimmers in the light of day, she presents me with a dazzling white robe.

She responds to my puzzled look by saying, "Yes, Meelah, this robe is for you. Have you forgotten that you have travelled here without clothing?"

Lightheaded from lack of oxygen, I did forget that I am naked, and I'm surprised to realize that I'm now sitting in cold water in a shallow river bed. Crossing one of my arms across my chest and pulling my knees in toward my body, I do my best to cover up.

Now with dignity, again, I gaze over my shoulder. With my free arm, I reach behind me and the pleasant stranger hands me the much-needed robe. "Thank you," I say to her. My lips are quivering. Wet and quite cool, I welcome the dry robe. Slipping the garment over my head then threading my arms into each sleeve, I am again dressed. I'm unsure what I'm wearing and don't care. Looking down, I see that gravity has drawn the balance of my new attire onto the chilly water. Not wishing to soak the bottom half of my clothing, I press my hands against the slippery rocks on either side of me and attempt to stand. Nearly vertical, every part of me begins to tremble. My legs seem to stop working. Like a heavy rock dropped into water, I plunk right back down. Sitting upright, I watch as the older female kneels before me. She's speaking, I can see her mouth moving, but I hear nothing. I see her eyes focus just over my shoulder, perhaps at someone or something behind me. I try to follow her focus with my head but I can't move. Weak, dizzy, breathless and no longer able to remain erect, I fall backward. As a dark haze fills the space before me, I feel someone holding me in their arms. I look up to see who or what is cradling me but there is no clarity. There is only ambiguous fog.

I don't know where I am. Unable to move and blanketed in silence, I muster up courage for whatever this moment may bring. Quiet, peaceful, I'm slipping into utter darkness. I can't stop it. Unable to resist—I surrender.

I hear voices all around me—voices I cannot identify. My eyelids feel heavy and my body, weighty. I remain in this state for what seems like hours, or has it been days?

I'm able to open my eyes. When I do, I see the face of a young man sitting in a chair beside me. When his eyes meet mine, he smiles. His expression illustrates a sense of relief. I watch as, seeming lost in his silence, he stares into my eyes. His eyes are the color of milk chocolate with a hint of cinnamon, and are familiar to me. As with Mikiel, I feel as though he knows me and I know him. His complexion is olive and his long hair blacker than the night sky of a new moon. He is quite handsome.

I try to sit up and instantly experience a headache so piercing that it lowers me back down.

"No, Meelah. You mustn't sit up yet. Wait for Shria," he says, using only his thoughts.

My happiness at understanding his silent communication is quickly replaced by dizziness. I am nauseous. I feel awful.

"Where am I?" I ask telepathically.

"No questions, Meelah. Close your eyes and rest. Shria is making a tincture for you to drink. It will assist you. Close your eyes; you are safe here."

Closing my eyes, all I can do is rest. I feel safe in the company of this young man. As long as I can recall I have had a fear that I could not understand but here it seems to have faded away. Perhaps I have been sensitive to my father's fears. Regardless of where my fright has originated, I feel protected and thankfully, I fall asleep.

While sleeping I see an image of something beautiful. It is in the shape of a diamond and seems to be made of four stones. The stone on the top is clear, the one on the left is an iridescent green, on the right is a bright red stone and the stone on the bottom is deep blue. This object shines before me as it is suspended in midair. Drawn to its beauty and purity, I reach out to touch it.

"You must drink this, Meelah," I hear a soft voice say.

Feeling a connection to this rather spectacular object, I lean closer. I wish for nothing more than to hold it. I wish to listen to it as if it has a story to tell me.

"Wake up, dear. You must swallow this."

The persistent voice succeeds in waking me and the object that I was so close to reaching disappears. Upon opening my eyes, I see the same older female I met earlier. She is the same woman who appeared when the still water of my shower created a window to a different space. She looks kindly at me like a mother would to a daughter. Yet, I'm certain I am a stranger to her.

"No, you certainly are not, Meelah. I know you as well as I know myself. In time, you will know me, too. I am Shria. I am the head elder here on Churria, and, my dear, you must swallow this. It is what we call a tincture. Sit up for me."

I push myself up, feeling weak and heavy. Shria hands me a tiny cup filled with a thick liquid. The viscous nature of this is not appetizing.

"This tincture will nourish and heal you. I teleported to each of the four quadrants of Churria and gathered herbs to make this specific recipe. Your body will recognize it. Drink, Meelah."

Allowing my instincts to guide me as I navigate into new territory, I swallow the thick mixture. It runs down my throat. At first it is quite bitter, but soon it changes into a divine sweetness that coats my mouth. My insides are warmed and begin to rejuvenate. How is it that a sip of liquid can have such an effect?

"Are you asking me a question, my dear, or do you wish to answer it yourself?"

"I'm sorry, I'm still adjusting to telepathic communication and not used to every thought being heard so readily. Shria, I have many questions for you."

"I have many answers for you. Where do you wish to begin?"

"Where am I and why am I here?"

"You are on Churria. Churria is a star that resides within the same universe as earth. As to why you are here, that is quite simple. This is your true home. You were born Churrian though you are more than that, and here you will live out your destiny."

"I am Churrian? What is Churrian? What does that mean?" I look around me and then state, "This is not my home. Earth is my home, where my father and I live. That is where I will return."

"Yes, you will return to earth temporarily. And how is Samuel? He is missed by many here on Churria. He is missed especially by his father."

"You know my father?"

"I know Samuel well. I was there when he was born. But, Meelah, he is not your birth parent. They are also here on Churria."

Feeling stronger, I stand. My light, white gown moves with the soft, warm breeze that pours through a window-like opening in the room. This information is a great deal for me to digest. Shria remains quiet and still as I process. I can feel her watching me as I pace back and forth in the small room. I find myself at the window. The air is so sweet and the view is breathtaking. The abundant thriving flora outside is striking. If my father is indeed a Churrian, then I understand where his passion for all things "green" derives. I think of him. I bet he's worried about me.

"How can I return home? How long have I been here?"

"You have the power within you to leave at anytime, but since your powers haven't fully awakened, I suggest that you leave the way you came. I will bring you back to Calla as soon as you wish. Calla is like an earth river. But here, she is one of us. Now, as to how long you have been here: You have been here for four rotations, which is equivalent to four earth days. Mikiel has advised Samuel of your location. You needn't worry."

"Four days; how has it been four days?" I ask quietly. Perhaps this is simply a dream. Then I recall the four stones; they are somehow connected to me.

"You saw the amulet!" Shria exclaims, while delving into my reeling thoughts.

Her eyes become bright and alive with this news.

"What amulet?" I inquire.

"I will show you," she answers as she leaves the room.

"I must master the art of shielding my thoughts. It is not as though I have secrets, but I need some privacy."

"You will, dear, all in due time," Shria exclaims from the other room.

Curious, I follow her voice, first by proceeding down a narrow corridor then into a rather large sitting room. This room is open to the green outside. This foreign oasis is magnificent.

The aromatic air hits me. Magically, it seems to lift my conflicted spirit. The lush vegetation is abundant.

Shria draws my attention as she flips through several books strewn about a wooden table. She seems intent on her task of discovery. Strands of her white hair have escaped the tight bun of hair atop her head. They frame her round face and bounce about as she flips through the pages that look like aged parchment. The writing is in a language that I do not know. But perhaps I do. Nothing would surprise me now.

Her passion continues to pique my interest. I try to read her thoughts, but only the sound of the outside wildlife is audible. Closing my eyes, I try again. I focus. But still, all I hear comes from the surrounding nature. I don't give up. Then, there is no sound at all. Everything falls silent. Upon opening my eyes, I see Shria standing before me. Her light-brown eyes are soft and filled with kindness. Her smile exudes love and compassion. I cannot help but smile back at this sweet stranger. Perhaps *stranger* isn't the correct word. Though I've only just met Shria, she is no stranger, she feels like family.

"Thank you, dear. Now let me show you something."

I follow her over to the table. Upon it is a hefty weathered book. Its yellow and thick pages appear ripened by time. It's open and I look down, curious. But it's blank. Not a word or a picture. There is nothing more than empty, aged parchment.

"Meelah, only you can see the image upon this page. Tell me, what do you see?"

"I see nothing, Shria, nothing on the pages," I answer in a frustrated tone.

She doesn't say another word. I can feel from her that she knows I can see whatever is here, but perhaps I need time to develop this skill. So I continue to stare at the blank pages. I run my hands over the book's surface and feel an intimate connection to it. Closing my eyes, I rest my hands upon its aged pages.

Then I see something—no, someone. They are ahead of me. I look around and I am no longer surrounded by green life. I'm now encircled by sand, which is, seemingly, devoid of all life.

A being stands with its back toward me and a large book open in its hands. It is winged like Mikiel, but the wings are a pure white. I watch as its white gown, similar to the gown I am now wearing, moves in the arid breeze.

I am drawn to step forward and I do just that. I wonder; am I having a vision? The tepid dry air wafts by me and my hair dances about in it. The heat from what appears to be the sun warms my skin. The cerulean atmosphere is similar to a perfect afternoon on earth.

Inching closer to the winged being, I am unsure of what I'll learn. Somehow I know that this is my path. This being can tell me what I need to know. Something here will make all of this clear to me.

I stop and now am directly behind the winged being. As I stand in the being's shadow, I notice that its wings are similar to that of a massive white dove. They are beautiful.

"What am I to learn from this?" I state out loud.

No sooner did those words leave my lips, than the being turns around and faces me. I look at the open book in its hands. It is the same ancient book that Shria showed me, but it is newer. Reaching forward, I touch the thick, white pages. As I do this, a map appears upon its surface. I do not understand it. Unfamiliar with the language it's written in, I study it for I wish to leave wiser. I yearn for understanding. Below the written text are icons to paths that eventually lead to a golden being holding four stones—the amulet. It is just like what I saw in my dream.

"But I do not know where this is," I say to the figure.

Its face is shadowed by the sunlight from behind us. How could it not be my first instinct to see who it is holding this map? Who is this winged being, similar to Mikiel? I struggle to get a clear image. With the sun streaming into my eyes, I come closer and the being does the same. As it enters into plain sight, the clarity that I wished for vanishes.

Catching a glimpse of this being, I am shocked! I cannot believe my eyes. Not only is the being wearing the amulet on a fine chain necklace, the winged being is me. I continue to gaze into my mirror image and she does the same. She possesses a powerful confidence that I seem to lack. I watch a tear journey down her face and drop into the dry sand at our feet. I discern true emotional pain in her eyes. "Retrieve the amulet. It holds the key to your power. You must recover it before your eighteenth year on earth," the voice similar to mine says. "He looks for it. He must not find it before you do. All life as you know it will fall, if he does. This is the only way to afford all beings a chance of a future—a future that honors free will."

"Who is looking for the amulet? Who is he?"

"You have already seen his darkness. But you have not yet witnessed his true power. It is a part of you. Use it to your advantage."

"What do you mean it is a part of me?"

"We now embody both the light and the dark. There was no other way. Recover our amulet. Your time to do so is short. Fulfill our destiny. Soon you will remember—everything...."

With those words, my winged image fades into air. I continue to hear, "Recover the amulet. Your time in which to do so is short," over and over again. Those haunting words envelop me.

As I open my eyes, I see Shria, her attention focused on me. I wonder if she saw what I did. I wonder if she knows who I used to be. She continues to stare at me and I understand from the expression on her face that she can no longer read my mind. I don't know how this happened, but it feels wonderful to be alone with my own thoughts.

I look again at the yellowed parchment before me. It remains blank, and I now understand why. I have hidden the amulet and I must retrieve it. Now I am ready to use it.

"I must return to earth, Shria," I say with a stronger sense of inner power.

"Then you shall," she answers.

Shria doesn't ask what I know or if I saw the location of the amulet. I trust her.

A translucent channel descends and we teleport to the river, Calla. Shria radiates contentment. Over her shoulder I see a young man running toward me in the near distance. His eyes are upon me as he races in my direction. I notice that he breathes heavily as if he has been running for quite some time. His black hair glistens in the light of day as does the sweat beading up on his forehead. He is the same young man who sat next to my bed. He continues to stare as he nears me. His essence awakens something deep within me.

Shria turns to see who or what has captured my attention. I sense that she doesn't want me to connect with this Churrian.

"You must be leaving now, dear," she states.

"Who is he, Shria?"

"He is Kriyo. But Meelah, Calla is waiting for you."

I turn back to a raging river. The fast-moving water obscures a view of its depths. I have no idea how to travel using the river. I look over my shoulder and see Shria's kind face. I glance past her and no longer see Kriyo, but I sense his presence.

"You know what to do, Meelah. Listen to your instincts. I will see you when you return. You have a great deal more to learn."

I lower my head in respect to Shria then I step into the cool, surging water. Its aggressive current pulls at my gown and I almost lose my balance. Then I begin to understand. Churrians are connected to all living things. Calla is a living being, not simply a torrential river.

"Calla, I apologize for not asking your permission prior to entering you. May I remain?"

With those spoken words the water around me changes. I now stand up to my knees in a small pool of placid water though the river still rages about me. Using only my instinct as a guide, I nod my head to the animated river and give her my thanks. Spreading my arms, I open my heart and fall into her still surface. As if I had stepped through a doorway, I return home; at least home for now.

Chapter Six

Upon opening my eyes, I see the concerned face of my father. His worried expression illustrates his genuine affection for me. I gaze downward, curious if, this time, I travelled with my clothing. Thank goodness the answer is yes. This moment might be quite awkward if my white gown remained on Churria. Travel between realities, dimensions or worlds (I'm not sure which is more accurate at this point), is so new to me.

I am eager to get out of the bathtub, though the water temperature is quite pleasant. I believe that my father has been keeping it warm for me. By the look of the dark circles under his eyes, this may have been an all-night and all-day feat since he didn't know when I'd be returning.

"I'll give you time to do whatever you need to," my father says awkwardly. He rises to leave and then stops. "Oh, Meelah, I will make a tincture for you. I believe this mixture will assist you," he assures me as he closes my bathroom door.

To my utter surprise I feel pretty good. I'm wet, but not nearly as exhausted as when I arrived in Churria. With ease, I stand. My gown is heavy in its saturated state. Water cascades from it as I remain standing in the tub. It makes the sound of a summer rainstorm. All that is missing is the boom of thunder.

I pull the heavy gown off over my head and wring it out, release the drain in the tub and watch the translucent water, which had acted as a doorway, disappear. I will never look at water in the same manner again. After drying off, I slip into my comfy pink-patterned pajama bottoms, my cherished sweatshirt and cozy pink slippers. These are my favorite earthly possessions, though my treasured books are a close second.

I am anxious to comfort my father. The last exchange we had was unsettling to us both. I now see that he was only trying to keep me safe and innocent for as long as he could.

At present, I carry a great weight with me; the knowledge of who I was and the amulet that I hid and must find, Churria and inter-dimensional travel. There is much that I must understand, but first I wish to give Father a hug.

Upon entering the kitchen, I see him grinding herbs by hand. The plants release a clean and distinctive aroma. It is soothing and reminiscent of the aromatic, abundant greenery at Shria's place.

I can feel that he senses me standing behind him. My father faces me with a kindhearted smile. I go in for my hug and he squeezes me in return. He is my everything. He is my best friend; for much of my life, my only friend.

I can feel that he, too, is carrying a great weight. He pulls back and lovingly studies me. His eyes say so much. In them is guilt that he didn't share what he knew. I also see sadness. He wishes that this path was not mine to walk. Then there is fear. He is unsure if I am prepared for such a task. He worries that he will lose me in its pursuit.

"I love you, Dad. You have raised me well. I will do what I must and I will walk the path destined to me. I am not afraid."

"Meelah, you understand why I couldn't tell you?"

"You were protecting my free will. Every action that I make must be my choice and mine alone."

"Yes," he answers.

My thoughts rebound to Churria. I see its magnificence in my mind. This was my father's home. This is what he left in order to guide and protect me. What a sacrifice he has made.

"Father, Churria is beautiful. I saw you in every part of the flourishing plant life. The air is so clean and pure. The atmosphere is unpolluted and clear. I now understand your passion here on earth. There *is* another way. Churria is a living example."

"Yes, there is another way. Now drink this, Meelah. It is fresh and already losing its nutrients. It will nourish you."

I swallow the green, thick and mild-flavored liquid. It feeds me. Though it was only about two ounces of fluid, it rejuvenates me.

"Father, do you miss Churria?"

"Yes, but," he pauses and I wait for his spoken words. I respect his reflective moment of quiet and am careful not to read him telepathically. However, his pause continues and he answers me in this silence—without using words or thoughts. Silence is powerful. I feel his answer; it fills the space around me. I feel his longing for Churria, but realize that his loving attachment to me tethers him here to earth.

This profound moment is broken by a strident banging on our door, as the persistent and increasingly louder knocking rudely interrupts us. Knock, knock, knock! Knock, knock, knock!

"It must be Luther. He has been worried about you," my father says while walking to the door.

I follow my father with my eyes. Before opening the door he turns to me. At first he seems still uncertain of what to say to me. We needn't say a word to one another. My gratitude for what he has given up is written on my face. I know he feels and sees it. He smiles at me and I return the heartfelt gesture.

The loud knocking breaks our silent communication again. With no words exchanged the energy between and around us is lifted. My father opens the door still wearing a smile.

"Meelah! You've returned and you've come out of the closet," Luther spouts while rushing over to give me a rather tight hug.

"I've been waiting for this day," Luther continues.

"What day would that be, and what closet have I stepped out from?" I ask while smirking at my father.

He continues to hug me. He doesn't let go even though I am no longer hugging him back. Though his embrace is becoming a little awkward, it does feel good to know that I am loved.

"Now, now, Luther, let poor Meelah take a breath," my father says as he fills the kettle with water.

"Of course, yes, yes, I mean no disrespect, your queen, no, your leader, your royalty. Samuel, what do I call her now?"

I can hardly contain my urge to laugh. I watch as my father studies his disheveled friend. Luther's button-down shirt is incorrectly buttoned and half of it is hanging out. His shoes don't even match. On his left foot is a worn black-and-white sneaker and on his right a black shiny dress shoe. His hair is wild and crazy.

Both my father and I remain quiet as Luther struggles to figure out how he should address me. Imagine that, it's not as though I married into a royal family. I am the same person I have always been, but now I have purpose. Perhaps I am making light of what I've learned about my past or even what may await me in the near future. But one thing I'm not is egotistical.

"What? Why are the two of you just looking at me? Have I offended you? Samuel, have I offended her? Why are you two doing this?"

Like a child about to have a temper tantrum, Luther's face flushes bright red. He seems disconnected from the silent communication between me and my father. He cannot read either of us and runs his hands through his already wild hair to leave it standing on end like a male peacock displaying his feathers. He paces about awaiting an answer—a reaction, anything from either one of us.

My father can no longer restrain the mirth welling within him. His face is as crimson as his hair and his lips are tightly pursed. Like a volcano on the verge of an eruption, he can't contain his hilarity and bursts into laughter. My father roars in peals of laughter harder and louder than I knew possible. It is one of those contagious laughs that make your eyes tear and nose run. I have the giggles so bad that my stomach muscles begin to ache. The fact that Luther has no idea what is so funny makes the joyous moment persist. Perhaps our enjoyment is simply a form of energetic release, but it is still fun, especially since Luther has no idea why we are laughing.

The high-pitched siren of the boiling teakettle brings my father and me back to reality. Luther stares at the two of us with his mouth agape and a perplexed look on his face. I find his innocence endearing.

"What kind of tea do you want, Luther?" my father asks while drying his eyes.

"I don't know. What tea have the two of you had? Perhaps I should have some of that."

"Yes, my dear friend, perhaps you should," my father answers.

"Luther, I am still Meelah, so please address me as such," I say to him. "I have not changed just because I have been given information."

Luther stares at me with his bright blue eyes. His demeanor becomes grave. He places his warm, rough hand over mine.

"Who you are is more than who you used to be. You have a destiny. You don't understand yet, and for all of our sakes, I hope that you do soon."

"She will, Luther," my father states adamantly. "She will," he repeats as if he is now convincing himself.

"Meelah, what do you know about your eighteenth birthday?" my father asks.

The energy has shifted from a brief light moment to a serious reflection. Luther and my father embody this change with their intense demeanor and rigid body language. They seem to mimic each other. Though I wish to return to our moment of gaiety, I know that this shift is where I must be. But I can't help myself.

"I suppose I won't be having an eighteenth birthday party then?"

"Meelah," they both say in unison.

My father hands both Luther and me a steaming mug of herbal tea, then sits down. It is about a month until my eighteenth birthday. I know that I must locate the amulet before then, but I can feel that there is far more to my eighteenth. I see it on their faces.

"Father, what is it?"

He pauses as if he doesn't want to tell me—as if he wants to protect me from whatever lies ahead. But he can't. He knows that what will happen on my eighteenth birthday is also fated.

"What is it? I would much rather hear you say it."

"Once you locate your amulet, at the moment of your eighteenth year on earth, your powers will activate."

"That doesn't sound too bad. What powers will I have?"

"I do not know."

"Samuel, you must tell her."

"Luther, what is it?" I ask.

"No, Luther, I will tell her," my father says somberly. "Meelah, you needn't focus on what will occur on your eighteenth. You must focus on locating the amulet prior to your eighteenth. The Dark Force also seeks the amulet. It holds the key to awakening your powers and he knows that you'll be vulnerable without it. Only you can read your map. Only you can remember where you hid it."

"But why am I being told about the amulet now? Why has everyone held this from me for so long? I do not understand this logic. I have a little more than a month. I could have been searching for it my whole life."

Again Luther takes my hand into his. He stares into my eyes and I eventually look into his.

"Meelah, you were not ready. I feel that when you were a Light Warrior you knew exactly what you were doing. You timed all of these events precisely. Though one month may seem like an insufficient amount of time, it won't be. Last week you walked as an ordinary earthling. This week you walk with a powerful sense of purpose. And right now, you are being reminded that you are not alone."

He is correct. I am not alone, though the burden of all that I know is only mine to carry. My father sits contemplative. With still more that he wishes to say, he holds it back. Though I find this trait utterly frustrating, I do my best to let it go. In time I will possess the knowledge I seek.

It's dark outside and all the events of the day begin to weigh on me. I see it's already 11:22 in the evening. I wonder how I'll begin to locate the amulet. I ponder what my next step should be, but fatigue trumps any other current desire.

"Go to sleep, my Meelah," my father murmurs.

He, too, looks exhausted. The circles around his eyes have become darker and his overall energy seems heavy. Luther rubs his eyes as if our fatigue is somehow contagious.

"You have an early day, Meelah, and before we know it tomorrow will be here," my father says while clearing our mugs from the table. "Luther, I'll get a blanket for you. It is late," he adds.

"The couch is calling to me. I'll keep watch over Meelah while you get some shut eye, Samuel. The statues are powerful, but so am I."

"Thank you, dear friend," I hear my father say in response.

Before I head to my room, I speak from my heart. "Thank you both. Thank you for everything."

Both men lower their heads to me and I do the same. My father walks into his room then closes his door. Luther fumbles with his blanket. He repeatedly attempts to cover himself though his blanket isn't fully unfolded. He struggles and I smile to think that he is the one protecting me. I cannot stand seeing the needless battle with his blanket, so I go over to unfold it and tuck him in. I wonder if he, too, is Churrian; he is seemingly opposite from my father in so many ways.

"Luther, are you a Churrian, as well?" I ask.

"Oh, no, why?" he responds, as if that notion was somehow implausible.

"Are you human?" I ask again.

"No, I not human, either. I am a Galidrome. Would you like to see my true form?"

"Yes," I answer, curious.

"Stand back then. Oh, I should move this coffee table. We wouldn't want to break it, though that might be an improvement," he jokes.

The idea of Luther concealing his true form is intriguing. It opens my mind to unlimited possibilities. If he can transform, then who else is like this on earth? How many others walk alongside me on the streets of New York hidden in plain sight?

"Meelah, you're ruining my thunder with all of your analyzing. I can see it in your eyes. Now, are you ready?"

"Yes, I am," I answer eagerly.

I watch as Luther first runs his hands through his wayward wisps of hair. Then he closes his eyes. His clothes deflate and fall to the floor.

I wonder where he went and what he has become. He certainly is no longer human as his clothing lies devoid of his body. Then I see something rustle about in Luther's clothes. I move closer. Something shoots from his clothing and bounces across the dimly lit room. A vase crashes and breaks. In no time my father is in the living room standing by my side. He sees the deflated pile of Luther's clothing.

"Really, Luther, you have to do this now? Are you out of your mind? Do you know what time it is? We have neighbors. Contain yourself!"

Both my father and I duck down as Luther flies past us. Whatever he has become zooms around our living room knocking pictures and other items onto the floor. Crashing sounds fill the air. Luther seems to be having the time of his life, while my father is becoming increasingly agitated.

There is a soft, but audible knock on our door. With my father distracted, I head over to open the door. I can't help but watch my father as he has words with the rather zealous Luther who is still zipping around the room. My father jumps into the air attempting to catch him. The sight before me is so funny, I want to stay and watch. But as I walk past the statues toward the door, for the first time in my life they speak to me. Not audibly, but telepathically.

"Meelah, you may proceed," they say in unison as I pass them.

"Thank you," I say in return, rather surprised.

Before opening the door, I close my eyes to sense who or what stands outside in the hallway. I feel their presence. It is Desitere. Without further delay, I open the door and see that my instincts were correct. Desitere, rotund and stout, looks past me and begins to chuckle.

"What is Luther doing? I was worried that something else was occurring up here. As soon as I heard the banging, I came up."

"You heard this all the way from the lobby?"

"Of course I did. This is what I've been trained for."

"Would you like to come in, Desitere?"

"Thank you, Meelah, but I can't."

"Of course you may. Perhaps you can help us catch Luther."

In the background Luther continues to zip back and forth. He moves so quickly that I still cannot see what he is. My father persists in jumping about attempting to catch him.

"Please come in. You don't see this every day."

"No, you certainly don't. But Meelah, you don't seem to understand that I cannot come in. Allow me to show you."

Desitere begins to step over the threshold, but when he tries, a white translucent shield blocks him from entering. He touches the shield and pushes on it with all his might, demonstrating its protective nature. I realize that this force field is emanating from our stone statues.

The rucus behind me falls silent and I look at my father who is holding Luther. His arm is tugged up then down as Luther tries to evade my father's grasp.

"Hello, Desitere," Father says politely. "I apologize for all the noise. It was Luther, though I assume you've figured that out."

Desitere nods and says, "Well then, I'll take leave of you all. Have a good night, at least what is left of it." He pauses as he studies me. His kind demeanor brings a smile to my lips. He lowers his head and I do the same in respect. As he takes a step back, the white shield dissolves like a magic trick. I close the door and turn to inspect these rather amazing statues.

"Only you, your father and I can come through them once they have been activated," a high-pitched Luther states.

My father is still holding whatever Luther is against his will. His arm is pulled in every direction, but somehow he continues to hold him tightly.

"What is he?" I ask.

"I already told you. I am a Galidrome," Luther squeals.

"Luther, do you promise not to misbehave again?" my father asks.

"Yes, yes, I promise," Luther squeaks.

My father lets him go and I get a good look. Suspended in mid-air is a creature like no other I have ever seen. In totality he looks like nothing here on earth. He is like a cross between a hawk and a weasel. My father pets his head and Luther leans into every stroke. He is about the size of a full-grown bald eagle and has a hair-covered tail about twelve inches long. His face is furry and his eyes are still big and blue. His ears move in every direction as they tune into the sounds of the city at 12:32 in the morning. I think he's cute. I touch the top of his head and he makes a purring sound like a cat. His tail moves around like a fur-coated snake. His wings move quick as a humming bird's.

"I found Luther at Ameira," my father says. "His planet and many of his kind have been destroyed. We bonded immediately and he asked to come with me here to earth to find and then protect you."

"But how does he change back into human form?"

"It took practice, let me tell you. But a Galidrome is able to shift into other cellular forms. He is my friend and has been since I was about sixty Churrian years of age."

"But you look no older than forty."

"In earth years I am about thirty-eight. Everything here on earth is so dense. My time here has aged me considerably. In Churrian years, I am almost 300 years of age."

"What?" I gasp. "How long do most Churrians live?"

"My father, Trall, is nearing 600 now. I miss him. Did you see him? He and Shria are quite close."

"No, I didn't, but I'll make sure I do the next time I go. Why don't you come with me?"

"Perhaps one day, but now you'd better get some rest. The sun will be up soon and you must continue to go to Religards for the time being. There is a great deal for you to learn."

"Really? I am flying around and the two of you are talking about Religards?" Luther says in a squeaky tone.

"Now, now, Luther, that will be enough. Meelah must get some rest."

I pet Luther's head. He flies upward, nuzzling his head into my hand. The notion that the majority of his kind were somehow destroyed or eliminated pains me. Who or what would do such a revolting thing? This touches a chord deep within me. The needless destruction of innocent beings infuriates me. My mind begins to race. There is so much I need to understand. Mining Ms. Lucy's wisdom is a great place to begin. I know that she holds many answers, especially because she is not as close to me. My father's familiarity creates a barrier—an impenetrable wall. Perhaps he justifies it by feeling that it is for my own protection. With a little more than six weeks before my eighteenth birthday, I can no longer afford to be hindered.

I watch the continuing interaction between Luther and my father and grin. In the living room, picture frames and bits and pieces of glass are strewn about. It looks like someone played a game of racquet ball in here. I go into the kitchen to retrieve the garbage can. As I return, I see Luther curling into a fury little ball on the couch. His brown-feathered wing covers his sweet little face. He is thoroughly tuckered out. With a yawn, I begin to straighten things up.

"No, you need sleep. Luther and I will take care of this in the morning. Meelah, you must take care of yourself; your strength depends on it."

My father's words have never been more true. Exhausted, I proceed back to my room. After another yawn, I crawl into my bed. My mind is too fatigued to process anything else. I close my eyes then sleep overtakes me.

Chapter Seven

The cold brisk morning air chills me. The winter wind is so arid it seems to strip my skin of its moisture upon contact. Though spring is right around the corner, winter holds on tenaciously. I walk swiftly to Religards, seamlessly blending into the mass of pedestrians who are also beginning their day. But very close behind me is a familiar presence.

As soon as I stepped out of my apartment building, I felt the company of Mikiel. He remains invisible to all others. He is here for me and me alone. He follows me and does not say a word, nor does he need to. The more my essence awakens, or perhaps simply matures, the more I appreciate the power of stillness and silence. Even though I am encircled by humans and other beings trying to camouflage into earth life, I block all of them out. I choose not to hear their thoughts or read their energy. I walk amongst many only aware of one.

I stop to wait for the traffic light. Patiently, we all wait as if we are conditioned to do so. Some are listening to their iPods and are moving to a song that's only audible to them. Others are talking on their phones or reading e-mails on their tiny electronics.

I am still. I have no distractions; well, that's not true. I have Mikiel and I can't help but close my eyes as I sense him move closer to me. As the space between us diminishes, I feel my back warm. I have an inexplicable connection to him, and feel his breath on my neck. I sense his love for me, though he grapples to restrain it. I am still unsure of my feelings toward him. But regardless, these moments are wonderful. Standing surrounded by strangers but only sentient of one being is a tremendous experience.

I open my eyes and look around me as if awakening from a dream. I am drawn to a toddler all bundled up in a stroller right beside me. Only a small part of her face is exposed to the cold air. Her soft dark brown eyes affect me. They are pure innocence. To me, at this moment, this small human embodies hope. Our eyes connect and her spirit touches mine. In this simple moment, another part of me awakens. It is passion. Not romantic fervor, but dedication to my higher purpose. My higher calling must take precedence. I feel myself emit this vibration, this message. Mikiel takes a step back, putting distance between us, acknowledging this change.

As the mass of people around me begins to move forward, I watch the toddler. I don't want to disconnect from our moment. She turns around, also not wishing to sever our connection. But, like all such encounters, our exchange is temporary. Her parent pushes her onward while I remain in place. This small human has helped me become aware of my purpose. My inner drive, the momentum that has brought me to where I now stand, begins to stir deep within me. I must protect the innocent here and beyond.

I open my mind and tune into the humans surrounding me. Many are consumed by trivial matters, but some are filled with love and generosity. They, too, embody hope. They navigate through the crowds thinking not of their own needs or wants. They hold doors and pause in the frigid elements to give a stranger an authentic smile.

I become acutely aware of those who wish for positive change and others who choose to remain disconnected and self-involved. The simple act of making eye contact—a connection—is what actuates change. This change is critical here on earth.

Ready for more learning, hungry for knowledge, I continue onward. Religards is only a block away now. Somewhere in the last block, or perhaps during my profound epiphany, Mikiel has left. He is no longer behind me but I sense he is watching. Truthfully, I cannot afford distractions. I have only about six weeks. I wish no harm to come to any human, especially after feeling the profound virtue within that sweet little girl.

I do not know where the dark energy is, but I can sense that it is not near. I am connected to it. I realize that now. This is how it attempted to pull me from Religards. If I embodied only the light, like Mikiel, the Dark Force couldn't connect with me. I recall the message from when I was a Light Warrior, that I am both light and dark, and to use this to my advantage. Someday, I know that I'll require this knowledge and its application, but not today.

My enlightening walk to school ends as I open the academy doors. Students hurry past me as I head to the main office. I unravel my scarf and take off my gloves on the way. My hair bounces with each of my steps. I decided today to wear it down instead of in my usual twisted bun. It feels good to have it unrestrained and free for a change.

"Meelah, you're back," I hear Brandon Higgley say.

It is as if he has been waiting for my return. He pounces on me like a cat would a mouse. Something about him irks me.

I say not one word with my mouth. Instead, I turn and look at him intently and tell him, with my essence, to back off. I see the appearance of fear in his eyes, although I have no idea what he sees within the brown pools of mine. But without another word, he scurries off. I watch as he pushes through the crowd of his peers on their way down the hallway. They look like mice navigating through a maze, all hoping for a nibble of cheese.

"Now that wasn't kind, Meelah," I hear Ms. Lucy scold from behind me.

I'm not sure what she was referencing, the banishment of the odd Brandon or the condescending thought of mice.

"Both, dear," she answers, rather unimpressed.

Her energy is still so kind and pure, quite similar to Shria's. She continues to focus on me, exuding patience. Silence is her power. Not a thought or a word comes from her. I know what she is waiting for. Listening to my heart, I do feel a little remorse. Brandon certainly doesn't deserve whatever it was that I did.

Contrite, I acknowledge Ms. Lucy's truth and hear her say, "That's better, Meelah. We all expect more of you."

Joseph's friendly face surfaces from the stream of students flowing past the main office. He smiles at me, and then makes his way over to us. Today he's wearing a bright-red knitted winter cap; it looks handmade. Some of the loosely knit loops of yarn stick out, adding charm to his hat. His long brown hair juts out at the bottom of it. His dark brown eyes remind me of the sweet toddler from this morning, soft and full of presence.

"Meelah, are you better? Ms. Lucy said you had a bad case of the flu," he says with empathy.

"I am quite well, Joseph...Joseph Holmez," I answer with a smirk.

"Cute, Meelah. Perhaps next time I'll introduce myself not sounding like a newscaster. 'This is Joseph…Joseph Holmez.' Well, I'd better go to class. I'll see you later then?"

"Yes, you'd better be going, Joseph," Ms. Lucy adds. "Meelah, come into my office for a moment, dear. Again, I have a busy morning ahead of me."

I observe Joseph proceed on his way. He, too, personifies kindness. He stands out, but he doesn't seem to care. He nods hello to those he passes as he continues onward. I can see that many do not understand his benevolence but he knows who he is.

"Come on, dear. I have back-to-back meetings this morning," I hear Ms. Lucy direct.

I turn and follow her down a hallway then into her office. To my surprise her office only consists of a desk and three chairs. Upon her desk are neatly stacked piles of papers, and nothing else. There is not even one picture on the wall or knickknack of any kind. On the sill of her window is a single white orchid. While she fumbles around in her desk, I take a look out her window. Her view oversees the entrance to Religards. My warm breath fogs a small section of glass in front of me. I am so close that my nose is almost touching the cool pane. Cold air from the frost outside makes it through the old and inefficient window.

In my mind I see symbols—three of them. I breathe onto the glass again, fogging it over, and I draw them just as I picture them in my mind. No sooner do I finish than I hear Ms. Lucy from behind me.

"My dear! Do you know what you've said?" she asks with enthusiasm.

"No," I answer, curious. "They simply appeared to me. What do they mean?"

"It is the white orchid beneath you. I'm sure of it! White orchids are pure. They speak directly to one's soul if they, too, are pure. This orchid sees your next step and knows where it is."

"Where what is?"

"Your amulet, dear," she answers in a whisper.

"You know of the amulet, Ms. Lucy?"

"We all know," she says mysteriously and still in a whisper.

"In what language are these symbols?"

"Meelah, these are ancient Churrian symbols. You cannot read it?"

"No," I answer while looking at them. "Are you Churrian, as well, Ms. Lucy?"

"Yes, I am. I arrived at the same time as your father and Luther. They worked on locating you, my dear, where many others began their work to protect you. No one has come or gone from earth since. Well, with some exceptions, beings whose vibrations are quite high and don't need to use vortexes in order to travel."

"Beings like Mikiel?" I ask.

"Yes, and others," she answers vaguely. "There is a great deal for you to understand," she says with a sigh. "Mikiel is the only one who is permitted to travel to and from earth at this time."

"What is Mikiel? I know that he is a Light Warrior, but what is that?"

"I am not sure how to best answer you," she replies with a chuckle.

"Please don't laugh at me."

"I'm not, dear. It's just difficult for me to explain what your soul already knows. You lived and walked as a Light Warrior for more than 10,000 years, Meelah. You should answer this and if you have questions regarding who you were, perhaps Mikiel is better suited to answer them.”

I continue to gaze out the window then at the three symbols. I run my pointer finger over them, outlining their form. I do this a few times. Then I read—no, I feel—their meaning.

“The first symbol means earth, the second means water, the third means the golden beings.”

Anxious, I look at Ms. Lucy, who is also processing. I am still familiarizing myself with how quickly communication happens when the other being sees your emotions as plainly as a reflection in a mirror.

“Who are the golden beings?” I ask, though I already know from her perplexed expression that she, too, is thrown by the last symbol.

After another close examination, I perceive that she has deciphered its meaning. Her energy becomes filled with a sense of contentment.

“This symbol is for the Timeera. They have two purposes. They are known as the record keepers and, most importantly, they maintain balance between the Light Force and the Dark Force. They are impartial beings and are mysterious. Meelah, I do not comprehend why they would be involved with your amulet.”

Swiftly, she rubs the window, erasing any evidence of the symbols. I listen to her sleeve squeak against the glass as she polishes them away vigorously. Then she hands me the single white orchid.

“Take it. It will assist you in remembering not only who you are, but all the knowledge from your last incarnation. And Meelah, trust no one, not even me, with the location of your amulet. He wants it. More important, he doesn’t want you to locate it. Trust no one with this information.”

I breathe onto the window again, right where I drew the three symbols. Though I just watched Ms. Lucy wipe them clean, they still exist as if they are imprinted into the surface of the glass. I close my eyes and run my hand over the window's cool surface. The area fogged by my breath, the symbols—all of it erases. All of it disappears.

"That should do it then," I say out loud.

"Yes, that will do. Your visit back to Churria was quite fruitful, I see. Your powers are awakening," she states. "Oh, dear, look at the time. I must keep up appearances. However, I yearn for Churria. I, above all, long for my son and my Faro, but I am enjoying my time here, especially since you have finally arrived. Your father was supposed to have you here a year ago, but he did what he thought was best."

She shuffles through papers at the top of the pile. Then she opens a drawer and takes out a clip. After fastening the ornamental clip to the sheets of paper, she hands them to me. With her calm and always warm energy, she takes hold of my hand and again, she peers into my eyes. I feel so humbled by the many having left their homes for me. I now stand before one who, like my father, is making a difference here on earth.

"Take these, dear, this is your true schedule. Remember, appearances are quite important. If you can blend in and not make waves it will be more difficult for the other four 'humans' who have been overtaken by the Dark Force to locate you. The one that Mikiel killed has been on you and your father's trail for some time. But you already know that, Meelah," she says with a gentle voice. "I really must be off now and so should you. Enjoy your advanced placement classes," she says while winking.

With my new schedule and white orchid in hand, I make my way down the hallway. These passageways are quiet and empty, and I ruminate on how nice this is. I make a quick stop to the lady's room.

But I realize that I am not alone. From right outside my stall I hear giggling. I look under the stall door and see no feet, no legs; I see nothing, but I continue to hear the condescending laughter.

I pull up then zip and button my pants and open the stall door.

"She doesn't even have the courtesy of flushing," the unfamiliar voice spouts.

As I step out of my stall, I am picked up and flung across the room. My back slams against the wall hard; so hard that I am breathless. I lift my hand to freeze time.

"Look at her now," the invisible presence says with a hint of contempt. "And she is the one chosen to defeat the army of the Dark Force? Meelah, little Meelah, your trick of freezing time—it doesn't work on me!" the voice says, now in front of me.

Grabbing the sink, I pull myself to my feet. Immediately, I take another blow, but this time it is to my face. Again, the strike sends me clear across the room. Landing with a resounding thud, I slide to a stop. Anger rises within as I taste my own blood. I remove my hair from my face. Some of it sticks to my lip, pasted with blood. Pulling it back, I tuck it behind my ears. To say that I am pissed is an understatement.

"Anger, finally! But let's look at you! You're still lying on the floor—pathetic! I guess he chose wrong. Too bad for all these humans, I suppose that they really don't deserve this planet anyway."

"Who are you?" I shout. "Show yourself, you coward!"

"Who am I? That's your question? Shouldn't you be wondering what you can learn from this, oh chosen one?"

Then I see her. The being stands before the middle mirror. She appears as a human, but obviously is not. Her thick, shiny brown locks frame her face. Dressed in black leather boots, a long skirt and a tight blue sweater, she fixes her hair and applies red lipstick. She purses her lips then blows herself an obnoxious kiss. Sauntering past me, she tosses me her lipstick.

"Oh, I suppose you really don't need this. Look at you, your lip is already red, bloody, but red. Thanks, Meelah, this has been fun," she says with a laugh as she proceeds into the hallway.

I try to pull myself together both emotionally and physically. Coming to a stand, I grab paper towels and dab my bloody and swollen bottom lip. It seems to be getting bigger by the second. I feel pain everywhere! What just happened?

I didn't believe a body could endure such blows. This creature would have crumpled a human. Her sheer might was incredible. I look around the bathroom and see the collateral damage. The wall looks dented in the shape of my upper body. As I stretch and move around, nothing feels broken, nothing but my ego. Again, I stare at my face and stand in utter shock. My lip has healed! The red marks on my cheeks are gone! Everything is repaired, leaving no evidence of what just occurred. I stand in awe.

I move my body around again and it, too, has mended itself. Thinking back, far back, to my childhood, I begin to wonder. Have I ever been injured, or even sick, for that matter? I have been fatigued but no, I have never been plagued by illness, disease or injury.

I see a broken shard of glass from the far left mirror. I remember flying past it when I was flung across the room. My body must have hit it somehow, shattering its corner. Walking over, I pick up and hold the small piece in my hand. I open the palm of my left hand and deliberately cut a diagonal line into it. The line runs from my pointer finger all the way down to the right side of my palm. Instantly, I begin to bleed. My entire palm fills with thick, deep red blood. Though this experiment has pained me, I am willing to risk not using my left hand if my theory is erroneous. My blood overflows my palm and runs down both sides of my left hand. Eventually, gravity draws it into the white porcelain sink. Each drip changes shape as it expands and dilutes into the wetness already present in the sink basin. The dripping ceases and I bring my attention back to the palm of my hand. There is a residual pool of blood within my palm. I wipe it away and reveal my findings. I marvel at this new revelation. My palm has healed. Only a minimal amount of blood remains and I rinse it away. While drying my hand, I scrutinize it again. Not a mark—no evidence of tearing into it remains. I move my fingers around in the air. There is no soft tissue injury, nor any residual pain.

Again I inspect my face, especially my lip. All has been restored, all but a few strands of my hair that are still matted with blood. I rinse them, removing the last physical evidence of my brawl with whatever that being is. Just the wall and mirror damage remain.

Having gained this incredible knowledge, I am almost grateful for this experience. I hold my bag deliberately with my left hand and open it. Upon inspection, I see that the white orchid remains safe and unharmed. Beside the dainty orchid is my new schedule from Ms. Lucy. As I pull it out the bell conveniently fires off and the hallway outside the bathroom fills with the clamorous sounds of students.

"What happened here?" a brunette asks casually as she and two other girls come into the bathroom.

"Perhaps the janitors had a fight. It was probably Joseph Holmez's father. You do know that he works here at the school?" the obnoxious redhead retorts.

"Well, I don't care what his father does, he's hot. As long as my parents don't know that he's poor, I'd do him." Gazing at her reflection in the mirror, the blonde adds, "But let's be real, my parents only know what I want them to know."

Hearing them laugh amongst themselves, I continue to wrap the precious white orchid. I secure it again in my bag. Wanting nothing more than to quickly head off, I hurry. I wish not to engage with them especially after they continue to put down Joseph's father. Moving hastily, I gather my things.

"You're Meelah, right?" the bouncy blonde asks.

All three girls look at me, awaiting my response. I am not sure if she asked or stated who I am. Rising, I come to a stand.

"Yes, I am Meelah," I answer them.

"She's pretty. I wish my hair looked like that," I hear the fair-skinned redhead say in her mind.

"I don't like her. She's too skinny and damn, she's tall. Bloomingdale's sells her bag. I remember it from last year's sale," the rude blonde mumbles in her mind.

But I hear nothing from the brunette. This intrigues me. I continue to stand there delving deeper into her thoughts, but still there is only silence.

"I like your accent, Meelah. Where are you from?" the blonde asks while fixing her makeup.

"I am from South Africa," I answer.

I still wait for a thought from the brunette to come through. Feeling as though I am somehow tuning an antenna, I wait for something. I expect something.

"But you're not black, or African American. I know how touchy people can be if you don't use the correct term," the blonde says, revealing her ignorance.

I don't dignify her with an answer; instead, I continue to probe the brunette's mind but still there is nothing. Only silence. This intriguing girl doesn't even look at me. Her expression appears blank. Unfortunately, it's time for me to go since the bell will sound any second. Answers will have to wait, for now.

Reluctantly, I turn to leave. About to open the door, I hear the blonde spout, "Oh, my name is Sharon." Then she points to the redhead, "This is Sally." Finally her bony little finger points to the brunette, "This is Shelly. We are the S's, here at Religards."

I pause, I can't help myself. I was so close to putting distance between me and the pretentious Sharon. But I ask anyway. "Are you telling me that you three are the only seniors, no, students here at Religards with names that begin with an S?"

"The only ones that matter," Sally answers.

They laugh amongst themselves though that was hardly a comedic answer. Again I try to read Shelly's thoughts and again retrieve nothing. It is as if she blocks me somehow. *What is she, I wonder?*

"Are you going stand in front of the door, Meelah? Perhaps her English is limited, being from South Africa, after all. Please move...we have to go to class...now," Sharon drawls, extending the words as if I can't understand her.

Truthfully, I am blocking the door but I do it to read, hear or even feel something from Shelly. Opening the door, I remain holding it open for them to exit. I wait for Shelly to walk past me, in hopes of receiving something. She walks by me without a glance my way. I find her silent concealed energy intriguing.

"Meelah," a kind familiar voice says to me.

I overhear Sharon say hello to Joseph as she strolls by him. She flips her hair and purses her lips while Joseph simply nods his head to the group. Still the mystery of who Shelly is captivates me. Again, I wonder how she blocked me from hearing her thoughts.

"Meelah, hello there, wake up," Joseph jokes, while standing beside me. "Why are you holding the ladies room door open? Wow, what happened in there?" he continues, while looking past me and into the wrecked bathroom.

Stepping forward, I allow the door to close. In my hand is my schedule and I become aware that Joseph is reading it. I watch him as he tries to make sense of some of the class titles. It's probably better to allow him to see my classes instead of hiding them and piquing his interest. Also, I want to hear his thoughts. I wonder if he's questioning who I am. I want to trust him. My instincts trust him, but I must be sure. I tune in to his mind.

"She smells so sweet, kind of like cotton candy. Two more periods before lunch. I can't wait. Damn, I'm hungry!"

Okay then. He's not reading my classes. Unable to restrain my smile, my face beams. He's so funny and also quite famished. He's a friend and I don't use that word loosely. Still wearing his vibrant red knitted hat, he stands out and doesn't care. He is authentic and genuine.

The bell rings again signaling that the start of a new class. Joseph still acts like he's reading my schedule, but he's not. However, to my surprise, he points to the place on my schedule indicating my third period.

"You have to go to room H-6—what room is that?" he asks.

"I'll find my way. Go ahead, you're already late."

"Are you sure? I don't even know where that room is, Meelah."

"I'll find it."

"I'll see you for lunch, then? I'm starving!"

"Yes, I'll see you then, Joseph," I answer.

With a grin, he turns then darts down the hall, the hall that is rapidly clearing of all students. Again, I find myself alone and late for my next class. Looking down at my schedule, I see, "Ms. Maya, room H-6, Advanced Theoretical Studies." Closing my eyes, I allow some sort of inner navigational force to guide me. This pull brings me down four flights of stairs then a long hallway. Finally, I stand before a door. Upon opening my eyes, I read its number, H-6, so I open the door and see her! The same being that gave me a beating about ten minutes ago. Well, she has the same face, but her hair is slicked straight back and pulled up in a tight bun. She's now wearing thin black-rimmed glasses and a conservative grey pantssuit. Her energy is different, as well.

"Come in, come in, Meelah. You are late, you know. You'd better not make a habit of that. I have a great deal for you to remember in a short amount of time. Now take a seat and open the book I have provided for you to page sixty-two."

"Who are you?" I inquire as I look around the empty class-room. "I'm pretty sure that you are the one who just threw me around in the bathroom. I will not just take a seat. I expect some kind of explanation, apology—something!"

"Oh my, I'm so sorry," she answers while approaching me.

Instinctively, I brace myself. Making fists with my hands as if I'm a boxer, I'm ready. I will not be a victim again!

"That was my...that was Tali. She can be quite crass, but I assure you, once you gain her respect she will be a devoted ally. Did she injure you?"

"Only my ego," I answer, still suspicious. "What are you two?"

"We are the same, all three of us. Pasha, or Ms. Lucy as you know her, calls us the 'sisters.' "

"All three of you, what do you mean?"

"I am Maya, you met Tali, and then there is Riya. She has always been the most liked of us all. I represent knowledge; Tali, strength and tactical maneuvers; Riya, camouflage. Riya can blend into any social scene anywhere and do it flawlessly. Don't ever underestimate the power of camouflage."

"Are you schizophrenic?"

"Oh no, that is a human condition. We are not human. Tali isn't terribly fond of humans, but I am indifferent regarding them. Riya *loves* humans, finds them entertaining, especially the males."

I move closer, inspecting her. I am still unsure of how to react. *How does she change into these other personalities? I wonder.*

"You must really work harder on consistently blocking your thoughts and your mind. Riya can help you with this. But to answer your question, my other sisters are NOT personalities; they are quite physical, in fact."

"Are you triplets?" I ask in audible words.

"No. Your reasoning is extremely limited," she answers, chuckling at me. "We are one. Only one of us comes into form at a time, though. Since this is an intellectual query, I am the one who must explain it; therefore, I am in physical form. If Tali were here, she would most likely knock you around some more, and Riya, she would be encouraging you find out who Shelly Ranoe truly is," she says. Delving briefly into my thoughts, she continues. "You've already lost your curiosity regarding Shelly from the bathroom? We do have a tremendous job before us. Take a seat and open your book to page sixty-two. Perhaps I should do it for you?"

With a wave of her thin feminine hand, I notice the book in front of me open then flip to the correct page. I take a seat and see her write on the chalkboard, but she has no chalk. She has nothing in her hand. Casually, she turns around and picks up a big mug, with the word *LOVE* on it. While she sips, words—no, symbols—are appearing on the chalkboard. She seems to manifest them with her mind.

Gazing at page sixty-two, I see that the text consists of symbols like the ones she is writing—like the symbols I saw earlier in my mind. I realize that I just gave her the information. With my one loose thought she knows that the amulet is here on earth. I look at Maya. She rolls her eyes at me.

Closing my eyes for a brief moment, I deliberately shield both my thoughts and mind. I visualize a translucent wrap enveloping me. Then I open my eyes with confidence, and I feel an innate connection to something bigger than me.

Again I look at the symbols on the page, and this time I hear their meaning. In amazement, I look up at Ms. Maya, who is smiling at me. From my expression and body language, she intuits that I understand the ancient language but in a breath's time her smile shifts into a more serious expression. I can sense her trying to enter my thoughts, but she's unable to do so. Her energy pokes into my invisible shield like one would poke at a balloon. My protection is pliable and yielding but, most importantly, she cannot penetrate it.

Proud of myself, I read—no, I hear the meaning of the Churrian symbols. I sense profound pain within them—great adversity. These symbols communicate directly to me. They touch a place deep within my soul, stirring it, awakening it.

The secret language speaks of wars upon wars, death, destruction and pure annihilation of innocent beings—planets destroyed leaving nothing behind but charred matter. Intense sadness is infused in this story.

The next symbols continue to pain me. In my mind, I even hear the cries from unsuspecting beings. They were innocent creatures consumed by a Dark Force that brutally slaughtered them. This grotesque effort to annihilate all such pure-hearted beings is beyond ruthless. The cries of these beings consume me. Their agony overcomes me.

Their plight is real as is their anguish. My logical mind cannot comprehend the senseless nature of what I'm seeing and hearing. I become voracious for more information.

With my eyes closed, I continue to run my hand across each symbol. I flip rapidly through the pages of this primordial Churrian book. These symbols no longer communicate to my rational mind. There is *nothing* sane about this destruction, death and agony. The communication speaks only to my heart.

I continue to hear the cries from the unsuspecting pure beings, but more and more suffer a horrific fate. They fall to their demise. Fainter and softer become their pleas for help. Then, silence. There is no life. An entire kind has been destroyed. All that remains are the menacing creatures. Their grotesque forms have taken all life here. Though my heart is filled with sorrow for the fallen innocent, something else begins to consume me. It is not merely anger, but fury. The symbols representing these venomous beings controlled by darkness become repugnant to me, revolting. Each time my hand goes over their symbol I feel the wicked force within them.

"How dare they? What gives them this right? They must be stopped. THEY MUST BE STOPPED!" I shout.

As passion overwhelms me, I raise my eyes and see Ms. Maya lower her head to me. She doesn't speak as she comes over to where I am sitting. Leaning forward, she closes the ancient Churrian book in front of me. Her features are perfect and her face pale, like that of a porcelain doll. Her black-rimmed glasses somehow fit her academic persona. Her hazel-colored eyes behind her glasses pierce me as if she wishes for me to see something within them.

Then I feel it. I see the connection. I know why she chose these symbols to tell this unbelievable story. This is her story. She is the last of her kind. She abruptly turns away in a failed attempt at concealing her pain, Tali's pain and Riya's pain. Green tears cascade down her face, framing it. She cries for herself. She cries for her family. She cries for all of her kind that no longer number among the living. She mourns them all.

I place my hand over hers. I feel her grief as if it were mine. She uses her other hand to wipe her emerald tears. They smudge her face, leaving a jade-tinted mark behind. Though her tears are beautiful, they are overflowing with tangible angst.

There is more to this story; I sense it. I know that I am strong enough to delve into her thoughts and see it, but I don't. I respect her, her sorrow and the plight of all her kind. They were pure-hearted. There exists no rational way to accept destruction such as this.

She is ready to continue on with the story. But this time the book remains closed. She wishes for me to see what happened within her eyes, in an intimate connection between us.

I see white light. It descends over the creatures that destroyed her kind. The light spreads, it is the Light Warriors. They viciously take down the creatures. They embody my drive, my revulsion toward the iniquitous Dark Force and the vile creatures that are controlled by it.

When the Light Warriors realize they are too late, this fuels them. They eliminate all the contemptible beings, but they stand defeated. None of the Light Warriors have fallen, but they have lost this battle. They stand knee-deep in the needless slaughter of innocents.

An inexplicable shift has occurred. A single Light Warrior flies across this now desolate planet. Hope is now replacing utter loss. They land and I watch; I feel them listen. I also hear a faint sound. There is life.

I walk as one of the Light Warriors. I see through their eyes and hear with their senses. I feel powerful and driven like I have never felt before. Physically, I am as strong as a Light Warrior—more powerful than I feel in this form. With this prevailing dynamism, I search through the debris, through the bodies of the fallen pure. One remains, I know it. Continuing my search, other Light Warriors join me curious, as to what I am sensing.

I stop. Here it is. I lift one of the bodies among the many, the dead, but I still feel life near it. Holding one of my hands over the deceased form, I scan it for life and again I sense a heartbeat. As reverently as I can I unwrap its clothing. Another Light Warrior lands beside me. I feel her question my unusual actions. Gently, I lower the deceased down and come to a stand. Spreading my tremendous white wings, I emit a power I never knew I possessed. The young Light Warrior drops to her knees and bows to me. Another Light Warrior lands beside me with a resounding thud, it is Mikiel. He, too, drops to his knees in my presence. All of the remaining Light Warriors land around me. Their impact vibrates the surface beneath my feet. One by one, they drop to their knees and lower their heads. Eventually, I am the only one standing. I retract my wings, which are stained with blood and charred from battle. I am surrounded by my remaining kind. They, too, have diminished over time. We have suffered great loss in our pursuit. We were once 10,000 Light Warriors. They have passionately battled against the Dark Force; now, we are no more than one thousand.

I kneel back down and the other Light Warriors rise to a stand. I can feel it. My senses must be more acute than theirs. Life is present; I know it and I will find it. Life gives hope. One life saved, one life...I repeat to myself.

I unwrap the dead being's clothing. Beneath layers upon layers of blood-saturated linen, is a small swaddled bundle. I unwrap the innocent youngster. Its parent saved her by concealing her deep within its clothing. Soaked in her parent's blood, one survives. I take this last being into my arms. This young one doesn't cry; it doesn't make a sound.

I set her down and she stands among my magnificent kind. She is surrounded by both Light and destruction. I reach down and take her hand into mine.

"Though you must leave with us, you mustn't forget your kind or this day," I say to her.

The vision ends and again I am looking into Ms. Maya's eyes. They are filled with tears. But this time her iridescent green tears come from a place of gratitude. She removes her glasses and lowers her head to me.

I am the one who saved her. With this epiphany, I am overwhelmed with emotion. I come to a stand and, as soon as I do, Maya drops to her knees. Her head is still bowed. I place my hands together at my chest and give her the bow of my head. I ask that she rise.

"What does one say?" I ask in a whisper.

"I would like to say thank you," she answers.

Chapter Eight

The bell sounds. It is the end of another day at Religards. Ms. Maya wipes her face with a tissue. She works hard to erase all evidence of her tears, though their green residue has stained her flawless fair complexion.

The day has flown by. I even missed lunch! But I'm grateful that I remained here, immersed in this knowledge, with Ms. Maya. I realize now how much I need to learn; how much I want to learn. The gap between who I was and who I am baffles me. I need answers.

"Ms. Maya, may I continue to read the Churrian book?"

Still wiping her face, she replies, "Meelah, please address me as Maya. As for the Churrian book, this will be all for today. You have another teacher who is waiting to meet you. You should be on your way. I look forward to tomorrow," she says with love.

Then she disappears from sight. She's gone! I turn to look all around me and, again, I find myself alone. I glance around for the Churrian book wishing to learn more, but it, too, has vanished. The symbols on the board have faded. The classroom is as it was when I arrived—empty.

I pull out my schedule and see that I have another class at 2:35 in the basement. A regular school day ends at 2:20, but I am again reminded that I am not "normal." This class is my last for the day and it has no ending time. I have fifteen minutes to eat the fruit I brought, drink a little water and find the place. I have to go to the very bowels of Religards. I wonder what's down there.

While biting into my delicious, sweet apple, I remember that I also missed Joseph at lunch. Though it feels nice to meet a genuine person like Joseph, I have so much to learn. My plate is beyond full.

Continuing down the steps, I finally reach the bottom. I take a swig of water then shove my apple core into my backpack. This is a disgusting habit, but I wish not to litter. This little practice of mine has backfired on me. Many times I have reached into my backpack and touched gross rot that I have forgotten to place in the trash. If this is the least of my problems, I'm pretty fortunate.

While standing at the base of the steps, I sense something. The fluorescent lights above me flicker. Uncertain of what to expect, I place my bag on the floor. Ahead of me is a door and behind me are the stairs that ascend up the many levels of Religards.

Using my instincts, I open the door before me. Mindfully, I enter an enormous dimly lit room. The floor and the walls are gray concrete. Above me are pipes that run as far I as can see. Moisture trickles down from them adding even more character to this wide-open space.

Someone else is here with me. Sensing a presence, I look around the room and see something lying on the concrete floor. It glows as it draws me closer. I wonder if this is a trap; the glimmering thing acting as bait. But like a rabbit drawn to carrots,

I cautiously approach. My favorite boots make noise with each step. I try to walk on the balls of my feet in an effort to muffle the noise. Instinctively, I quickly twist my hair up into a bun. If something is going to happen I don't need it in my way.

After tiptoeing over to the gleaming metal object, I can see that it is a sword. Looking down, I see my reflection in its burnished surface. I also see Tali's reflection from behind me.

I roll onto the hard, unyielding concrete floor and take hold of the sword. Both of us are surprised by my little move. I see her smile; she likes the challenge. Tali strikes at me with her sword and I raise mine into the air, blocking her. Our swords make a loud clatter when they strike against one another. My sword is heavy, or perhaps I am weak. Regardless, Tali continues to come at me. Her wild curls fly as she attempts to thrash me. Her hair is reminiscent of angered snakes. She resembles Medusa. Despite becoming winded, I defend myself.

That is all I am doing, I am only defending myself. Blocking her every strike, I am increasingly fatigued as a result. My sword becomes more of a challenge to wield. It has only been five minutes—a long five minutes.

Tali laughs at me. I realize that, in my weakened physical state, I have dropped the shield guarding my thoughts. I try to both protect my thoughts and myself but this fatigues me even faster.

Then she hits me. Her sword slices into my arm like a knife into warm butter. Immediately, I feel heat then pain in my left shoulder. I glance down to assess my injury. The sight of my blood infuriates me!

Raising my sword with my right hand, I lunge at her with all of my might. I didn't even know that this power was in my exhausted body. She takes steps back for the first time and I continue at her. Her expression changes from a smug smile to a grave expression. For a moment, I see fear in her eyes as something takes over me. I wield my sword and finally her back is against the wall.

Breathless, I strike again but deliberately hit the wall behind her. She disappears from sight. I sense her, I hear her belittling giggles.

With my sword raised, I shift left then right, wondering where she has gone. I glance at my wound and see it's beginning to heal. The sleeve of my shirt is ripped and my entire arm is drenched in my own blood. This is the second time I've met this nasty Tali and the second time she's caused me to bleed—all in one day!

I feel her all around me. She mocks me. Moving into the very center of the room, I then close my eyes. Collecting myself, I make sure that my shield is raised so that my thoughts are protected as well.

I raise my sword in front of me. My razor-sharp blade measures from the top of my head down to the handle that rests at my waist. I wait for her to approach me. I can feel that she is unsure of what I'm doing—unsure of what I'm capable of. Self-doubt opens her telepathic thoughts to me. She becomes vulnerable and now, I'm able read her mind. I know what her next step will be.

I grin as I sense her behind me. Turning around as quick as the crack of a whip, I clutch my sword and press it into her neck. She smirks and drops her blade. I lower my sword and catch my breath.

"You're sloppy, Meelah," she criticizes, wiping her sweat.

"I'm out of shape," I answer, thoroughly winded and exhausted.

She picks up her sword and stands beside me. I don't trust her, not at all. I am on guard. She raises her sword then places her weight forward as she thrusts her sword into the air beside me. She walks back to me and does it again and again. Parry, parry, thrust, thrust. I watch, and I do the same. I drive forward over and over again. My arm burns, it is weak but I continue as does she. Watching her, I then mimic her. I work through my pain; I use my pain. I don't let it stop me even though it tries. The mere thought of her kind being annihilated fuels me. Tali can no longer read my thoughts, but I know she feels this fresh surge of determination within me. I begin to earn a little respect. This process is as sluggish as a snail but I remain steadfast.

We continue until neither of us can move. Hours have passed and the two of us are saturated with sweat. She sits down and I do the same.

Exhausted doesn't equate to how I feel. My body is heavy and every muscle aches. I examine my arm and see it has healed. Only my ripped and bloody shirt illustrates that something happened. I look over at Tali who is running her hands through her hair, which is dampened by sweat. Her long, lush, almost frizzy locks cover her face.

"This has been fun. You'd better get some rest. Tomorrow is another day," she says in earnest.

Aching, I rise to a stand and say, "Here's your sword, Tali." The sword becomes heavy as she simply looks at me. I continue to hold it for her until I can no longer do so.

"It's yours, Meelah. It has always been yours," she answers. She lowers her head to me, grins, and then vanishes. She is no longer here. I can't sense her at all.

I must learn how to travel like her—no, like them. Are all of the "sisters" a singular being or are they a plural? Unsure, I continue on my way to the door with my sword in hand. How am I going to travel the streets of New York with an ancient golden sword? It is about three feet long; too big to conceal. It is definitely a conversation starter.

Nonetheless, I wrap my coat around it and stick it into my bag. It obviously doesn't fit, but it is less apparent. I drag myself up the endless flights of stairs. With each step my muscles complain in a new area of my physical form, but I persist. I make it up to the main floor. Opening the doors, I see that the hallway is still lit. The empty and quiet halls are pleasing after the day I've had. Pushing the front door open, I leave school to begin my cold journey home.

Truly the streets of New York never sleep. People are always walking and cars travelling. Lights from stores create a radiance that spills out onto the sidewalks. While waiting for a signal light to change, I become aware of the panic from the stranger beside me. She stares at my bloody sleeve. This is not easy to explain. I walk off, darting between the cars. If I can handle Tali for four hours, I can navigate around slow-moving cars.

At last, I am home. Desitere is waiting outside as if he knew I was on my way. Perhaps he did.

"Have a fun day, Meelah? Looks like you'll need a new shirt for tomorrow."

"That I will," I say to him. "You look nice and fresh, Desitere."

"Thank you. I just began my shift. Have a good evening, Meelah."

As I wait for the elevator, I become acutely aware of the door to the stairs right behind me. "Get moving, Meelah," I tell myself.

I am a glutton for punishment! Opening the door, I begin to haul myself up more flights of stairs. My bag, still holding my sword, becomes increasingly heavy. The strap to my bag feels like it's permanently indented in my shoulder.

The first flight is brutal! My legs are burning and heavy to lift. But progressively, my aching muscles begin to move with more ease. With this alleviation, I increase my pace from the speed of a tortoise to the swiftness of a cat and not just any cat, a feline that is bounding away from a predator. Now at the seventh floor, I feel joy as I move even more effortlessly up the stairs. I grab the railing and use it to propel me forward more rapidly. Who thought that stairs could be so much fun?

I am there. I made it, and I feel great! Striding down the hallway and arriving at my door, I seriously cannot believe how good I feel. An hour ago I was racked with pain—all of me, even my fingers. Well, perhaps that's a bit of an exaggeration. But I was hurting in a way that I never felt before, at least not in this physical form.

Ecstatic, I reach out to open the door, but it's locked. For fun, I try a little experiment. As I close my eyes, I visualize the dead bolt turning to the unlocked position. Then I do the same to the lower lock. They both unlock and I open the door. I have so much to share with my father and Luther.

The statues greet me as I walk past them. Their high frequency vibration almost tickles me. I cannot believe that I was once so unaware of their power and resonance. I have spent far too much time in my life asleep. But I realize now that I must become aware. I must fully awaken.

I breeze into my room and change out of my bloody clothing. I toss aside the destroyed Religards uniform and pull on my jeans and a white T-shirt. Glancing over at my obtrusive sword still in my bag, I wonder how it is that no one commented on it as I walked home. Perhaps someone did and I didn't notice because I was too consumed with arriving at my destination. I reach into my bag, lift out the delicate white orchid and place it on my window sill. While looking at the pristine flower, I feel it. Something is wrong. The pit of my stomach begins to ache. Something has happened. My energy shifts. I must find my father, I must....

Sensing that he is in his bedroom, I move quickly to him. The door is open and I see him sitting on the corner of his bed. He's leaning over Luther and dabbing his side with what looks like an herbal concoction. Luther has been injured and quite badly. In his human form, there is a gash in his side running from his armpit down to the bottom of his ribs.

"What has happened, Father?" I yell.

He doesn't answer and his reticent presence begins to enrage me. Tali has helped me awaken an inner strength. I now understand that I required anger today to be able to fight. Fury fuels me. Being passive will no longer protect any of us. The Dark Force will step on then crush me if I allow it but here and now something has occurred. With a tad calmer tone to my voice, I ask him again.

"Father, being silent will no longer help anyone. You must stop trying to protect me. What has happened here?"

"Meelah, come with me into the kitchen," my father answers.

I hear Luther whimper like a wounded animal. My father leaves the room and I am drawn to Luther's side. The pathetic sounds he's emitting break my heart. My eyes fill with tears. He begins to writhe in pain. The herbs that my father just slathered into his wound seem to be adding to that agony.

"Luther, it's Meelah, I'm here with you," I say in a soft voice while trying to keep him still.

I place one of my hands on his head and the other on his hip. This seems to stabilize him. He nuzzles his head into my hand in the same way he did when he shifted into a Galidrome. I sense he simply wishes not to be alone.

I continue to hold my hands on him, but suddenly he becomes still, too still. His breathing also becomes shallower. I lean over to see his face. It is pale and off color.

"Father!" I scream telepathically. "Come here!"

My father runs back in with his hands full of supplies. As he rushes over to his dear friend, I move over to the other side of the bed. I watch my father tend to him with medical training I never knew he had.

"It is the herbs, they are working. I gave him a sedative so that I can thoroughly clean out then sew up his wound. But he's still burning up. This is not good. Meelah, get me some wet towels."

Dashing into my bathroom, I saturate three towels. On my way back to my father's room I hear, "You possess the power to save him, Meelah." This high and intense pure energy makes all the hair on my arms stand on end. This voice out of nowhere overwhelms me—stopping me in place. I have never felt energy as powerful as this.

"Meelah, hurry!" I hear my father shout.

Instinctively, almost as if someone is steering me, I drop the towels into a big wet heap. Then I rush into the kitchen and open a drawer. I take out the sharpest knife we have. It is a just-sharpened paring knife. I proceed back to my father's room holding the four-inch knife pointed down in my right hand. When I enter the bedroom, my father looks at me almost as if he doesn't recognize me.

"What are you doing? Where are the towels, Meelah? We're losing him." His face takes on a look of horror as he asks, as if in a panic, "Is that a knife?"

With my mind, I tell him that everything will be okay—that I'm being driven by another force, a white force. I communicate to him that this is divine and that it wants to help Luther.

My father scrutinizes me, seeking the truth of my message. He loves his dear devoted friend and he doesn't want to risk losing him.

Then he sees it. I have been pushed aside, while an unusual bright light utilizes my physical form. He tells me later that my eyes turned white as light radiated out from them. My father is quick to step back and allows me, as I'm guided by this intense energy, to approach Luther.

I'm aware that the life force in Luther is tenuous. The injury is robbing him of strength. He no longer makes a sound. There is little breath within him now. But Luther doesn't want to leave. He wants to remain with me and my father, and the light that consumes me has a purpose for him. I watch from behind this magnificent force. It raises my left hand and, in slow motion, it slices a deep cut into the palm of my right hand. I feel the burning from the incision. Then the presence runs the knife across the palm of my right hand again, slow and deep—to form an X. The pain is intense. The gashes in my hand are so deep that it takes a moment for my blood to start seeping out. But in a flash, my hand begins to bleed profusely. The light holds my bleeding hand over Luther's wound. I watch as my blood drops into his deep gash. The entire wound receives droplets of my blood until my hand begins to self heal, ceasing the flow.

The brilliant power within me pulls upward as it dissipates. I feel myself fall to the floor as soon as the white light vacates my body. I am heavy and temporarily stunned. My body feels like it's going into shock. All of me shakes; I feel intense heat then profound cold. My body struggles to rebalance itself. I lie there and finally, I experience peace. I feel warmth again as I promptly normalize.

Anxious, I sit up, wondering if Luther is okay. I see my father. He is kneeling right by my side. Quickly, I bound to my feet and over to Luther. I smile at the sight of him. His wound is healing right before our eyes. His deep tissue and muscles repair and the gash that once was, begins to close.

I look at my father and see that he is also smiling at this miracle. His relief is almost tangible. He glances at me with love, but that look swiftly changes. He takes my face with his hands and peers into my eyes.

"Meelah, your eyes," he says, astonished. "Look at them," he urges.

I walk over to the small mirror above my father's dresser. My hair is still up in a bun, though several loose strands frame my face. I curl them behind my ears. Then I see it. My eyes! What has happened to my eyes? They are a very light green. Moments ago, they were a dark brown. For the last seventeen, almost eighteen, years, my eyes have been dark—dark as night. Now they look bleached. Perhaps the tremendous white force that flowed into my form altered them. I turn back to my father, uncertain how I feel about this dramatic change.

"You're beautiful, Meelah," he says tenderly. "You saved Luther. Come and see. His injury has almost completely closed. His temperature has also stabilized. How is your hand?"

I almost forgot about my hand. Turning it over, I examine my palm. I don't feel the injury but I have a large scar. In the shape of an X, it covers the palm of my right hand. I show my father and he outlines it with a finger.

"I don't know what to say, Meelah. I didn't initially trust you, and I ask for your forgiveness," he admits, lowering his head. "I foolishly forgot who you are, who you are destined to become," he adds, with deep emotion in his words. He looks into my new, light green-shaded eyes while tears fill his. "Meelah, I have to let you go. You are no longer a little girl. I have to let you go," he repeats, in a poignant tone.

"Father, I hope that you never let me go; just allow me to follow my path."

"Samuel, Meelah, what are you doing over there? I'm so hungry," Luther says.

My father and I cannot help but chuckle. One moment Luther's on the verge of death and the next he's ravenous. We both go to him. His wound has healed, leaving no trace of a scar or any obvious residual damage. Luther sits up and stretches as if he's just awakened from a restful nap. His hair is as disheveled as ever.

"Luther, what happened to you?" I ask in earnest.

"Meelah, your eyes, they're beautiful," he answers while touching my face. "What happened to them? How did they change? They're so bright and full of light," he continues with a gentle smile.

"Luther, Father, you really must tell me what happened! Luther almost died. He would have died if I didn't give my blood. Stop protecting me! This tactic will no longer work. We must work together," I say with force.

"I was trying to protect your father. It was after him. It happened right in the lobby," Luther explains.

"Meelah," my father adds, getting my attention. "They are here in New York."

"Who is?" I ask, feeling like I'm finally making some headway.

"They are," my father answers, disquieted.

All three of us sit in silence. We exchange not a word or a thought. I know who "they" are. My father needn't explain or define them. They are here in New York. They are the last of four. They are the reason why my father has moved us all around the world. They embody him, they personify the Dark Force. This malevolent force has again taken control of beings' free will and this time these beings are humans. He sent five essences in total to earth the day I arrived. Mikiel has taken one down in front of Religards.

My presence here on earth has affected so many lives. I close my eyes. I feel my breath. I honor the changes to me and within me.

Mikiel, I need you, I state telepathically, in a manner meant only for him to hear.

I feel his presence, but his essence is subdued. Then I get it, the statues have blocked him. He has not been in this apartment since they were set up. This is a flaw! I bring my energy to the statues and ask them—no, tell them, to permit Mikiel's passage. With this action—my action—he physically rushes into my father's bedroom. Still adorned in a golden outfit suited for battle, he is here.

"Mikiel," Luther shouts in an excited and childlike manner.

Mikiel bows to everyone. My father looks at me and shakes his head. He knows that it was me who granted his entry. His disapproving expression tells me that it was he who blocked Mikiel. My father abruptly gets up and leaves. I know where he's going. He's going to the statues, but they now obey me. Honestly, I don't understand his action. Mikiel will help us, he is our ally. I mean no disrespect to my father, but I must trust my instincts.

Luther is rambling on to Mikiel about what he gallantly did for my father and how he almost died. He retells the story with ease to Mikiel, but was tight-lipped with me.

Mikiel steps closer to me. He is always drawn to me like a bee to a newly blossomed flower. He takes my right hand and turns it over and examines the X mark. He gently outlines it with his pointer finger. I look up at his face while smelling his sweet natural aroma. His energy is alluring. His eyes meet my new green eyes and, for the first time, I feel like one of his kind.

I feel like a Light Warrior. My body, mind and spirit personify this incarnation and I savor my strength.

He sees my newfound inner and outer strength and grins at me. His face changes when he smiles, his eyes soften as does his demeanor. Still holding my hand, he lowers down to one knee and looks up to me.

Luther prattles on in the background, oblivious to the profound reverence Mikiel is bestowing on me. Mikiel lowers his head and I can't help but close my eyes. I have been here before, in this precise position. I can almost feel the wings I once had. I experience their indescribable weight upon my back as if they are real. I honor their need to spread and extend them like a human would stretch her arms and body upon waking in the early morning. They fan out, consuming the space behind me. I hear each feather. My wings sound like an accordion fan when it opens. They are rejoicing at being free.

The sound of Luther's banter falls silent and I acutely feel the presence of my father, as well. I raise my head and open my eyes. Luther and my father have also lowered down and bowed to me.

My hair has come loose and tumbles down my back. I again feel my wings behind me. Embracing their innate power, I stand in a physical form similar to that of a human being, but I am not human. I do not feel Churrian. At this moment, I am like a Light Warrior. I recognize that I embody all three. I, for the first time in this life, in this form, which seemed stuck between three realities, comprehend what I am. I possess the mind of a Churrian, the body of a Light Warrior and the heart of a human being. I am all three.

I ask my father to raise his head and within his eyes, I see my mirror image. What I make out is bright white light outlining my wings within this reflection.

Reaching over my shoulder, I stretch to touch my wings—the wings that I see within my father's eyes. But when I turn around, there is only light. Touching this light with curiosity, I feel intense vibration, but nothing more.

"Father, this bright light could be quite difficult to explain to the average human being, assuming that they, too, can see it. If they can, I guess continuing at Religards is out of the question."

With these doubts, the white outlines of my wings diminish. I see them fade from the reflection in my father's eyes. It is only me that I now see. My doubts and ill-humor have dissolved my wings. I see that Mikiel, Luther and my father are still kneeling down and I don't feel worthy of this honor. I am not yet a leader.

"Please, all of you, stand up," I state. I am flooded with emotions yet I am unclear of which emotions they might be. They surge over me all at once.

One by one all three come to their feet. Mikiel sees through me. I feel a profound sense of loss or perhaps it's weakness. There is doubt and insecurity that resides in my human-like heart and I must overcome it. He is witness to all of my imperfections, and there are many. I have not mastered blocking him from my thoughts. I turn and move away from the group. Immediately, I overhear Luther speak to my father. He expresses how delighted he is that my father allowed Mikiel here.

"This was not of my doing," I hear my father say. His tone denotes how displeased he is by my actions.

"Enough!" I command, feeling frustrated. "We must be unified. We must work together. There is no time for whatever this is, Father. They are here, remember? How long do you think it will be before they come through the veil of protection from the statues? Come to think of it, if the Light Force that came through me and guided me to help Luther can come through, why can't the Dark Force? What is holding that force back?"

"Meelah, be careful with your words," my father answers in a frightened voice.

"Luther, Mikiel, please talk to him. My father has to understand that we must be cohesive. Without this, all of us will fail."

I turn and stride out of his room. I leave them all behind. Though there is admittedly an attraction to Mikiel, that is not what I need right now. I want and need a friend. My father is too frenzied with controlling my fate, a destiny that has already been written. His inner fight, the fight to let me go, is his weakness.

I cannot afford further limitations. I need a plan. If the beings possessed by the Dark Force are here, what is my next step? For starters I must come up with a name for these things.

"They are called Shadows," Mikiel says from behind me.

I sense him circle around to stand directly before me. He reaches his hand out and takes hold of my right hand again. He turns it over and re-examines the mark. I watch him study the scar on my palm as if he can read it.

"This is a key," he says in his cool voice.

"This mark is a key? A key to what?" I ask.

"You will know when you are meant to use it," he answers. He folds my hand and holds it within his. "Meelah, the Dark Force is not permitted here on earth, but that will change the moment you have been here for eighteen years," he explains. He then continues, "As for the current power of the Dark Force, he slipped in five Shadows here on earth before the vortexes stopped spinning upon your arrival. These Shadows only embody a portion of his power. Do you understand what I am telling you?" he asks, reading me with intent—reading my essence.

I see everything in his eyes. I look away. I see his fear. He is uncertain that I am ready for what I face and, most relevant, he wishes not to lose me again.

"How am I to conquer what even you feel I cannot?"

He pulls me into his arms and holds me. His arms cinch tightly around me like a belt. I feel his bare arm against my face. His scent is so sweet. I close my eyes and stand within his energy, within his embrace. He wants nothing from me. He just holds me close.

Chapter Nine

I open my eyes. I must have fallen asleep after my words with my father and Mikiel's much-needed squeeze. The dark of night coats all around me. I sit up. Once my eyes adjust, I see that I am on our living room couch.

"Your eyes are quite beautiful," I hear Mikiel say from somewhere in the dim room.

"Where are my father and Luther?" I ask, ignoring his compliment.

"They, too, are resting. They are in your father's bedroom," he answers serenely.

"How is Luther? Has he recovered?"

"He is quite well. You healed him."

"I'm so hungry," I say as I head into the kitchen. I don't remember the last time I ate. I have been on an adrenaline high all night. Now my body requires food!

I turn on the kitchen light switch and Mikiel is right in front of me with that look of his—that distracting gaze that makes my face blush red. "Really, I need to eat something. Do you eat?"

"No," he answers in his composed voice.

"Do you sleep?"

"No, not like you require," he answers, inching closer.

Opening the fridge I pull out a loaf of whole grain organic bread. The slices are as heavy as cement. I take out one and place it on a plate. Mikiel watches me like a tiger waiting to jump on its prey. His eyes follow every move I make. I smother the single piece of bread with peanut butter then drizzle it with honey. I run my finger over the honey, blending it with the peanut butter. He continues to watch. He closes his eyes and swallows when I bring my finger to my mouth and taste my creation.

Slowly, and I mean slowly, I take bites, chew then swallow my small meal. He watches me and waits for me to finish. I take my time as I revel in the moment.

After I eat the last bite, he walks over to me, takes my plate from my hand and places it on the counter. We are alone, and I feel his longing for me. In a moment of weakness, I give in to it. I reach up and touch his face. It is warm and supple. He presses his face into my hand then takes my hand in his and holds it to his heart. He closes his eyes as he touches the tip of his nose against the surface of my face. His warm breath grazes my skin. He places his forehead to mine then draws my body nearer.

Am I too young to feel this way? I ask myself. But, of course, he hears even my weakest of thoughts.

"You are more than 150 Churrian years of age. You are about the equivalent of twenty in human years. You are also exactly the age that I remember you," he states in whisper.

"How am I nearing twenty? I am turning eighteen!" I am adamant.

He redirects my forehead back to his then he closes his eyes again. He does not answer me, though I know he will.

I bookmark this; I will ask him again. But his warm steamy breath caressing the surface of my face is a valid distraction.

He places his arms around me and draws me even closer, narrowing the space between us. Everything around us seems to disappear. His lips touch mine. They are soft and filled with passion. He clutches the back of my shirt tight in his hands and pulls me against him. I can feel our hearts begin to race as he fervently kisses me.

He pulls back and runs his hand through my hair, then caresses the side of my face. I can feel him struggle to restrain his fervor, but I do not. I bring my lips to his and again, we connect.

He lifts me into his arms and carries me into my bedroom. I kiss him with every step. I feel his thousands of years of unbridled passion for me—the vehemence that was never satisfied moves closer to a head. He closes the door behind us then lowers me down and onto my bed. I watch him unhook his armor and place it on the floor. He stands wearing only his tight-fitted bottoms. His chest is muscular and smooth. He is beautiful and perfect. He stares at me. If his eyes could talk, I know what they would say.

He smiles at me when he feels my flattering thoughts, then crawls into my bed. I am on my back and he on his side. Again, he strokes the side of my face. I lift my lips to meet his and we kiss. Our breathing becomes heavier. He lifts my shirt over my head leaving only my bra. The skin of our bodies touches. I want more. I can feel that he does, too.

But he stops. Lifting his lips away from mine, the ephemeral moment ends as soon as it began. He places his head on my chest and listens to my heartbeat. I feel my rapid breath begin to regularize and my heartbeat return to normal. I honor his restraint as I feel his profound respect for me.

With me running my fingers through his silky, flaxen hair, we remain in this space. This intimate moment needn't go any further. This, whatever this is, satisfies us both. But now curious, I wonder if a Light Warrior can do more. Does he have the same equipment as a male human?

Mikiel raises his head and looks at me with his endearing smirk and says, "You better believe I do."

I can hardly contain my grin. Even a Light Warrior feels the need to defend his masculinity. Though I know he heard my thought, he has no other comment. But I have another question stirring within me. "Mikiel, were we romantic when I was a Light Warrior?"

He lowers his head back to my chest. His silence causes me to believe that there was some sort of past between us. "You are more than a Light Warrior, Meelah. You are our reincarnated leader. For 10,000 years, we battled alongside one another. For 11,000 years, I have loved you."

I feel his tangible angst. I believe that he never had me though he always wished he had. I yearn to remember all of my past life as this leader, his leader. Again, I am aware that he hears my thoughts, yet he chooses not to face them.

We simply lie together in this reflective stillness. With Mikiel's head resting on my chest, the sun ushering in a new day begins to rise. Everything around us is gilded with the sun's ensuing light. A selfish part of me wishes to freeze time and remain in this quiet tranquility. But I don't.

If the sun has already begun to rise, I will soon be late to Religards. I must get up. I have a great deal to learn. I work with the "sisters" today. I needn't say a word. Mikiel also knows this moment must end.

"If you already know what I'm thinking, please answer my question from earlier last night," I say to him.

"And what question would that be?"

"Perhaps I asked you more than one question last night. I'll give you a hint...my age."

Lying on his side he continues to be quiet. I must learn how to do this. He conceals his thoughts flawlessly.

"Mikiel, must I ask you twice?"

"No, you mustn't," he answers as he sits up and fans out his wings. "Will you always begin the day as if yesterday never ended?" he asks.

After sitting up I wait for my answer wearing only a smile, my black bra and blue jeans. I swear he waits only to draw out the moment—the wonderful, yet innocent moment from last night—the moment that now must come to an end. As I stand up, he snatches my wrist, halting my steps forward.

"You came to earth when you were about the equivalent of two human years of age. Do you truly have no memories of your time on Churria?"

"I don't remember anything before I met my father here on earth. What does this mean regarding my age, Mikiel? Will I be turning twenty in a few weeks?"

"No, you're already the equivalent of twenty in earth years," he answers.

"Then I'm the oldest senior at Religards," I say, trying to use humor to mask my pain.

As the truth of my age sinks in, everything that I knew to be real begins to unravel like a ball of yarn. The powers that be are like a cat pulling on that ball of yarn. They toy with my veracity.

My identity, who I thought I was, even how old I thought I was, everything has fallen apart. Within the last few days, my reality has turned upside down and the very ground that I'm standing on is giving way.

"Why are you upset, Meelah?" he asks, also coming to a stand. "I answered your question," he states.

"Yes, you did, Mikiel," I reply, trying to hold back my tears.

He's truly perplexed by my rather emotional response. He wipes my tears then embraces me. I stand in his arms yet again. Perhaps he has no frame of reference regarding my emotions. I feel so betrayed by the consistent lack of honesty all around me. I didn't even know my factual age. Every birthday that I celebrated was false and my Churrian birthparents? Where do I begin with them? They spent the equivalent of two human years with me. What is that in Churrian years, about twenty! They just let me go. How could they do that? What of my current existence is true?

"Being with the humans as long as you have has diminished you, Meelah," Mikiel chides me.

I pull away from him with fire in my eyes. How would he know what it is like to be human or live amongst them? I was thrown to earth and now I smell of them?

"What a condescending and ignorant thing to say, Mikiel. Human are not pliable. They are not solely emotion-driven beings, either. I have seen their kindness, I have seen their purity. If I embody them, then I am proud. Do not mock what you do not understand," I declare as I pad in bare feet toward my bathroom—alone!

Again, I look into my mirror as if it is a crystal ball. But anger wells up in me. Perhaps I am experiencing the emotional processes of a death; my death. The loss of who I thought I was. First I was in denial, now I'm mad as hell, and perhaps tomorrow I'll feel sad then finally acceptance will settle in. Regardless of whatever process I might be experiencing, resentment and anger are welling in me. I feel ready to explode. My entire life has been an untruth. No more lies. No more! I fling open the bathroom door and see Mikiel fastening his armor. I run to him.

"What else have I not had the privilege of knowing? What else are you concealing from me? I feel it, Mikiel, what else?" My anger vents with a resounding punch into his pristine golden armor, denting it.

He looks at me with shock registered on his face while touching the dent that my fist just created. He searches my eyes wondering where his Meelah has gone. His silent and passive reaction infuriates me even more. Ferocity rages through my veins. I feel betrayed and abandoned. Venting my anger again, but this time on my bedroom wall, I punch my wrath out, bam, bam, bam, then again, bam. I see my blood. Blood from my knuckles has smeared the indentations in the wall. I'm getting stronger. I smashed the sheetrock with such fury that I've exposed the wood beams behind it.

"What is going on?" my father yells as he bursts into my bedroom. Luther follows him, close on his heels.

He witnesses Mikiel continuing to fasten up his gear and me in only my bra and jeans. My father reacts as if he breathed in my rage the moment he stepped into the room. I know what he thinks has happened between Mikiel and me and I DON'T CARE. My father rushes over to him—to do what? He is a mere Churrian and Mikiel's a warrior. Regardless of what my father thinks he should do, this is not his place; not anymore.

I stand between them. A power within me bursts to the surface. My arms rise above my head. From the palms of my hands energy issues out, creating a translucent shield that surrounds Mikiel and me. I have no idea what I'm doing, but thankfully, this barrier remains between my father and Mikiel. If anyone is going to give Mikiel a beating, it will be me! There is so much that this Light Warrior still must tell me. I will no longer tolerate the lies or the untruths. I feel like the universe, my life and the lives of millions of humans lie in the balance. This balance is not in my favor without the knowledge of who I was, who I am and what I must do. Enough of all of this, enough!

"Meelah, what are you doing? What is this?" my father exclaims.

"Look, it's so beautiful," Luther says from the background. He's completely detached from the moment.

"You needn't protect me," Mikiel says from behind me.

"I'm not," I answer. "I don't want you to disappear on me," I snap at him as I glare in his direction.

I observe my father. He has hurt me more deeply than he knows by concealing everything that I am. Even my age is a lie. What is authentic; what is real? What other information will I learn that he has?

My father can no longer hear, read or pry into my thoughts, though he tries with all his energy. He does not understand why I am angry, nor does he realize what he has done.

"What did you do to her, Mikiel? Did you steal her innocence, her honor?" my father cries with contempt.

I sense Mikiel place his hand on the handle of his sword. My father has struck a sensitive chord.

"No, Mikiel. He is not your enemy. He is just a pathetic Churrian."

My father looks at me with hurt in his eyes. At that moment, I regret my stinging words. Though I am angry with him, wounding his heart seems to have injured mine more.

"That wasn't kind, Meelah," I hear Luther say. "Come on, Samuel, leave her be. She needs time," Luther adds, trying to console his friend.

"Why, Meelah? Why are you so angry with me?" my father asks with profound emotion.

"I have been lied to. The moment I stepped foot here and tried to blend into this life on earth, I was deceived. What part of my life here has been based on truth?" I ask with sorrow in my voice.

"You know why I couldn't reveal these truths," he answers.

"You couldn't even reveal my true age? When you sang happy birthday to me each year, you lied."

"I love singing happy birthday. I can't wait to sing it next month for you, Meelah. We'll have balloons and cake, too," Luther utters quite innocently.

"Luther, March 21st only marks the anniversary of my arrival here on earth. As for my factual birthday, who knows when that is and who cares anyway? Luther, tell me; how old am I in earth years?"

"I know, I know," Luther shouts as if he's playing on a game show. "You'll be eighteen, isn't that right, Samuel?"

"No, it isn't," my father answers. "She is already the equivalent of twenty earth years of age," my father says like every word stabs at his heart.

"Then why were we going to sing happy eighteenth birthday?" Luther asks like a child.

My father stands before me. My translucent shield separates us. He waits for me to look at him and, in time, I do.

"My love for you is real, do you know that? I love you like you are my birth daughter. You are my daughter," he affirms.

My father places his hands up to mine, which I rest on the face of the barrier. I feel warmth from the palms of his hands through my shield. He smiles at me hoping that I believe him, and deep down I do. I begin to weaken my shield and lower it, but something within me halts this process.

Instinctively, I look to my left, and see the water in my glass begin to vibrate. The floor beneath my feet also feels strange, it begins to shake.

"What is it, Meelah?" my father asks.

Mikiel spreads his wings out behind me and pulls me close to him. My father turns around as if to shield me. The door to my room blasts off the hinges along with a vast part of my wall. My father drops before me and Luther is thrown across the room like a doll and lies unconscious. Within this moment, my world as I know it begins to fall apart.

I abruptly lower my arms and drop to the floor. Mikiel steps forward and draws his sword. He fans his massive wings, creating a barrier between me and whatever has breached the power of the statues.

I pull my father onto my lap. A piece of wood has impaled his chest. Blood runs from the corner of his mouth. Everything falls silent. Nothing else matters. I feel helpless. I feel my father's life force rapidly diminishing. He's dying right before my eyes.

"Wake up, wake up," I murmur in his ear.

But he lies unresponsive and unconscious. Reaching behind me I grab my sword from my bag then slice a gash into my hand. I drip my blood into his mouth and onto the wound to his chest. Desperate, I attempt to remove the piece of wood lodged in his chest. The entire area is now saturated with blood. The bleeding gets worse as I try to dislodge it. I stop and apply pressure. My blood still drips into his wound.

"Meelah, we must leave. I must get you out of here!" Mikiel shouts.

Then I hear Mikiel's sword strike against something. A battle has begun, but my broken heart immobilizes me. Mikiel's words fall away. I will not leave my father here. I will not let him go, not like this. I hold him in my arms and rock him back and forth.

"Don't give up! Don't leave me here," I howl.

His arm slips from my lap and hits the floor, lifeless. My blood didn't repair a thing. He's gone! Though chaos is erupting around me, it doesn't matter. One second my father was looking into my eyes and now I hold his body. I bring my head to his chest, there is no sound.

Then I feel them. The malevolent presence of the Shadows is ubiquitous. The Shadows remain invisible to the naked eye but they're very much here, all four of them. They're in my home, my bedroom. They have killed my father.

With all the love in my heart, I lie my father down. I close his eyes and remove the sharp piece of wood from his chest. I rest his hands, still warm though rapidly cooling, upon his chest.

I come to a stand. Covered in my father's blood, I step in front of Mikiel. He reaches for my hand to stop me, but I won't be stopped. I raise my blood-soaked hands in the air while moving forward. From both my heart center and my hands a bright light emits and fills the room. The Shadows shriek and scream. I feel two slither away before my light can trap them. Two still remain and I will end them. I direct my intense light onto them, forcing them to materialize into physical form. Mikiel strikes at one of the Shadows and the other Shadow is mine. I advance on this putrid-smelling, deformed creature. This being may have once been human, but the Shadow's presence has altered it into something else. Its face is covered in boils oozing with black tainted pus. I push it up against the wall, holding it by its neck. I glare into its black eyes. It has the nerve to smile at me.

"When you see your maker, tell him that I will also see him soon," I scream while spitting in its face.

Something wells up in me and I allow it to surge through me. All I see is pure white light. I hear the Shadow squeal. I feel him writhe in pain. Then there is silence.

I see my hand squeezing nothing. The Shadow has left a residual outline of his essence. I destroyed him. I run back to my father and, as I do, I see Mikiel, appearing stunned by my actions. I don't care.

I hold my father in my arms. The surface of his skin has cooled. I embrace him, drawing him close to me.

"We must be going, Meelah," Mikiel says.

"Luther...have you checked on him?" I ask.

"Yes, he has a bump on his head, but he'll be fine when he comes to."

"No, he won't. Today he lost his brother; his best friend. Today I lost my father. Nothing will be fine!"

"We really must go, Meelah. Humans will soon be coming. You cannot be here when they do."

"Why can't I be here, because I am not one of them?"

"No, you cannot explain what has happened. They are not ready to understand this! We must go!"

"And Luther and my father, we should just leave them?"

"I must protect you, Meelah!"

I see Mikiel follow the sound of the approaching humans. I will not leave my father or Luther behind.

"Bring Luther to the basement of Religards. We will be there," I state.

Mikiel tilts his head as if he can't comprehend what I'm saying. Though I'm uncertain how to travel as instantly as the "sisters" do, I know that I must. I close my eyes and my father and I leave.

Once I arrive I call to Ms. Lucy with every bit of my heart. I feel her acknowledge me and I wait. Still holding my father, I wait.

"Dear, oh dear! What happened?" she shouts, darting across the dark room.

I become overwrought with remorse. I feel like a tanker truck has hit me and torn out my heart at the same time.

"Let him go, Meelah," she repeats over and over again.

I can't do it. I can't let him go, though I know I must. I just cry deeper and harder than I thought I ever could. I hear other voices and see Luther, Maya and a small stranger all running my way. Behind them stands Mikiel.

"Samuel, Samuel, NO!" Luther shouts.

Luther drops to the hard cold floor and kneels by his fallen friend. I see a hand reach down to me. I look up and into Ms. Lucy's eyes. My shaking hand takes hers and I stand. I let my father go.

Ms. Lucy holds me and I sob into her shoulder. While wiping my face, I see Mikiel still standing in the distance. I see that he wants to take my sorrow away, yet he doesn't move. He holds himself back.

A small stranger taps on Ms. Lucy's leg. He stands no higher than my elbows. He lowers his small tweed fedora and says, "He is deceased, madam. My sincere condolences."

"Thank you, Mr. Giblet," Ms. Lucy returns.

I feel that she, too, is injured by the loss of my father. I look back at my father and watch as Luther continues to weep over his friend's body. This sight is like salt to my wound.

"I'm quite sorry for the two of you," a feminine voice says.

"Thank you, Riya," Ms. Lucy states.

"Here is my proposal," Riya says, while handing Ms. Lucy a folded piece of paper.

As Ms. Lucy opens the paper, I stand on my own. My emotional weight causes me to relearn to balance myself. I look in Mikiel's direction and see that he is gone. I wonder why he has chosen this moment to distance himself. It hurts.

I feel Riya take stock of me. She appears quite different than the other "sisters." She has an air of sophistication about her. Her manner is elegant, as is the way she speaks. Her silky straight black hair frames her face. Wearing a deep red lipstick, she looks like a perfect china doll. She continues to stare at me with genuine sensitivity in her eyes.

"This is what we will do. Thank you, Riya, thank you," Ms. Lucy repeats. "Could I have your attention, please? Today we have lost a person who was dear to all of us. Sadly, he has moved on—not the Churrian way, but nonetheless he has left us all. The best way to handle this unfortunate situation has been proposed to me."

"The best way to handle what?" I ask.

"We have sent a team out to smooth over the damage to your apartment, Meelah. The blood was removed and it now appears that the explosion was linked to a gas leak in your apartment."

"And...?" I ask, already certain that I'm not going to like the rest.

"We will have Samuel cremated. There will be a car waiting after dark. They will take his body to the crematorium and, when the vortexes resume, I will bring his ashes home to his father."

"No! No!" I shout. "You will not do that to him."

"Meelah, I understand your concern, but here on earth his body will break down, to put it gently."

"I understand the process. I know what happens to a deceased body," I answer. "But I will bring him home. I will have him buried on Churria. I must do this, I must!"

"Meelah, your intentions are good. But this is not possible."

"Yes, it is," I answer. "I have travelled to Churria. I will bring him with me."

"That is not possible, Meelah," Ms. Lucy answers again.

"You don't know if it's possible. You would just prefer that I don't try."

"It might be possible," Mr. Giblet offers.

"We will understand more of Meelah's power if we allow her to try. It is worth a shot, especially under the cover of darkness," Riya adds.

I look over at my father's body. Luther seems to have run out of tears. He just rests his forehead against my father's.

"Riya, notify who you must. If Meelah feels that she can do this, I will honor her attempt. Mr. Giblet, please prepare Samuel. I don't wish for his father to see him this way. And Riya, please get a blouse for Meelah. She seems to have misplaced hers." I lower my head to Ms. Lucy and she reverently lowers her head in return.

Chapter Ten

I stand on the very top of the bridge. The night conceals what I'm about to do. Riya has somehow halted all traffic. No human eyes shall see my actions.

And I fall.... But this journey I do not make alone. I hold him in my arms. I hold him close as gravity draws us downward. The fall seems endless, but it is not. I can see what I believe to be the imminent-appearing surface. I never thought that my destiny would commence with his ending. With profound regret, I bring him home.

We plummet into the vast cold water and slide into a parallel plane of existence. I gasp for air as I rise to the surface of Calla. My arms are growing heavy, but I don't let go of my father's body.

I look up and see many Churrians, all wearing white robes. They are waiting for me; they are waiting for my father. As soon as they see me rise to the surface, they run into the water. Dragging their wet and heavy robes, they make their way to us.

"My Samuel, my dear son, I am here now," I hear an older Churrian cry. He repeats his heartfelt words as he passionately wades into the waist-deep waters of Calla.

Exhausted, I move forward still holding my father. Finally, they reach me and I let my father go. They lovingly take hold of his corpse.

"Kriyo, I need your help," the older Churrian cries, though there are many others already assisting him.

Kriyo races into the water to join me and my father. His silky black hair bounces around his face. He, too, is adorned in a white robe, but he moves with ease through the water. Our eyes connect for a fleeting moment. Then he takes hold of my father's body and assists in carrying him to shore.

Their white robes are saturated and appear to be weighted. Reverently they carry him; two Churrians on each side of my father's body.

I, too, am assisted to shore. I drop to my knees as soon as my feet touch land. Every part of me experiences profound sorrow. Looking up, I see Kriyo extend a hand to me. I vaguely remember him carrying my father and now he's here with me. Too fatigued to stand or try to figure out why Kriyo is here, I remain in a crumpled heap. He kneels beside me and says nothing, he just sits there. I hear the voices of several other Churrians who have come to my side to help me, but he dismisses them. The two of us sit on the shores of Calla, alone. It is quiet, and the darkness blankets everything.

I don't care. I wish not to move. My broken heart again has immobilized me. The reality of living without my father has hit me with great force.

In my mind I see the four Churrians carrying my father. This image haunts me, as it was at this moment that I let him go. I cry and begin to release my profound loss. Not only was he a father to me, he was my friend—my only true friend.

I feel the weight of something covering me. Kriyo has enveloped me with the dry warmth of a blanket, and then again sits near me, still not exchanging even a thought. He remains here as if he's protecting me. In a weird way his presence affords me comfort. Exhaustion overtakes me as I slip into sleep.

I don't know how much time has passed when I open my eyes again. I remember the events of the previous day and can only hope that my father's death was just a bad dream. As I sit up, pain jolts my legs. They are tingling and feel weighted, having fallen beyond asleep from my prolonged odd position. The restriction of adequate blood flow makes them prickle.

My thoughts return to yesterday; it *was* real. I wish to bury myself within the warmth of the blanket. Denial is a valid option, right? I become aware of the sweet-smelling breeze. I feel the air stream through my hair and touch my face. It calms me. My pain-filled thoughts float away within it and I willingly let them go. Again, I become still and peaceful. The absence of thought and quiet of the mind gives me a taste of peace. I wish to stay here and remain within this sacred space I have created.

I see a hand before me. It waits for me to take hold of it and, in time, I do. It is Kriyo, he pulls me up and I stand as my legs wake up. Again, the light wind strokes my face. I inhale its sweet, rejuvenating goodness. My legs give out and Kriyo catches me. I look up at him and his eyes are already locked on mine. He pulls me up to a stand again then lifts me into his arms and steps forward.

"I will take you to head elder Shria," he tells me with a re-assuring voice.

I nod then relax in Kriyo's arms.

"Thank you, Meelah. Thank you for bringing him home," he says. "We should go; the head elder is waiting. I can sense her. And Meelah, your eyes are quite beautiful. I overheard Mikiel speak with Shria regarding their change. It is my opinion that they now suit you."

"Thank you, but I should stand. You can put me down."

"Perhaps I don't want to," he answers sweetly, and then he lowers me down.

I stand close to a being I just met and it feels as natural as breath. He moves a strand of hair from my face and places it behind my ear. His energy and presence is so familiar to me. I wouldn't allow just anyone to be this close to me. But here we are.

"Did you stay with me all night?" I ask.

"I did," he answers.

"Why?"

"Because you needed me, Meelah," he answers as a matter of fact.

I have no response. He's right. I did need him. His silent, yet protective energy was what I required. How strange is it to need the presence of someone you just met?

"Thank you," I say to him from my heart. He takes my hand and we teleport to Shria's.

"Kriyo, where is Mikshe? I sent her for Meelah at yesterday's nightfall," Shria asks while looking around. She appears to have been waiting for me. "I thought that you were in Ralta with Trall," she continues. "Were you with Meelah all night, Kriyo?" she asks in an annoyed tone.

"Yes, Kriyo was with me, Shria. He sat by me all night. Have we done something wrong?" I ask directly.

"Well, you're here now, Meelah," she abruptly answers, changing the subject. "Let's get you cleaned up. Today we will honor Samuel. Kriyo, I'm sure Trall would appreciate your help. Thank you," Shria concludes.

Taking my hand, Shria guides me into her welcoming home. I look over my shoulder at Kriyo. He waited as though he knew I would. As our eyes meet, he teleports and fades from my sight. I follow Shria into a small washroom. She has filled a huge basin with steamy water. I watch her peel the emerald-colored petals from a flower and drop them onto the surface of the water. She gives thanks to the flower and its essence. I observe this reverent action, thinking it is beautiful.

Then I feel it. The wretched agony deep within my heart wells to the surface again. I try to hold it in, but I can't. Tears stream down my face.

"Good, the silvera flower is working. The essence of this flower opens the heart center. You must release your grief, dear," Shria says while squeezing my hand. "Immerse yourself in the water, Meelah, and permit the silvera to help you. Be in the moment and commence your healing process. Samuel loved you, this is what he would want," she adds with love.

She steps out of the room, closes the door behind her and I am alone—alone with my emotions and thoughts. I take off the shirt that Riya gave me then see smears of my father's blood dried on my chest. I sob with every movement I make. My bra, jeans then my underwear all come off. Everything is stained in dark dried blood. Tears run down my face as I step into the hot soothing water. The green silvera petals float around me. They seem to gather in front of me. I hold my head and bawl. I release and release. I feel the guilt. I relive the last exchange my father and I had, and realize that I was cruel. I called him pathetic. I vented all of my frustrations into one hurtful statement. I wounded him selfishly and now he's gone. My father, my support, my only friend, is gone.

"Please forgive me. I love you, Father," I say out loud before I submerge into the water.

I try to escape. I try to hide beneath the warm water's surface. But I can't. The silvera opens my heart and draws out all that I do not wish to face. From beneath the water I release my worries and fears and fall into a state of deep inner calm. The surface of the water above me becomes as still as my essence. Once I do not give power or energy to my thoughts, I slip into another place and it is wonderful. I feel my love for my father and I feel his love for me.

Honoring my physical need for breath, I rise. Drawing my knees to my chest, I rest my head on them. Then something catches my attention at the foot of my small tub. I bring my gaze up and see my father. I rub my eyes and he still remains. He is adorned in a white Churrian robe. With his palms together at his chest, he bows to me. As his head rises, I see his peaceful smile.

"I will always love you, Meelah, and I will always be with you," he speaks earnestly in his soft voice. "Feel me in the wind, feel me when you laugh. My ending is also a beginning," he whispers as he fades from sight.

A light wind flows past me and I feel his presence within this breeze. I sense his energy. I am surrounded by his love. What a gift he has just given me. Though my heart is scarred, it has also begun to heal. I again submerge into the cleansing water. As I rise for air, I see that all of the silvera petals are gone. Perhaps they disintegrated or perhaps they have fulfilled their purpose. I feel my heart center fully open; there is minimal residual sorrow. My anguish has been replaced by love.

Clean and comforted, I step out of the tub and slip into the robe Shria left for me. Shria meets me at the door like she knows I am finished. Her round face exudes compassion. She brings me into her sleeping chamber and sits me down. Sitting behind me, she brushes my hair like a mother would after her daughter had a bad day. Her actions bring a reminder of my birthparents. They are here somewhere on Churria. Did they ever love me?

"You will meet your birthparents, Meelah, but at the right time. Everything occurs as it is destined. This I believe," she says. "Today, we will honor Samuel. That is enough for any heart to bear."

I turn around and face this kindhearted being. Adorned in her distinctive gilded robe, she radiates compassion. Her gray hair is pulled up into a bun atop her head and soft brown eyes are infused with love. Wearing the most brilliant smile, I see wrinkles gently framing her mouth.

"Thank you, Shria," I denote, lowering my head.

"No, dear, it is we who should be thanking you. That said, hundreds of Churrians wish to express gratitude to you, especially one."

"Kriyo?" I ask.

"No. I am speaking of Trall, Samuel's father. Why would you say Kriyo?" she asks.

"I don't know. His was the first name that came to mind, I suppose. Shria, may I ask you a question?"

"Of course, dear, what is it?"

"What is it with Kriyo? Do you not like him?"

"Kriyo is an honorable Dristan. He is from the quadrant of Drista. Churria has four quadrants, each quite different from the other. Soon we will depart to Ralta, where Samuel was born. It is in Ralta that we will honor his journey."

"You still have not answered my question."

"Meelah, you can't afford distractions. You have a destiny—"

"And you wish for no other Churrian to die as my destiny unfolds," I say, interrupting her.

"No, Meelah, you don't understand. You are Churrian, my dear. You are one of us. This is your home and yes, I do wish for no one else to have a fate like Samuel's, but his fate was his choice. He would have lived his life no other way. He loves you."

"Do you know my destiny?"

"I know that you are still connected to earth. It possesses something that you require. I know that there will be a war. Churria will provide you with temporary protection upon your return, but this war will take place, Meelah. Balance between the forces must be restored and this you will do. Again, dear, everything occurs as it's fated. I have faith in this," she states. "Focus on locating your amulet. Be in the present and feel your next move."

Honesty, candid truthfulness, this is what I've been longing for. I appreciate her answer even if it's still a little vague. I'm certain that the future has not yet been written. If I can stop this war, I will. No one else needs to live with such loss.

"It is time, Meelah. I have head elder duties, so we must be leaving," she gently urges.

I acknowledge her with a nod and walk back into the washroom. I run fresh water over Riya's shirt and use it to wash the surface of my boots. Squeezing the soiled linen shirt out I remove the last of my father's blood. I embrace the love he still has for me.

Slipping on my favorite boots, I silently thank Riya for ascribing her shirt to further my healing. Standing in my boots and adorned in a Churrian white robe, I am quite the sight. I twist my hair up, fasten it and then I am ready.

As I step out, I see Shria waiting for me. While standing in the room that houses all of her ancient tomes, I hear messages from the surrounding books. They speak to me, bestowing their knowledge. Closing my eyes, I breathe in their wisdom. I become engulfed by their words, their stories, their images.

"Meelah," I hear Shria say tenderly.

Shria's gentle nudging brings me back. I feel great honor as the lasting impressions from the various tomes drift around me. They remind me that I still have much to learn.

"Indeed, you do. Meelah, these journals only communicate with the head elder. I find it telling that they spoke to you. Perhaps it will be my robe that you wear," she states.

Head elder, former leader of the Light Warriors, at this moment both titles are meaningless. I choose to embrace the present, not the future or even the past. Today I am here on Churria and in Bursa. Today I will honor my father and now I must learn how to travel like a Churrian.

"Shria, how does teleporting work?"

"It is easy. Just visualize where you wish to go then the portal takes you there. You are Churrian, Meelah. Your physical body resonates at the vibration required for teleporting. All you must do is try."

"Shria, I have no idea where we're going."

"Yes, this is true, but you'll find your way. I'll see you in Ralta, at Trall's home," she assures me as she teleports from sight.

Alone, I am left to master this means of travel. Closing my eyes, I see a blue light where Shria was just standing. It leads to a conduit above me. It is like a pathway, an energetic trail from her. Who thought that I could see more clearly with my eyes closed? I seem to use another eye. I envision this pathway and now I bring my intentions to this channel.

Upon opening my eyes, I see the luminous quality of Ralta. I did it! Teleporting is as natural as breathing. The Churrians who live here in this quadrant are called Raltans. I'll try to address them properly. As I prepare myself to meet the Raltans, my attention is redirected to the unusual yet incredulous sight encircling me.

The magnificent omnipresent energy within this landscape is exceptional. Moving onward, I wonder where everyone has gone. While pondering this, I cannot help but place my hands on one of the many massive clear quartz crystals that protrude from the ground. The crystal vibrates as if singing an inaudible tune. Both stones and crystals lend a shining glow to this land.

I can feel the reverence that Raltans have for all life even within the seemingly inanimate minerals and crystals. The Raltans have built their homes seamlessly into their magnificent landscape. Their dwellings are camouflaged amid the crystal and stone backdrop. Progressing forward, I am now before a residence that flawlessly blends into the colossal clear quartz stone. I stand before Trall's home. My father's energy is here. I visualize him as a child running over the unique surface. I even hear his giggling; playfully it dances in the air. I also see him as a man, the man whom I know as my father. His love for his home is very much present. He lives on—not only in my memories, but within this stunning landscape. The crystals seem to have captured his exceptional essence. He will be eternally present here.

The presence of many rouses me from my reverie. On my walk I have arrived at a side entrance of Trall's abode. No doubt Shria chose this entrance in order to make her way in. I can now sense many Churrians are waiting for me. I am attuned to their energy.

As I pass through the threshold, I appreciate the beauty of Trall's home. I can see through it, but obscurely. His residence is composed of an enormous quartz crystal with striation of tourmaline running through it like lightning bolts. Nothing is like this on earth. The vibrations that surround me are inexplicable. I place my hand on the smooth, outside surface of his home. It is filled with loving emotion. It draws out my residual pain.

"Meelah," a pleasing female voice interrupts my thoughts. "I am Mikshe. I have been asked to collect you," she explains.

Before me stands a female Churrian. Her gaze is down as she lowers her head in my direction—her palms together at her chest. I wait for her head to rise and when it does, I see her, a tad shorter than me with her brown hair swept up, and she radiates honor. Her face is simply beautiful. Without uttering another word, she proceeds and I follow. She leads me back outside then around the massive quartz. She makes no sound when she walks. Beneath the rim of her robe, I catch a glimpse of what look like sandals. But it's not what she wearing, it is how she's moving—as fluid as water. In contrast, my boots clomp and clatter with every step I take. I alter my step and shift more of my weight onto the tips of my toes to mute the sounds from my boots.

Though I feel the presence of many others, oddly I still don't see anyone else. I follow her as we walk away from what I thought was Trall's house. She takes me down a narrow pathway between two colossal pieces of quartz. I gaze up and see that the opaque rock is about forty feet high on either side of me. These magnificent stones form an entryway. Journeying past them, we enter a coliseum of sorts filled with a sea of white-robed Churrians.

I trail Mikshe as we continue down a center aisle. Though everyone is silent, they all turn and look at me as I pass. They study me and it feels rather disconcerting. We proceed onward for all to see and I begin to wonder where it is that Mikshe is leading me. I'd much rather blend into the sea of beings than to stand out as I am. The walk feels endless with the many scrutinizing eyes fixed on me.

Then I see him. I see my father's body ahead of me on a platform. On his back, dressed in a white robe, he lies upon a grand flat crystal. He's home. His people encircle him. The love they feel for him surrounds me. I also see Shria. Mikshe moves her arm like a feather, as she indicates where she would like for me to stand.

I fill the spot between Shria and a male whom I believe to be Trall. Mikshe bows then seamlessly blends into the mass of Churrians. I have never seen so many people in one place. Even Times Square in NYC on New Year's Eve pales in comparison. My father was loved.

The energy here is different than that of a funeral on earth. Though there is a body, there is no grief. I sense the acceptance and reverence for my father's journey, and the admiration.

I am drawn to look to my left and, as I do, my eyes are met by my father's father. I know who he is, though we have not been formally introduced. Trall lowers his head to me. I do not feel worthy of his reverence. It was my fated journey that ended his son's life. I am the reason why he stands where he does.

"No, Meelah," he answers my thought with his denial of my guilt. "Though you are destined to lead us all, you have much to learn," he adds.

His long gray hair gives him a distinguished look. I notice how it moves in rhythm with the light breeze. His face is reminiscent of my father's and his eyes are consumed with emotion, none of which is anger or sadness.

"Thank you for bringing my son home, Meelah," he whispers. He takes my hand.

I lower my head to him and, as I raise my gaze, I see Mikiel in the background. He stands out with his golden armor and massive wings. He tries to connect with me, I feel it and turn away. Trall squeezes my hand before he and Shria approach my father.

Shria begins to speak lovingly about him and his journey that is everlasting. She speaks of the work that he will still do and the lives he will still affect. The perception of existence and growth after death is fascinating though her words ring true to my core. I am certain that my father will be with me always. I feel him now.

Trall touches everyone's heart as he speaks of his son's early childhood. His love for his son is tangible. I crave more anecdotes of my father, especially from when he was young and learning. I enjoy hearing them, but they, too, come to an end. Trall thanks everyone for making his son's life as wonderful as it was. Then he thanks me again.

"Samuel was a father to me. He was all I had and I will forever love him," I state with conviction. I then bow to Trall.

That he thanks me in this public forum is overwhelming. His acknowledgment that I somehow made his son's life better touches my heart. No words can describe the purity of these people.

Shria signals for me to join them. Out of respect for Shria, Trall and my father, I hesitantly join them. I do not feel that this is my place, but when I see my father's peaceful face, I know that it is. Standing before thousands, I for the last time gaze down at my father's physical form.

Shria stands at his feet, Trall at his head and I on the side facing the many honoring my father. With no words spoken and no words needed, we all say goodbye. Both Trall and Shria raise their arms and, as they do, the crystal base beneath my father grows around him, encasing his physical form. He appears cocooned in a semi-translucent crystal shell.

"Meelah, place your hands on Samuel," Shria says telepathically. "Help him ascend."

I place my hands on the crystal shell. I feel Shria and Trall do the same. My eyes immediately close. I feel warmth beneath the palms of my hands. Every part of my essence feels love. Then I see a soft white light. Even though my eyes are closed, I'm aware that this radiance fills the space around us.

My thoughts are consumed by this luminescence. I witness my father leave with the light. It takes him to where he will continue to grow and thrive.

I open my eyes and see that my hands are suspended in midair. The crystal shell is gone, so is my father's physical body. Only his white robe remains on the platform.

Trall picks up his son's robe and lovingly begins to fold it. I sense something coming. I instinctively look up and over to Mikiel and see that he, too, feels it. He is also looking upward and then our eyes meet. I can see within his expression that this is not good.

"Shria, take Trall and leave!" I scream, disrupting the surrounding stillness.

Darkness begins to cover the space above me. Its murky ink spreads over Ralta, shading all light. Instantly, there is chaos. Mikiel flies over to me with his sword drawn.

"What is this?" I hear Kriyo yell from behind me.

"Go, Kriyo!"

"No," he answers, also drawing a sword.

A face begins to press through the ominous gloom with malevolence in its eyes—in its essence. Its face is not human. It's not Churrian. It's not like anything I have ever seen. It's pure darkness. It's the Dark Force, himself.

"Is this soon enough, Meelah?" it spouts at me.

I see Mikiel disappear from sight. The force tosses away Kriyo effortlessly then it encircles me. It only wants me. I stand surrounded by its malice. I am unafraid. Something rises within me. Though I am connected to this force, this is not the power that resonates with my essence. A light surges through me and pushes the darkness back.

"You have power, and without the amulet? This is quite intriguing," it says from all around me. "Too bad that's all you possess."

I hold the light around me. My arms are extended and I push as hard as I can against the looming Dark Force. My white light whips around me and my physical body begins to weaken. I feel my nose bleed. Then from above me I see something as powerful as the Dark Force, but it is pure light. The Dark Force also feels its presence. I can sense him weaken as his brother, the Light Force, approaches.

"I will smite you, you pathetic creation of my father. If my Shadows don't get you, Meelah, I will take control of every being necessary. You will never defeat me," the darkness spews. "And Light Warrior, you're just as pitiable. I relish the thought of your wings being torn off. Soon, Light Warrior, soon."

Mikiel lands beside me. I can feel him close, but I remain focused on the battle above me. I watch as the Dark Force is forcibly removed by his brother. The skies clear and I maintain my column of white light. I see that it's connected to the divine Light Force. Somehow I am channeling his power, his force and his light.

"Meelah," I hear Mikiel call.

I don't know how to disconnect from the channel I have created. It flows through me and up into the upper dimensions. My nose continues to bleed, coloring the front of my white robe red.

"Look at me, Meelah!" I hear Kriyo shout. "LOOK INTO MY EYES!"

"You can't touch her, Kriyo," Mikiel cautions. "Only she can cease the flow of light."

I bring my head down and examine Kriyo's eyes. I see him try to lower my arms, but he cannot touch the channel that surrounds me. It appears as though its energy and vibration burns his hands each time he tries. He brings his eyes back to mine. I watch his hair tossed about in every direction from the channel's residual force.

"Lower your arms!" Kriyo orders. "You can stop this. You must, Meelah, it's killing you."

With everything I have, I lower my arms. The taste of blood fills my mouth as I exert my physical self. The channel of light begins to subside. Kriyo reaches into the diminishing light and, with his help, my arms relax at my side and the channel dissipates. I stand for a brief moment then everything fades to black.

Chapter Eleven

As I open my eyes the intense light all around me overwhelms my senses.

"Meelah, how do you feel?" I hear Mikshe ask.

I feel her presence, though my physical eyes do not see her. I squint and try to locate her. The radiance filling this chamber is brighter than a sunny day.

"Where am I?"

"You are in Ralta, at Trall's home. I will advise the head elder of your awakening."

"Thank you, Mikshe."

My eyes begin to adjust to the overpowering bright light. The chamber's walls, ceiling and floor are clear quartz. The daylight amplifies the innate energy of the quartz. I am embraced in its serene vibration.

I sense Mikiel. I know he is here, though I don't see him. Getting up, I move slowly around this amazing room. Running my hands over the smooth, temperate walls, I sense life within the crystal. The soles of my feet vibrate. My feet are bare! Where are my boots?

"They have been cleaned," I hear Mikiel answer.

I follow the sound of his voice. He still chooses to remain invisible, so why should I interact with him? If he doesn't have the courtesy to reveal himself then I will not acknowledge him. Time passes and I wait. No Shria and no further words from Mikiel.

"What am I doing?" I ask out loud. "I have no time for games. After I get my boots, I must leave. I will not endanger anyone else," I state.

Walking over to what I believe to be the door of this room, I note that it's perfectly camouflaged into this crystal chamber. Leaving might prove more difficult than I imagined. I place my hand on the door as I remember Mikshe doing and Mikiel takes hold of my wrist.

"What are you doing, Mikiel?"

"I don't know, Meelah. When it comes to you, I don't know what I'm doing," he murmurs.

I can sense him move closer behind me. He pulls me back one step to ensure that I don't leave, then he spins me around and there he is, no longer invisible. I'm facing him. He fervently gazes into my eyes and I look away.

"You have found him again," Mikiel affirms.

"Found who? Mikiel, I need answers from you, not riddles. You are well aware of what I face. The Dark Force just revealed himself to me; I have an amulet to locate and a war to stop. I DON'T HAVE TIME FOR THIS! So, if you can't answer me, then I must leave!"

I wait for a moment then turn around. I attempt to place my hand upon the door again, but again he stops me. I turn around and stare into his deep blue eyes. I don't understand his reluctance to be forthcoming with me.

"Have I lost you again, Meelah?"

"You can't lose what you never had," I answer. "Mikiel, I can't do this because I don't know what this even is! We have a connection, I admit, but..."

"But what, Meelah? Is it Kriyo?"

"What about Kriyo? Is he who you were referring to before? You need to talk to me! I demand a stop to these games."

He lowers his forehead to meet mine. His energy and connection to me feels restrained, like a dam holding back rising water. He takes my hand in his and his breath wafts over my face.

"Mikiel, why are you here?"

"The Dark Force... Meelah you should not have taunted him as you did. You must be wiser than this."

"Thank you, Mikiel. Is there anything else?"

"Yes, there is. Your powers, I have never seen anything like them."

"I must be awakening them from my last incarnation."

"No, Meelah. You were never able to tap into the Light Force's power. No one can; and that is what you did. Once you find the amulet, I fear that your Churrian form will not be strong enough to house you."

"What are you saying?"

"As your powers develop, your physical form adapts and your vibration increases as a result. When you connect with the amulet, there will be such an increase to your frequency that we are unsure of what will happen to you."

"I will stop the Dark Force," I answer.

"No, Meelah. The Dark Force can never be destroyed. He is a part of the duality that exists in all things."

"I know that and I appreciate the need for this balance. This precise polarity also resides within me. And I didn't say that I wish to destroy the Dark Force himself, but I will destroy every being he possesses. He will no longer violate the universal law of free will. Too many innocents have died. It is enough."

"There you are," Mikiel says with a smirk. "My liege is back in true form."

"Mikiel, where are my other Light Warriors?"

"They are waiting for you to lead them. They are well rested and able."

"I would like to see them before I return to earth."

"As you wish," he answers, lowering his head.

He reaches out, and as I take hold of his hand, I feel such an attraction to him. Every part of me wants to kiss him but.... He grins at me as he hears my thoughts.

"Mikiel, what about Kriyo? Who is he?"

"So much of your memory has been lost."

"As your leader, I order you to answer me."

"I will show you. Come closer, Meelah," he says, grudgingly.

I take a small step toward him, closing the gap between us. He places his hand underneath my chin and raises my head so that our foreheads rest against one another's. I feel his sultry breath against my lips. He wants our lips to touch, but he, too, restrains himself.

"Close your eyes," he states.

In my mind I begin to see another foreign land. I hear the sounds of wildlife all around me, like a jungle teeming with life. I see Kriyo. He strides over to me with fervor. It's as though he's been waiting for me and I for him. He loves me and I love him in return. When our lips connect, it feels like time stops. Our ardor makes me buckle at the knees and I fall into the arms of Mikiel. His embrace disconnects my passionate vision. Mikiel respectfully stands me to my feet.

"I loved him."

"Yes, you did."

"I loved him when I was a Light Warrior?"

"You have only had one other incarnation, Meelah, and you were never just a Light Warrior. You were our leader."

"What happened to him, Mikiel?"

Mikiel avoids the question. He turns away but I don't allow him to stop there.

"Mikiel, answer me. What happened to him?"

"He was killed. All on his planet were extinguished, Meelah! Why do you want to know this? It will only bring you more sorrow."

"Does Kriyo know that we were once connected?"

Again he attempts to avoid the question. Then his eyes almost sear mine as they connect. He pushes me against the wall, holds my hands above my head and peers feverishly into my eyes. His breath is shallow and quick like he's been running. Running to where I now stand.

"Do you wish to further injure me?" he asks.

"No," I answer. "But I'm certain that Shria is waiting for me. Mikshe went to find her."

"I requested a moment alone with you."

I close my eyes, giving him permission to linger in this close proximity to me.

"Meelah, no one has told Kriyo of your connection, but I know he feels it. I have been watching him, listening to him," he whispers in my ear.

"Isn't that stalker-like of you?" I ask, inching my lips closer to his. "Tell me again why we were never together."

"I never said that."

"Then what happened?"

"Can't we just have this, together, now? Meelah, out of respect for you, I hold myself back. I want you but...I want you to long for me in return," he says, while searching my eyes.

He feels the confusion within me. He releases my wrists and lowers my arms. Then he runs his hand through his blond locks, pushing them from his face.

"I understand, Meelah."

"Mikiel, I just can't. I don't know why."

And with those words, the exchange between us shifts again. I watch as he paces back then forth. I don't want to wound him. I do have feelings for him but....

He nods his head in acknowledgment. Again he has delved into my thoughts. Seriously, I must use my shield.

"Meelah, I need to say something."

"Yes, Mikiel?"

"I am sorry. I should have protected Samuel. Your pain equally grieved me. Please forgive me."

"I never blamed you, Mikiel. I simply wished that you remained to support me."

"I left earth to come here. It was necessary that the head elder knew what occurred."

"And I appreciate your actions; still, my heart wished for more. But, all things occur as they are fated. Is there anything else that you wish to convey?"

He remains still as if I pressed the pause button on a remote. I know that he's just processing and he doesn't want to leave. He doesn't want to be away from me. He raises his head.

"Meelah, two Shadows remain on earth. They wait for you. All at Religards are prepared for your arrival. Before you leave, I will return with the other Light Warriors," he informs me as he bows.

"Thank you, Mikiel. Will I see you on earth, as well?"

"I will not leave you again. I have also left a gift for you with Tali."

"Tali! Really? What will I have to do to get it?" I quip.

"You have nothing to worry about." He laughs. "She will help you actualize who you truly are."

"I must speak with Shria and Trall. Thank you, Mikiel."

Bowing again, he disappears from my sight. Behind where he stood, I see a small basin filled with water and I use it to freshen up. While I splatter water on my face, every cell in my body feels an itch to return to earth. It is time for me to leave, but first I must speak with those who are waiting for me. I hastily run my fingers through my hair and twist it up.

Now I stand before this peculiar door. I vaguely remember Mikshe leaving through it, but I didn't pay any mind as to how she did it. It's flush with the quartz wall and has no apparent door handle. I run both of my hands over its smooth surface. The striations of tourmaline glimmer deep within the quartz. It is so beautiful.

Then I sense the energy existing within the crystal. Every Churrian is innately connected to their environment. I, too, am Churrian. So now I will embrace this manner of existence. I bring my thoughts to reflect what I want.

"Please open," I command telepathically.

The door slides open when it feels and hears my intentions. It moves silently and I eagerly walk through its opening. Before I go too far, I give thanks to the sentient crystal.

Since I see only a wall to my left, I journey to my right. My bare feet are surprisingly warm as I travel down this amazing corridor. It appears to be a hollowed-out, brightly illuminated tunnel. I run my hand along its surface as I continue. When the hallway comes to an end, I again take another right and see a grand room. Trall and Shria come to a stand when they see me. I approach them, bring my palms to my chest and reverently bow to them both. As I rise, I am greeted by their welcoming energies.

"Meelah, I have made a tincture for you," Trall announces as he abruptly scampers off.

I watch Shria, who is following Trall's every move with her eyes. He goes into his yall, which earthlings would consider to be a kitchen. I hear him babble to himself and I observe Shria enamored by his every move. Then she senses me watching her and her demeanor changes.

Continuing to smile at her, I ask, "Shria, have you ever been married? Actually that's an earthly expression. Are Churrians monogamous?"

"Of course we are. We are evolved beings, after all."

"Why haven't you married?"

"I am the head elder. Once you are voted into this position, your life becomes dedicated to Churria."

"So you deny your heart? That doesn't sound very evolved."

"Meelah, you have a great deal to learn," she returns, appearing rather agitated.

"I am sorry for offending you, Shria. That was not my intention," I say as humbly as I can.

"Meelah, these are yours," I hear Mikshe say from behind me. "I cleaned them for you."

"Thank you," I reply, my focus still on Shria. But in respect, I bring my attention to sweet Mikshe. Her head is lowered as she offers my boots. "Mikshe, they look like new! They're beautiful. How did you restore them?" I ask in amazement.

"Have I done something wrong?" she asks.

"You did nothing wrong. You are misunderstanding me."

"I will work harder to understand you," she states before she drops her head.

My heart and mind would much rather be talking with Shria. I watch as she muddles through a book as if she's not thinking about my words. Trall ambles forward with a tray in hand. But before me is Mikshe. Why does she feel inferior to me?

"Thank you, Mikshe. I appreciate all of your efforts. My boots look like new again," I repeat.

She raises her head and watches as I slip into my boots. As I rise she bows again to me. I am baffled by the Churrian traditions and customs so I bow in return but this doesn't work. Once Mikshe sees me bow to her, she again bows to me. I am stuck in some kind of reverence loop.

I remain standing and wonder what she'll do next. She, too, stands tall as if she's waiting for me to say or do something. I can't help but begin to laugh. This is so foreign to me and I don't know how to leave her without offending her. I look over to Shria. She is busy with Trall. So I act like a human; after all, that's how I was raised.

"Please join Trall, the head elder and myself at the table. Trall has made something for us. Come on," I say while coaxing her forward.

"Yes, please join us," I hear Trall sputter.

"That will be all, Mikshe," Shria commands.

Shria's words halt her steps instantly. Awkwardly, she bows to the group and abruptly strides off in another direction.

"We must have a meeting before Meelah is to leave. Time is short," Shria continues, as if not aware of the power of her words on Mikshe.

I watch Mikshe as she scurries away from her head elder's coarse rebuke. I feel that my invitation to the table has wounded her. That was rude of Shria.

"Yes, it was," Trall agrees, upon hearing my thoughts.

"She knows her place and Meelah must know hers," Shria insists.

"Shria, I will admit that I am unaware of your customs, but I was raised by a Churrian and he instilled in me respect and tolerance. I would have given Mikshe my tincture if enough was not prepared. I apologize for the open expression of my thoughts, but since you can hear them anyway, I believe it's more honorable to speak them face to face."

"Hear, hear," Trall enthused.

I see so much of my father in Trall. His mannerisms and his quirky sense of humor must have been ingrained in my father. And Trall speaks his truth. My father learned great qualities from him. I feel that I will, too.

"Are the two of you quite finished?" Shria asks.

"I am," I answer.

"Yes, my dear," Trall says to Shria with a mischievious grin.

Shria tries to conceal her desire to smile back as she struggles to compose herself.

"Meelah, please enjoy your tincture."

"Yes, yes," Trall agrees, animated. "It is my one of a kind herbal mixture. It will invigorate your spirit while nourishing every cell of your body. Please, drink up," he encourages, while passing me a small ceramic cup.

He seems so full of life. I can see that he has already had one, maybe three. His eyes sparkle and his aged form moves with ease. As I down the sweet mixture, I sense, then see, Kriyo walk into the room. He respectfully bows to all of us, and then asks to speak with Trall privately. I listen to their exchange. Curious about him, I observe them. He's the one with whom, in my past life, I had an intense romance. This is so peculiar. Well, I have learned to mindfully embrace the now. And now, I must speak with Shria. I feel the Light Warriors' imminent arrival. I take advantage of this moment alone with her.

Sitting next to her, I place my hand upon hers. Her kind eyes meet mine. Her presence is calming to me. She is the closest thing I have to a mother.

"That is quite kind of you," she replies as she hears my inner musings. "Now Meelah," she says, shaking her head.

"Shria, I will be fine. I will return to earth and do what my essence must. I will then rejoin you here and, when I do, I will learn the customs of the Churrians."

"My dear, you live from a pure place, never change that. About what occurred earlier, it was I who had a battle with my own ego. Mikshe was merely an innocent bystander. I will speak with her. Meelah, you were right," she concedes. "But what you don't understand yet is that my commitment to the Churrian way will always take precedence. Even if this means I deny my heart. I must remain focused on all Churrians, not one."

"This is your way, Shria, and I respect it, though I am not sure that I could deny my heart as you have. You are both dedicated and selfless."

"So are you, my dear. And Meelah, I have noticed the change of your eye color. They are as unique and beautiful as you are. "

"Thank you."

I can't help but look at Kriyo who is still conversing with Trall. His robe moves about as he talks and illustrates his story. His black hair is neatly pulled back into a low ponytail. His back is turned toward me and I wonder if he has deliberately faced this way. Perhaps he doesn't wish to communicate with me. Mikshe strolls into the yall and I observe Kriyo move out of her way. He lowers his head to her. As he rises, he senses my attention. Our eyes connect and his attention is more on me than on Trall, to whom he's speaking.

"Go to her," I hear Trall say. "But Kriyo, speak first with your father. As for me, you have my blessing," he adds.

Kriyo bows to Trall then ambles over to me. I feel Shria's disapproving energy and now I understand it. She has lived her entire life restraining her heart and she wishes that I not suffer as she has. Though she has not said these words, I feel them. On his approach, Kriyo lowers his head first to Shria and then to me, all the while his intent remains fixed on me.

"I will see you soon," I say to Shria as I come to a stand. "Trall, I see my father in your every move. He lives in you. Thank you for having me in your remarkable home."

"No, thank you," he replies, taking hold of my hands.

"I must be going. Thank you both. Kriyo, would you like to see me out?"

"Kriyo, please escort Meelah to the outskirts of Ameira," Shria orders. "Mikiel and the other Light Warriors will be arriving there."

"Take my hand, Meelah," Kriyo directs. "I will guide you."

Fireworks explode within me, flushing my cheeks. I see him close his eyes while reveling in our connection. When I feel the unique energy of teleporting envelop the two of us, I also close my eyes.

"There's no denying their connection," Trall insists.

"I don't wish her the heartache. That is what I have had to live with."

"Look into the eyes of an aged Churrian," Trall tenderly addresses her. "You only have to live with your own restrictions. You are head elder, after all. Who else can amend this rule?"

"Who am I to change a tradition that has been in place for thousands upon thousands of years?"

"You are our head elder," he answers.

***

In Drista, the driest quadrant of Churria, Kriyo and I arrive. Teleporting is so efficient. A hot, arid breeze comforts me as the sun warms my face. Upon opening my eyes, I see we stand on a precipice overlooking a vast desert. Directly below us is a clearing. It reflects the sunlight, making it difficult to view clearly.

"It is Ameira," Kriyo says. "It is the most powerful teleporting station within this universe."

I shade my eyes with my hand. Faintly, I see movement on its surface. Kriyo takes my hand and then steps closer to me. I remain confident and self assured. He's beautiful, quite exquisite. He also possesses a silent inner confidence.

I ponder the fact that, oddly, he's quiet. Then I understand it. He can't hear my thoughts. This is nice. I don't even try to hear his. Our silence is pleasant.

"You are like no one I have ever met, yet you are familiar to me," he says pensively.

"Perhaps it's simply that you are unable to hear my thoughts," I respond

"It's more than that, Meelah, though I find your silence intriguing. I perceive something profound, deep within you. I understand that you must leave, but I don't want you to go," he states ardently.

Despite his heartfelt words, I am fervently drawn to the atmosphere above me. Kriyo doesn't seem to discern anything, but I do. I take a few steps back. I sense that they're descending. Kriyo also moves back, anxious to learn what I'm sensing. I close my eyes and revel in their purity and judicious energy. Their intense vibrations resonate as one by one they land. Dust fills the air and I remain in place—honored by their dedication and presence. As the dust settles, I see my beloved Light Warriors. Standing in formation, they all drop to one knee as I approach them. Their wings remain retracted and I see the intricate beauty of the crests of their wings. Each possesses a distinctive pattern or design. Some are white with splotches of brown and black, while others are all one color. They are magnificent and striking and their reverence for me, for whom I once was to them, is inexplicable. Mikiel is at the head of the line. As he lowers his head, I catch him sneaking peeks at me and Kriyo.

I stand before each one and deferentially lower my head. I count only one hundred and thirty-nine female Light Warriors. So few remain from what once was. This army was once 10,000 and now only 576 in totality are here before me. This is why I now stand in this form, in Churrian form. I recall what I did and the agreement I made in an effort to protect them.

Mikiel looks up at me with his searing stare. Then I remember him pleading and imploring me. He knew what I was thinking of doing. He knew that I would choose the lives of my remaining kind over—my life. Light Warriors are eternal, but we are also mortal.

I remember dropping to my knees and I vowed that I'd find assistance. We could no longer fight the Dark Force alone. My army, my kind at this rate would soon be gone.

I was contacted by Head Elder Revil. He answered my plea for assistance. The Churrians were in need of a home. Their battle against the Dark Force's army had damaged their planet irreparably. These beings, highly skilled warriors, were part of the few that made it out with their lives. An agreement was forged between us. I contracted to reincarnate as a Churrian and lead the battle that would defeat the Dark Force's army, and thus a much-needed home was found. I fell to spare my remaining kind. I sacrificed who I was to save them and now, I again stand before them.

But why was I sent to earth? How did so much time elapse? Why am I now recalling who I was and what I must do? Even though I am inundated with questions, I thrust them aside, for, at this moment, I am fully present before the Light Warriors.

"Please rise," I command. "I am honored to again to be in your presence. I have been absent not only from you but from what we have been striving for our entire span of existence. I am here now and, when the time arises for battle, I would be honored if you will, once again, stand beside me. But this time we will not fight alone. We will be joined by the forces of the Churrians."

I place my hand to my chest and lower my head. All 576 Light Warriors bang against their armor in unity. The clanging reverberation encircles us. It unites us. Turning around, I focus on Kriyo who's standing behind me in absolute awe. My heart sings in rhythm with the ringing sound made by the pounding. I feel that I am moving forward in the right direction.

A Light Warrior with dark-brown, almost black wings saunters over to me. His dark skin beaded with sweat glistens in the daylight. With his helmet in hand, he bows. "Ruzi," I say to him. "It has been too long."

"It has, my liege," he says, while inspecting my new physical form. "You are the same, but without wings," he notes.

"Yes, Ruzi," I answer.

"But you are not yet who you once were," he says, while scrutinizing my eyes. "You are in there, though," he utters in thoughtful reflection. "We have missed you, my liege. No one could have replaced you, therefore no one did. We are honored to stand beside you again," he pledges, once more lowering his head.

"Ruzi, I have a request."

"Anything, my liege," he quickly answers.

"Train the Churrians. Prepare them for what lies ahead. I will advise Head Elder Shria." "Would you like me to send a Light Warrior to earth with you?"

"Mikiel has already agreed to the task. He is the only one permitted to travel there," I say while looking over in his direction. "Churria was once our home. Please prepare all on this star so that we can defend her."

Ruzi pounds his chest in acknowledgement. "On behalf of us all, it is wonderful to see you again," he says, before falling back into formation.

I turn around to briefly speak with Kriyo and see that he's gone. I scan all around me. I sense Mikiel's attention then I see Kriyo and Shria walking toward me.

"Meelah," Shria begins, "Kriyo advised me to meet with you. I can see that you have been quite busy," she continues, nodding at the mass of Light Warriors.

"With all due respect, Shria, I know that you are the head elder, but I have requested that the remaining Light Warriors remain here on Churria and help prepare for the battle that lies ahead," I say, then I lower my head in respect to her.

Shria is silent. She stands surrounded by the army of massive winged Light Warriors that I have asked to remain on Churria. I worry that I may have overstepped my power, trampling on the boundaries of her reign.

"Head Elder Shria, I would like to introduce you to Ruzi. He was and is a great warrior. He will aid in the training and preparations," I say instead, hoping to get a reaction from Shria. I fear that I have gravely disrespected her.

"Ruzi, it is my honor. I will advise the council of elders of your presence and your training skills," she promises him. Then she turns to Kriyo and adds, "Please teleport back to Ralta and notify Elder Trall that we will require an immediate gathering of the council in Bursa. Thank you, Kriyo."

Kriyo telepathically transmits to me, "Allow me to see you before you leave."

I nod my head. I can feel Mikiel in the background. He, too, hears Kriyo's request.

"Meelah, I expect you to attend this meeting in Bursa before you leave. It was, after all, your suggestion and there are channels that I, as head elder, must follow," she states. "Even if this suggestion is much needed and greatly appreciated," she concludes with a smile.

"It was never my intention to disrespect you," I affirm.

"I know," she answers. "I can see what a natural leader you are. Perhaps it is your path to lead all on Churria."

"You have rightfully donned the golden robe of the head elder. When your successor wears your robe, it will mean that you have ascended. Shria, my heart couldn't bear another loss."

"Meelah, everything is temporary, even my physical existence," she insists. "It is time for us to leave. I sense the council gathering in Bursa." Then to the Light Warriors she states, "It is our honor to have all of you return to Churria. Ruzi, I will be in touch."

She lowers her head then teleports from sight. Mikiel quickly makes his way to me. His blond locks shine in the sunlight. Dust covers part of his face. Before he utters a word, I follow the energetic trail from Shria and also teleport to Bursa.

Cobblestones, covered with moss, make up the surface beneath my feet. It's slippery and requires I make an adjustment to the way I walk. The air is thick and rich with moisture. Mature vegetation covers even the benches. I hear the sound of water and follow it. The stone pathway leads to a huge square, or meeting place, with a massive fountain dominating its center. I see Shria, Trall and other robed Churrians. They are all congregating beyond the fountain. I observe Shria as she steps up onto a stone platform. It, too, is swathed in greenery. Confident, I stand beside Trall.

Immediately I feel the stodgy and pompous energy of the elders that have gathered. It never occurred to me that I shouldn't be here. But it's clear they don't want me here and frankly, I don't care. What will transpire is bigger than their petty differences. I remain near Trall and he squeezes my hand and winks at me in encouragement.

Shria introduces Elder Jael and he gives a rather turgid and long-winded speech. If I had a watch, I would be looking at it impatiently. In summation, he wishes not to disrupt "the Churrian way." I become antsy. The energy of this Elder Jael is frustrating me. This attitude is futile against the Dark Force and any being that force controls. Out of respect for Shria, I bite my tongue.

Finally, she takes the platform again. I watch Elder Jael as he glares at me with obvious contempt before he takes his seat. What have I ever done to him? Again, Trall takes hold of my hand. He doesn't look at me. He remains fixed on Shria, but his warm hand affords me unspoken support. I feel my father's presence within the soft breeze. Perhaps this is why he chose to go to earth and find me. Perhaps he, too, was not like the older generation of elders. They possess an arrogance and anger that resides within. They appear to be rigid and resistant to change. But Trall is different. His honesty, authenticity and kind heart place him worlds apart from the elders surrounding me.

"I would like to bring Meelah to the platform," I hear Shria say.

Unsure if I heard Shria correctly, I look at Trall, hoping I misheard her but as he nods his head to me, he confirms that I didn't. Honoring Shria, I do as she asks. As I begin my walk to her, I feel like a succulent lamb entering a wolf's den. Tuning into the elders' thoughts, I quickly realize that they don't want to hear anything I have to say. They don't want me here!

I take the cobblestoned, moss-laden stairway, and all is silent, except for the thud of my boots on the stone beneath my feet. I stride over to Shria, my shoulders back and my chin held high. As I approach her, I am greeted by her genuine compassion. Her energy soothes my ragged nerves. I stand alongside her then look out into the moderate-sized crowd of robed Churrians, roughly one hundred and fifty in total. I find myself counting the tops of their heads. As soon as I get to about fifty, I hear Shria and so does everyone else. These "evolved" beings gasp at her words.

"I have designated Meelah an official elder of Bursa, making her the forty-third elder from this quadrant. I will personally educate her upon her return. It is my wish that Meelah don the robe of head elder when my time ends."

Her declaration causes me to forget where and who I am. Abruptly, I right my stance and regain my composure before I face Shria. Her announcement seems premature, especially since it evokes outrage amongst the elders. I do not wish for this disquiet prior to my departure. While observing her tranquil demeanor, I see how exemplary is her honor and integrity. She patiently waits for the elders to settle, though many never do. Rudely, they continue to exchange their livid outrage with one another in hushed tones. In spite of their impertinence, Shria continues with absolute power and divine certainty in her every word.

"The Light Warriors have returned to Churria. They will prepare our Churrians for the fated war that lies ahead of us. Without this concerted effort, all we know and love could fall," Shria warns. After a brief pause she continues. "I am your elected head elder. I have always done what is best for the inhabitants of this star. Each of you knows this," she states adamantly. "That being said, this meeting is now adjourned." She turns to me and nods her head then says, "It is time for you to return to earth."

"How can I leave you like this?" I ask, hearing the disconcerting murmuring of the elders.

"You must," she affirms. "Go to Calla, she's expecting you."

"It feels wrong to leave you, Shria."

"The only thing you have to fear is not locating the amulet. Find it, then return," she states resolutely.

At that moment, an immediate hush falls over the crowd. Sensing one of the Light Warriors approaching, I look upward and see Ruzi before he lands alongside Shria. He spreads his massive ebony wings before he retracts them comfortably behind him. His presence, as with all Light Warriors, demands respect.

"My liege," Ruzi says to honor me while lowering his head. "If it pleases you, I will remain with the Head Elder."

"Yes, Ruzi. Thank you."

Then I turn to Shria. It occurs to me that I didn't ask the Light Warriors to remain on Churria, she did. She premeditated all of this. I merely followed my instinct, which was precisely what she hoped I would do. Following my sense of duty, I validated her appointment of me as an elder and my subsequent promotion to head elder.

She again nods her head to me, but this time with a wink. As the elders begin to disburse, we are joined by Trall. He shakes his head at Shria.

"I sure hope you know what you're doing," he intones quietly to her.

"You know me better than that, Trall. I always have a plan," I hear her answer.

"Ruzi, please keep her safe, especially from Elder Jael. His resentment is almost tangible," I tell him.

"I will protect the head elder, and in particular, from your father."

"Elder Jael is my birth-father?" I blurt out, stunned. "Shria, my mother, is she similar to Jael?"

"No," she answers simply.

I sense Shria's attention on me as I digest the rather noxious revelation. I am in no way like that Churrian. He exudes such negativity and contempt.

I address Ruzi. "My father, Samuel Neegry, died on earth. I do not know Elder Jael nor do I wish to do so. Ruzi, thank you for keeping Shria safe. I will return as quickly as possible."

He bows to me, takes a step back and stands behind Shria and Trall. I reverently lower my head to all of them and teleport to Calla.

Standing on the shore of Calla, I inhale the clean sweet air. Across her water are impressive tall trees spanning her bank. They paint the landscape with beauty. Each tree has been individually influenced by Calla's surge crafting a distinctive bend to its main stem. Lofty branches weighed down by dense green foliage seem to bow to Calla, and to me. Lowing my head, I return the reverence.

Behind me, I feel the presence of a female and turn around. Positioned about twenty feet ahead of me is a Churrian with her hood raised. Her presence manifests as meek. She pushes her hood back, revealing a mild and quiet Churrian. Pieces of her graying brown hair frames her face. She looks over her shoulder as if she's worried that someone will see her meeting with me.

"Who are you?" I ask.

"Meelah, I am your mother, Raza," she answers in a whisper. "I am so sorry. I never wanted to let you go," she confirms, before glancing over her shoulder again.

"Why are you afraid?"

"Meelah, Jael never thought you would return, but I knew you would," she manages. "I must go. I am sorry that I have wounded you. If it brings you any solace, I still cry as I did the day you were sent to earth. That day you were torn not only from my arms but also from my heart."

Though she continues to peer over her shoulder, for a brief moment, her eyes connect with mine. It is here that I see the truth of her words. She teleports from sight. Her innocent yet sorrowful eyes singe my heart. She, too, was injured by my departure to earth. It doesn't make sense to me. Why was I sent to earth then reared by a Churrian? Regardless of the why and the how, I must be leaving. I hear Calla call to me. She has been waiting for me and she needn't wait any longer.

Beginning my journey, I step into her tepid water. Pleasantly greeted, I thank her for this unforeseen yet appreciated gift of warmth. After I am about seven steps in, the sound of swift striding footsteps from behind me seizes my attention. Turning around, I see it is Kriyo. He hurries toward me while I, still facing him, continue to move deeper. The water is not only lukewarm, it is also calm. Conversely, outside my small pool of peaceful serenity, Calla surges by violently. Entering the turbulent water, dragging his drenched heavy robe, Kriyo continues my way. He struggles against her force. I know she toys with him. She questions why he is here. If Calla wished to remove him she would; instead, she tests him. Steadfast and unfaltering, he fights against her strength, however, and steadily he proceeds. Appearing to have met the conditions of her trial assessment, she permits his fruitful persistent effort.

Nearly waist-deep, I stop. The water encircling me is placid and comforting, though outside my calm pool, she continues to rage fiercely. Kriyo finally reaches me. Now standing before me, also surrounded by stillness, here he is. I watch his chest heave as he catches his breath. Glistening droplets of water cascade down the sides of his attractive face. His moist lips separate as he continues to normalize his breathing. Standing taller than I as he faces me, no words or thoughts are exchanged. His eyes are alluring. He wishes to speak, I can sense it, but like the peaceful silence encircling us, he only continues to stare at me. Taking hold of my hands, he squeezes them with fervency. My soul feels this touch; it flushes my cheeks and they all but burn. Within his eyes I see his inexplicable connection to me. This intense feeling moves us closer to each other. His breath, still rapid, grazes the surface of my face. Within this closeness, I feel my heart as it begins to race, quickening my breath.

Memories of us and our past-life wash over me and I close my eyes to revel in them. But there was far more to us than heated exchanges, there was also profound love. Our souls mated, creating some kind of eternal union. Here and now I recall this bond. I experience this connection.

Opening my eyes, I see his eyes still boring into me. I know that he too feels this powerful binding unification. Though it appears still enigmatic to him, I witness him embrace it. Despite the profound bond forged in this moment, I hear her. Calla tells me that it's time for me to depart this world and gauging from his persistence, I gather that her message was solely for me. Though I am entranced by him, I smile then detach my hands from his grasp. Lowering my head, I say goodbye, then take a few steps backward. Again she prods me. I must leave. Closing my eyes, I fall into Calla. Just as I begin my descent, I feel Kriyo grab hold of my waist. Both of us submerge into her. Travelling through a flash of light connecting the two realities, I return to earth, but this time—I am not alone.

Chapter Twelve

It takes effort but I pull my saturated robe though the knee-deep water. "How are you able to travel with me, Kriyo? The vortexes are closed," I utter, attempting to make sense of what has just occurred.

"What's that unpleasant stench?" Kriyo calls out as he follows me to shore. "This water isn't potable! It reeks like nothing I have ever smelled before!"

Already at the rock-faced shore, I lean against one of the slippery outcrops and take off my boots. I dump out the water and see gross debris slithering out. Nightfall has touched the sky, but I can still observe Kriyo as he wrings the water out of his robe. He is comical as he gags from the foul odor of low tide. Then he sees the distant lights of New York City and is instantly mesmerized.

"We should go," I say. But he doesn't even hear me.

Again he appears affected by the disgusting pollution that surrounds us. As he leans against the rock next to me, I'm aware of his repulsion. No words are needed. He plainly illustrates what he's feeling as he bunches up his nose and furrows his brow while glaring at the slimy sludge covering his feet.

Where we stand has certainly altered the intense exchange of moments ago.

"Is this where you live?" I hear him ask.

"Not precisely here," I answer with a chuckle. "I live in the city over there."

"Is it also damaged like this ecosystem?"

"Kriyo, no city compares to Churria. But in some places here on earth humans live reverently with nature, just obviously not where we stand. We should be going."

"Can't we teleport?"

"No, we must walk, and our attire doesn't quite fit in here."

Kriyo looks down at his robe. I can tell that he already feels a bit lost.

"Kriyo, why did you come with me?" I ask, trying to capture his attention.

He reaches over and strokes the side of my face and says, "I didn't wish for you to leave again though I knew you must."

The natural comfort I feel with him is nice. His presence is like that of a true friend whereas Mikiel can be quite overpowering with fervor. I also love the fact that he cannot hear my jumbled thoughts and I respectfully don't delve into his. The lack of telepathic exchange is wonderful.

"Meelah," I hear a voice shout from above me.

Then I see Riya, who is happily waving to us from what appears to be a road. Instantly, she travels down to where we stand. This means of travel seems quicker than teleporting; I must master it.

"And you will, Meelah," she states. "But what have you brought to earth?" Riya asks while looking Kriyo over from head to toe. "He is both salty and yummy! Does he belong to you?"

"Riya, this is Kriyo. He came with me from Churria."

"Kriyo, that's an interesting name," she says, drooling over him.

Kriyo desperately tries to maintain eye contact with me. He takes a step back from her and slips on the wet slimy rocks. He struggles to get sound footing as tries to he avoid her charm.

"Meelah," she says while sauntering back toward me, "he's already taken. Apparently you haven't heard those reeling thoughts of his. Well, let's get both of you to Religards. Mr. Giblet will be especially interested in your guest. Too bad he's taken," she repeats. Disappearing into the ensuing darkness, I hear, "Come on, Meelah, let's do this today."

Again, she appears above us. Placing her hand on her hip she appears impatient. I almost hear the tapping of her foot as she wonders why we don't already stand beside her.

"We have two options, Kriyo. The first is try to travel as she did. The second option is a long and arduous climb."

"Option one, please," he says. "I already tried to teleport, but the energy here is far too dense." He steps carefully over to me, takes my hand and adds, "You can do it, Meelah. I believe in you."

And, indeed, he does. I close my eyes and bring my intention to arriving to where Riya is. Upon opening my eyes, I'm shocked to see where we are. Cars are coming directly at us! The sound of automobiles honking coupled with their bright headlights is overwhelming. We're going to be hit! Kriyo stands in front of me. A sweet gesture, but this will not be effective against cars careening toward us at sixty miles per hour. Quickly, I raise my hands and freeze everything, even Kriyo.

Catching my breath from the adrenaline rush, I gauge where we are and where we must go. In the distance, I see Riya standing beside a black car that is parked safely off the roadway. I place my hand upon Kriyo's shoulder. As he unfreezes, he releases a high-pitched scream. I restrain my laughter, yet a grin forms.

"What is happening?" he cries in a panic. "Where are we and what are these things attacking us?"

"Kriyo, I will explain. But now I must resume time. Let's go to Riya, she's over here," I say while moving off the roadway.

Once we're in the clear and standing beside Riya, I resume time. The cars that were careening at us skid and screech. But once the drivers see that we are no longer in the road, they swiftly continue on their way. One moment they saw two beings wearing white robes in front of them, the next they are gone. With my mind I send them a whisper of peace. I hope that this will pacify their steaming protest.

Riya shakes her head and raises her brow. "You need some work, Meelah," she says, rather unimpressed. "Great, more for me to do. While it was kind of you to send them serenity, a bottle of whisky would certainly be more effective. Well, get into the car, Ms. Lucy waits."

Slipping into the back seat of the sleek black Town Car, I instantly feel nasty in my wet robe. Kriyo still stands outside the vehicle. He inspects it thoroughly, unsure if he should get in.

"Hey, Kriyo, we don't have all night. You can look the car over when it's parked at the school. Now move it!" Riya shouts from the front seat.

He drops his head and, after a ready smile of encouragement from me, he awkwardly climbs into the car. Like before, I restrain my urge to laugh. I see Riya roll her eyes and signal to the driver. A calm thin man gets out of the driver's seat and closes Kriyo's door and I watch him shudder as the door slams shut. Looking every which way as he digests the new scenery, ultimately his eyes settle on me. I see him relax. This Churrian is somehow here with me on earth. Perhaps since my father departed, fate allowed one to replace him. Amid my pondering, a question for Riya arises.

"Riya, why use a car when you can..." I pause while looking at the driver.

"Oh, Raphael, Meelah; and Meelah, this is Raphael," she says while checking her lipstick in the small side mirror. "Raphael is cool. Though he's human, he is quite devoted and knowledgeable about all of this. Aren't you, babe?" she asks while stroking his leg. "Anyway, if he's not, he'll have another rousing meeting with Tali, right, honey?" she adds as her hand smacks his leg.

"It is nice to meet you, Raphael," I say to him.

"Yes, it is nice to meet you," Kriyo says, emulating me. His slow speech is creepy. I can't help but smile and, as I do, I inexplicably feel the presence of my father. At this moment, I feel happy. I haven't felt this way in, I can't remember when. Rather than dissect the moment, I decide to enjoy it.

The car moves forward and enters into the stream of traffic that only moments ago nearly flattened Kriyo and me. I look over and observe Kriyo. His senses seem severely overwhelmed while he stares out his window. I, too, get lost in the tremendous energy of New York City.

My wet robe now gives me chills. I rub my prune-skinned hands together. Kriyo takes my hands in his then brings them to his mouth. He blows into them for warmth and though I smile, I also shiver.

Sensing something else, something dark, I follow my intuition and look in the rearview mirror. I see Raphael intently glaring at me. His eyes darken. They become consumed by darkness—by a Shadow. The Shadow sneers at me and I hear the car accelerate.

"Riya, get out of here!" I yell.

Quickly, I take hold of Kriyo's hand. The traffic ahead of us is halted by a stoplight. We're going to crash into it! As soon as Riya disappears from sight, I close my eyes and, as if in slow motion, I feel Kriyo and I slip through and out of the careening Town Car. Once our feet are planted, we again dodge the oncoming traffic, but this time they're coming at us at a much slower rate, giving us the advantage.

Then I helplessly watch the Town Car forcibly crash into the cars stopped at the light. He used no brakes. The deafening sound from the Shadow smashing into the halted vehicles is intense. Shards of metal and debris fly into the air. Smoke and flames rise from several of the cars. The Town Car rests atop two other vehicles, wheels still spinning. I can feel innocent lives cry for help. Without another thought, I run over to them, but Ms. Lucy appears out of nowhere halting me. Just then, someone grabs my hand and forcibly holds me back. Struggling to move onward, following my heart, I remain restrained, frustrated and heartsick.

"No, Meelah! They have already seen too much. Mikiel, bring these two to Religards now, please," Ms. Lucy demands.

Mikiel remains invisible to the eye, but not to my senses. I feel him squeeze my arm and I see the indent on Kriyo's sleeve as he takes hold of his arm. Again, I see what my mere presence has created. I feel the lives of two humans slip away as we travel with Mikiel to Religards. My heart pangs and anger begin to overcome me.

We arrive at the rear of the building. I kick the door in and scream, "Again life is lost! I abhor them! I hate them," I scream then drop to my knees. In anger...no, rage, I run my fingers through my hair and pull, giving myself a taste of physical pain as a distraction.

Tali swaggers past me with an arrogant countenance.

"That's really effective, Meelah," she says with a snicker.

I stand to my feet and, with energy from my palms, I emit surges of power at her back, pushing her into the wall in front of her. She turns around and wipes the blood off her lip then appears before me and backhands my face. Surprising her, I remain in place. Again, I push her with energy from my hands.

Kriyo doesn't know how to respond. Nor does he understand where he is; he is lost. Tali and I throw each other around indenting walls, smashing light fixtures and everything else that comes into our path. Mikiel manifests into his physical form and stands beside Kriyo. He shakes his head as he watches the juvenile sight before him.

"ENOUGH!" Ms. Lucy shouts. "Meelah, I expect more of you," she scolds. "Tali, all of this must be repaired by morning. Students will be present and I already have enough to do! And I require the services of Riya, this instant! Mr. Giblet, in my office now!" she spouts.

From the corner of my eye, I see Mr. Giblet appear. His small stature was camouflaged in the school's dim lights after business hours. Always mindful of the environment, the Churrian way comes through Ms. Lucy.

"Meelah!" Mr. Giblet exclaims before he scurries down the hall.

I feel Mikiel approach me from behind. His intense presence is difficult to ignore. He captures my attention as he saunters by.

"Light Warrior," I hear Tali mutter under her breath.

"What's the deal with you, Tali?" I ask, getting in her face again. "We Light Warriors saved you. Did you forget?"

"No, I haven't," she says with contempt. "I also remember the Light Warriors not protecting my kind before they were all brutally slaughtered! Why did you save me? Do you think it's easy to live in the absence of all of your people?" She pauses as if to catch her breath. Her shoulders relax as I see her demeanor soften. "Why did you save me?" she asks as she holds back her tears.

The sadness in Tali is substantial. I recall saving her as a Light Warrior and, at that time, it never occurred to me that this rescue would bring with it bitter resentment.

"My actions were never meant to hurt you," I say to her back as she turns away from me. "Tali, finding life on your devastated planet gave me hope. It is ironic how an action that brought optimism not only to me but to all the Light Warriors caused you timeless anguish. This was never my intention," I state, affected by her distress.

With her back to me still, I see her shake vigorously back and forth. She moves so rapidly I can no longer see the detail of her form. From within the shaking and shuddering, I see vibrant-colored clothing emerge and, with it, a new being. Calm overtakes the altered figure now before me.

"Kriyo, you're still salty, a tad pale but...yum, yum," Riya says, leering at him.

"Hey, Meelah, thanks for the warning earlier. You saved us, again. Too bad for Raphael, though," she says while staring at her pastel-pink painted fingernails. "Not too many humans are open to our presence. Looks like I need another driver, but this time not a human. They are too vulnerable to the Shadows. Well, I must call Joaquin, the new young night janitor. He's delicious. Perhaps I'll turn up the heat so he has to take off his shirt. I must run; we have a great deal to smooth over."

"Riya!" I shout before she disappears from sight.

"Yes?"

"I am without words," I say as I struggle to find the right ones.

"I have lots do to, Meelah. What is it?" she asks impatiently.

"Riya, if my action of saving you has brought you the same amount of sorrow as it has to Tali, I am deeply sorry."

She strolls back over to me with her feminine little swagger. Searching my eyes for a connection, she answers me. "You have given us the opportunity to have a life. Tali is bitter, but I know that she appreciates your heartfelt words. Meelah, in this form you're different. You're more attuned to emotion and I like it," she adds with a genuine smile. "Now, I must be off. Oh man, it's already 4:23 a.m. The little minions will be flooding these hallways in no time. I have phone calls to make and several stories to fabricate. Gotta run," she explains as she hurries off. Though in a rush, she takes the time to look over her shoulder, while tossing her hair from side to side, and makes one last comment, "I'll see ya, Kriyo. I must go to Churria one day!"

Kriyo walks alongside me. His face is pale and his energy jumbled. He continues to watch Riya as she moseys down the long hallway in her three-inch black heels and sultry red dress. With his mouth agape, he finally faces me. I can't help but laugh, and he apparently doesn't find the humor in this.

"I'd walk off, teleport, leave, something, anything, but I have no idea where we are and what just happened!"

His words release my laughter. My eyes tear as I watch him look like a teakettle about to boil. I try to compose myself; I try.

"This is not funny, none of this is. We arrive on earth and I am bathed in scum then I meet Riya who looks at me as though she intends to devour me. Then, we are attacked by fast-moving objects. Then we enter one of these—"

"Cars," I answer, wiping my tears of hilarity.

"Cars, then we slip out of it and what happened? I have never been so confused in my life. Is this the way you live? This is no way to exist! Is this seriously the way you survive, Meelah?" he asks while pausing, breathless.

"Well, not all of my time on earth has been this way, just the last month," I return, seizing control of my amusement.

Kriyo paces the narrow hallway. The hem of his robe is covered in mud. Actually, most of his once-pristine white robe is covered in a variety of dark-colored smudges. The strap of his sandal is broken and, as he walks, his left foot slides out. He stops and I observe him trying to gather himself. He raises his shoulders and holds his head high.

"Now what, Meelah?" he asks with his regained composure.

"Let's find Ms. Lucy and the others. I need to go to my apartment and get a few things, like clothing for both of us. Though my robe is practically dry, I feel gross!"

"As do I. That is what we'll do. After you, then," he says, politely.

I move past him and feel him follow close behind me. With every step, his energy further relaxes. Taking a few lefts then a right, I navigate down the hallways like I've being doing this my entire life. In reality, I follow the residual energy of Riya. Finally, we arrive at the front office and I open its door. We hear voices in the back conference room and follow them. The door is open and Ms. Lucy is sitting at the head of the oval table. The rest of the many seats are filled with creatures I don't know.

Coming to a stand, Ms. Lucy welcomes us in. First she acknowledges me with a brief, but reverent bowing of her head. Then she stands before Kriyo. She grabs the back of his head and brings his forehead to hers. Curious, I tune into their exchange.

"It has been far too long, my son," Ms. Lucy communicates lovingly. "I apologize for not acknowledging you when you arrived. I told you not to come. It's far too dangerous here."

"I needed to see you."

"Faro is well?" she asks.

"He also misses you, Mother. He would have come if he was able."

"Soon, we will leave together and return to Drista."

"Mother, I came to warn you. Father has drawn—"

"What, Kriyo, what has he seen?"

"Darkness will come to earth."

"I know. The sooner we all leave earth the better it will be. No one wishes for these humans to suffer through any more violence. They have their own transformation to achieve. We needn't add anymore hardship to them."

Ms. Lucy turns and addresses the patiently waiting group. Though most are telepathic, some seem lost with the silent communication between her and Kriyo. As she talks, I watch Kriyo and wonder why he didn't tell me that Ms. Lucy was his mother. But this query must wait. Other pressing matters now take precedence.

"Meelah and Kriyo, please take a seat so I may introduce you to our Northeast Team. Some members you have already met, but others you have not." She pulls out the chair at the head of the table and tells me, "This seat is rightfully yours, Meelah."

"I don't need to sit at the head of the table."

"Meelah, you must begin to honor the leader that resides within," she states keenly. "Now sit so we may commence."

As I prepare to take the seat, I notice that every eye in the room is fixed on me, every eye but Kriyo's. I lower my head to those before me then hear Ms. Lucy begin.

"First, there is Mr. Giblet, whom you have already had the pleasure of meeting. Then we have Riya, whom you have also met." Behind Riya stands Mikiel. She pauses and lowers her head to him then moves on to the next member. There is no need to introduce Mikiel. I know him quite well. Continuing, she adds, "To your left is Dudley Kane, our media contact. He has influence in every media station here in the northeast. Next there is Roger Hedley and Rose Cummings. They head a team that cleans up after any beings leave physical evidence of our existence. They are known as 'the cleaners.' Next to them is Tamilia. Her skills have recently proved most effective, especially after today's earlier events. Tamilia mind sweeps, clearing specific memories from humans. Then there is Cal. He is the one who has surrounded Religards with an impenetrable field; well, impassable for now, anyway. But, as you all know, that soon will change. And finally, Kriyo, he is my son from Churria. His presence here must be investigated, Mr. Giblet. One of two phenomenons is occurring and we must know precisely which it is. First, the vortexes have begun to spin, allowing his entry, or Meelah's powers have exceeded our expectations. Regardless of which it is, please look into this. Now, let's continue our business; time is fleeting. Dudley, you have a firm grasp on the media feed, right?"

"Yes, the anchor on scene works directly for me. With the assistance of Tamilia, the fatal accident was deemed the result of drunk driving."

"All of this is quite unfortunate but thank you, Dudley. It's a shame that we lost Raphael. Did he have family, Riya?"

"No, he had no immediate family."

"Well, many human lives were lost this evening. How many perished?"

"Six," Dudley answers.

"Collateral damage. They died for the greater good," Ms. Lucy proclaims.

"The greater good?" I can't help but ask. "They all died because of me. I must find the amulet and leave these people alone."

"And this you will do," she answers. "Meelah, the entire universe hangs in the balance. The amulet is only the first step. But what you do with it will determine the very existence of this planet, every planet within this universe, and beyond. You are exhausted, perhaps this meeting at the present time is too much for our leader. Riya, please show Meelah to her room so she can change. I'm sure there will be clothing for Kriyo, as well. Samuel was about his size."

"Riya, please escort Kriyo," I state adamantly. "I know that he wishes to freshen up, but I wish to remain here. Thank you."

After giving me a pleased smile, Ms. Lucy adds one more request, "Oh Riya, free Luther from the trap again before school commences." Ms. Lucy brings her attention again to me and adds, "Miguel is determined to catch whatever is rifling through his supply room. Luther shifted back into Galidrome form the moment you left with Samuel. He has been a nuisance, to say the least. Perhaps your return will ease his mourning."

"Whatever happened to Desitere from my apartment building?"

"He was another unfortunate collateral loss. And Meelah, please address me as all of my peers do. I am Pasha to you. Ms. Lucy is the name of my earthling persona."

As I digest yet another loss, I bow my head to Pasha. After an additional hour of deliberating, making certain that all bases were covered to mask our arrival and the incidents that followed, the meeting is adjourned.

Coming to a stand, I lower my head to each member as they pass me. First is Tamilia. As she approaches me I observe her scrawny, gaunt form. Her light blonde hair is thinning and her complexion is a white as the walls. She appears as skittish as a scared mouse as she scoots by. Regardless of her appearance, I nod.

Then there is Dudley Kane. A healthy-looking man in his mid-forties, he stops and lowers his head. As he raises his eyes with an inappropriate smile, he winks at me. Slightly rotund, but seemingly light on his feet, he lingers with his awkward leer. I observe his just-dyed brown hair and unnaturally tan skin as he winks again.

"Thank you for your assistance, Mr. Kane," I say in an effort to get him moving.

Next is Mr. Giblet. As always, a smile brightens his sweet face. His stout, dimunitive stature suits the gently nature of his personality. Wearing a green flecked tweed ensemble, with a brown vest, a yellow bow tie, knotted tightly, and a matching hat in hand, he bows to me. The top of his small bald head gives charm to this kind-hearted creature. Reverently, I lower my head.

Before me now are Roger Hedley and Rose Cummings. Both possess an innate air of confidence. I can sense that they love what they do and they do it well. The two of them look like they fell out of the seventies. Roger, in human years, appears to be in his late thirties. His dark skin and neatly picked afro, shady sunglasses, bell bottom blue jeans and a form-fitting t-shirt cause him to stand apart from the others. But I'm certainly not judging. I'm wearing a filthy white robe and riding boots.

Rose, standing close at his side, is striking. She looks a little like one of the original Charlie's Angels. Her long blonde feathered hair, vibrant self-assured smile, pale blue eyes, along with her form-fitting, white t-shirt, skin-tight blue jeans and high-heeled black boots, showcase her femininity.

"Thank you," I say to the two of them.

Then last, but certainly not least, is Cal. His energy is calm, kind and simple. Physically he's large, tall, completely bald and quite pale-skinned. He definitely doesn't blend into the appearance of humans. He struggles to look directly into my eyes. I feel his energy; he is reluctant to express himself. Dressed in a grey cotton short-sleeved shirt and drab grey slacks that appear a tad too small, he remains standing before me, his head still bowed. I touch the surprisingly cold surface of Cal's hand. He immediately looks at me as if I woke him. We instantly forge a connection. The way his pale grey eyes meet mine touches me. His thoughts are simple and as soft as his demeanor. I smile at him and lower my head, and he swiftly raises my chin and brings my focus back to meet his. Then he takes a step back and bows forward to me. As he rises, he turns then ambles off. I follow him and observe Cal walk mindfully into the office and then straight into the wall. Shocked, I watch him seamlessly blend into the concrete surface. Going over to it, I place my hand on its surface and feel his unique energy residing within.

"Cal is short for Caltrimdon," Mikiel says from behind me. "Caltrimdons are very loyal yet uncomplicated beings."

"Is he the last of his kind too?" I ask.

"No."

"Please excuse me, Mikiel. May I have a few brief words with Meelah?" Pasha breaks in.

Mikiel nods his head then disappears from sight. Mysteriously, he comes then goes. Though many memories of who I was are resurfacing, I'm still acclimating to his silent means of travel.

"Meelah, I'm glad I caught you. School will soon commence. A few staff members are already here, which means that you must scoot. Get cleaned up and rest. After lunch, Mr. Giblet's day will be yours, in room F-2. Go, Meelah. Otherwise, your attire will be something else for me to explain," Ms. Lucy instructs.

"And where should I be off to?"

"Oh dear, I'm sorry. We moved all of the contents of your apartment into the basement. A room has been made up for you. Religards can more easily protect you and I thought it might be difficult for you to go back there."

"Thank you, Ms. Lucy, oh, excuse me, thank you, Pasha."

"You're quite welcome. Now off with you."

"Tina, good morning," Pasha says, looking past me.

I duck into the doorway leading to the steps. Picking up the hem of my long robe, I hurry down what feels like a never-ending stairway. Approaching the basement, I see Mikiel standing outside the door leading into my new room.

"My liege," he says, lowering his head to me.

"I'm sorry, Mikiel. I didn't mean to be rude earlier. Exhaustion only scrapes the surface of what I feel."

"No need to apologize, my liege."

"Mikiel, is that all you wish to say?" I ask, sensing his unspoken words.

"I will stand watch while you rest."

"Okay, Mikiel. Thank you," I return, resting my hand on his shoulder.

"Kriyo and Riya are in there, as well, Meelah."

I can't help but sigh. I am so exhausted that my body aches. The last thing I want to deal with is a party.

"Do you wish for me to clear the room for you?"

"No, Mikiel. I'll take care of it," I answer, knowing perfectly well how much he would love to kick Kriyo out of the room and even off earth.

I push the door open, the same door leading to the room where I battled Tali. I had no idea what it would look like with all the contents of my apartment now arranged in it. I am pleasantly surprised. The huge room is softly illuminated. Area rugs cover the majority of the concrete floor. I see my bed from across the room. It's just as I remember it in my apartment. I trudge over to it. Seeing my fluffy down comforter covered by my pink flannel duvet, I realize how much I missed my bed. And there's my pillow! My little pillow that has travelled the world with me and my father; how I missed it. Picking it up, I press it to my face. Then I glance around the room. On the far left of the room, I see Riya sitting, reading a newspaper. Part of the room has a partition dividing it. I don't remember this. Curious, I head over to Riya and the new structure. She brings her pointer finger to her lips signaling for me to be quiet. Aware of my noisy boots, I continue on as quietly as possible, unsure of what I'll find. I see something that I never thought I would. Chuckling under my breath, I creep over to get a better look. In another bed is Kriyo, dressed in a tuxedo—one of my father's tuxedos. Nuzzling his face is Luther. Still in Galidrome form, he nestles closer to Kriyo, undoubtedly to get warm. Sensing Riya walking alongside me, I turn and shake my head at her.

"I figured since he's never worn human clothing before, why not start with the best. Your father had fabulous taste."

"He sure did," I agree, looking first at Luther then at Kriyo, handsomely adorned in Calvin Klein.

"Meelah, we had an existing shower refurbished down here. It is open, as you can see."

"Let me guess, is that the reason why you remained down here?"

"I had to make sure that Kriyo was well taken care of, but the scenery from that shower was quite appealing."

"Riya, you didn't!"

"He also had no idea how to wear a tuxedo. I was only trying to help him."

"Of course you were."

"Oh, honey, he is SO YUMMY! Too bad he's also taken."

"Taken?"

"Like you don't already know. Well, Mikiel is always entertaining. A girl must have her fun. Ta, ta," she says and sashays to the door.

As the door slams behind her, I look back at Kriyo and Luther who are still passed out. I tiptoe over to my dresser, finding the drawers still filled with my clothes. I snatch some undergarments, something foreign to Churrians and a t-shirt and yoga pants. After slipping out off my boots, I pad barefoot to the shower and turn it on, all the way to hot. I peer out of the open bathroom, which is coincidently in view of Kriyo's bed. This will need to be changed. Taking off my soiled and heavy robe, I stand beneath the searing water. Riya was thorough enough to provide Kriyo with toiletries. I wonder if she offered to scrub his back. After luxuriating in my steamy, cleansing moment, I shampoo and condition my hair and, as I'm rinsing, I hear something fall to the floor. Swiftly I turn off the water and pick up my soiled robe.

"I didn't see anything!" I hear Kriyo call from right outside my shower.

"Meelah, are you all right?" I hear Mikiel shout in a protective manner.

"I'm fine! Will the both of you, please stand back?"

Then I see Luther sniff the air. When he sees me, he begins to happily scamper my way.

"You, too, get! I will come out when I am dressed!"

With a sad face, Luther turns around and waddles back. Feeling awful that I hurt his feelings, I quickly dress. When I come out from the shower, I see Kriyo pacing back and forth and Mikiel attentively watching his every move. No doubt he just wanted to make sure Kriyo didn't get a peek, if he hadn't already. Without a word, Mikiel returns to his post and I hear the heavy door slam closed again. Luther sits patiently on Kriyo's bed. His sweet, furry little face is attentive to me.

"I'm sorry, my dear friend," I say, while stroking the top of his head. "I didn't wish to leave you here. I know that you miss my father, as I do."

He perks up and begins to hover in the air. His plump new underbelly appears to be weighing him down.

"You gained a little weight there, Luther. No worries, we'll work that off. The next time I return to Churria, I will bring you."

His little ears perk up then he flies into my arms and nestles against me. Again, I follow Kriyo as he continues to pace back and forth dressed to the nine. At this point, I am too tired to even care if he saw me naked. I hurry over to my bed carrying sweet Luther. I can't wait to get into it. It seems to call to me. Then I hear Kriyo mumbling in the background.

"I may have seen you. This was not my intention, let me reassure you. I just heard the noise of the water and sat up."

"It's fine, Kriyo. I'm sure you're sorry and I am exhausted."

"Sleep well, Meelah, and no, I'm not," he says, returning to his bed.

"You're not what?" I ask, irritated.

"I'm not sorry," he says, loud enough for even Mikiel to hear.

Smiling at his response, I tell him, "Kriyo, look in the boxes next to your bed. While I was greeting Luther I saw a few of them labeled Samuel's clothing. You'll find pieces there that will be more comfortable than what you have on. Though, you look incredibly handsome in that tuxedo. It was my father's favorite."

"Thank you. Now try to get some rest, Meelah."

While climbing into my bed, I watch Luther curl into a small ball at the foot of it atop my plush comforter. His furry little body, though he has definitely grown a fat, but cute, belly, pulls into a tight fluffy ball. No sooner does my head touch my favorite pillow, than my eyes effortlessly close and the need for sleep overtakes me.

Chapter Thirteen

Hours pass and Kriyo lies upon his bed staring at the ceiling. All the eventful moments occurring in his short time on earth race through his head. On occasion, he tilts his head to the side, directing his attention to the partition that divides him from Meelah. The intense connection to her continues to confound him. He has been surrounded by other female Churrians throughout his life, but there has never been a spark with any of them. Then there is Meelah. In an instant, an indescribable bond was forged.

Still in the sexy, fitted tuxedo, he sits on the edge of his bed. He realizes that the closeness he feels to Meelah was not the only reason he was compelled to come to earth. There is more, but he struggles to make sense of the rash, yet fated decision that brought him to where he now sits. Though his mother is here, there is still more, his inner being knows it.

Closing his eyes, he reflects on his father, Faro. The two of them have always been close, especially in the absence of his mother. Kriyo recalls the first time he walked into his father's chambers and saw his prophetic paintings. Though he was quite young, he understood what he was viewing. In this memory, his father's newest painting illustrated that his mother would leave for earth. Faro's detailed paintings depicted Head Elder Shria's conflict in sending a young Churrian to earth. His drawings continued, showing that Head Elder Shria would travel to Drista and his mother would soon depart to earth along with Trall's son, Samuel. The reality of his father's pictures precisely foretelling those fated events still leaves him unsettled. Shortly after his father drew these creations, his mother did, indeed, leave. He avoided the sight of his father's work after that.

Moments before he grabbed onto Meelah as she travelled to earth, he visited his father. Like an invisible force had compelled him, he entered his father's chamber housing all of his paintings. He was shocked to see how his art had evolved. Faro's prophetic visions now covered all the walls of the chamber. Drawn to them, Kriyo studied the detailed illustrations. He was astonished to see that these pictures composed a timeline of his life. He remembered sensing his father's presence.

Turning around, he saw Faro, propped up against the threshold of the door. He appreciated how aged his father appeared. His long, white, neatly pulled-back hair exposed the wrinkles on the skin of his face. As always, his countenance was infused love. Resting his weight on his hand-forged walking stick, which for almost all of his life had helped him to be mobile, he silently remained in place. Though born with a partial left leg, Faro never allowed it to stop him from following his higher calling—his artistic talent. Every revelation that Faro'd had thus far had manifested into form.

Emotional to his core, Faro, welled up with tears as he saw his son appreciating his creations, especially since they were now centered upon him. Kriyo scrutinized the descriptive events that his father had seen. He witnessed the Dark Force making his presence known at Samuel's ascension ceremony.

Then two lines emerged. One showed that he travelled to earth and the other outlined him remaining on Churria as if the decision had not been solidified. He followed both lines and his father's visions stopped. Kriyo recalled his father's words.

"My son, both decisions lead to the same outcome—war. This fated war will not occur in the near future but it will happen. What is relevent to the present is that one decision possesses hope where the other does not," he said, while shaking his head. "I don't understand why you and my Pasha have been chosen. But I suppose time will answer this. Listen to your heart, son, you will know which path to choose."

The image of Faro's solemn face consumes Kriyo's mind. His father already knew what choice he would make and began to miss his son. Realizing now that his father wanted him to make this choice for himself, he acknowledges that the decision to come to earth is the one that will provide hope.

"Kriyo," a soft female voice whispers.

Coming to an immediate stand, he scans the area, wondering where the voice emanated. Suspiciously, he walks around the small space that he calls a room. Then he glances over at Meelah and sees her still resting.

"Help her," the voice adds.

Before him the atmosphere alters and a fair-haired sentient being begins to materialize. Dressed in a white, diaphanous form-fitted gown, the beautiful female coyly smiles at him. An ensuing breeze moves her golden locks, which tumble down to her tiny waistline. Her alluring yellow eyes draw Kriyo closer to her.

"It is here on earth. You must help her locate it before it's too late," she continues in a seductive tone.

"Locate what?"

"I will show you, come closer," she persists as she extends her arms out to him.

Her words float within the room before they move around him as if affected by the unusual gust of wind. Her magnetic presence encompasses him. Drawn closer to her, Kriyo sees golden scales over her brow line. They shimmer and glisten as he's lured further toward her.

"What are you?" he asks her telepathically.

"I am from the Realm of the Mystics," her voice sings as it journeys within the stream of air. "And my name is Rhana. You must help her, Kriyo. If she fails, our world, among many others that are connected to earth, will also fall. Come closer and I'll show you."

"Rhana, we should wake Meelah. You should speak directly to her."

"Other women and I don't mesh well. Look into my eyes, Kriyo, and I will show you what you need to know in order to be of great service to her."

Kriyo, under Rhana's spell, is pulled in by her enchantment. She places her shimmering hand on the top of his head. He feels a soft breeze encircle him. His eyelids grow heavy and close. In his mind, she shows him several of the worlds within this one. These worlds simultaneously exist here on earth and those who inhabit them are willing to defend her.

Rhana shows him beings that are half human and half aquatic. They swim within the ocean's waters. They whirl from the subterranean sea in harmony with others not originally from earth—the dolphins. Deep beneath the water he sees the earth's record keepers; they too are willing to defend earth. Humans recognize these beings as whales. All of the mammals have been sent here with a purpose. Kriyo can feel their pain as humans recklessly and selfishly damage their homes and, in turn, their purpose for being here. But all of these beings as a whole have not given up. They sense the change within humankind. They again take courage and will actively defend earth.

They vow to assist both Kriyo and Meelah. Honored, he bows to the sea and all that live beneath its sparkling surface.

Bringing his focus now to the land, he sees miniscule winged beings that have vowed to maintain balance upon earth's surface. Their essence produces greenery, while they restore some of the organic damage that humans have caused to this planet. They are everywhere. The green forest is teeming with these small winged beings. Their faces and bodies are reminiscent of a human's but their diminutive size, wings and dedication to preserving earth sets them apart from the humans Kriyo has learned about. These being have also vowed to assist both him and Meelah. Bowing his head, he shows reverence for their support.

Moving from the green forests, he travels to a city. Other diminutive beings, unknown and unseen by humans, also reside here, instilling their message of preservation. He sees them whispering in the ears of humans, reminding them to live in harmony with their mother. Then he sees a human child on a playground. This child is engaged in a conversation with a miniscule being. The child's parent sits oblivious to the interaction. The small winged being embodying pure light communicates to the young human, and he answers with a joyful chuckle. These beings also vow to give assistance. Again Kriyo bows in respect.

Rhana navigates the vision through the city, down crowded streets and eventually back to the polluted water in which he arrived.

"What she seeks is deep within these waters. She has already been given the key. The Shadows cannot travel beneath the surface of the water, but the Dark Force can. Kriyo, if Meelah doesn't get her amulet before he does, all will be lost and I am not only speaking of this world. You and Meelah have the full support of the Realm of the Mystics. I have come on behalf of Kune, our leader."

The sound of something hitting the floor behind him brings Kriyo back to where he stands. Though still mesmerized by Rhana, he glances over to witness Luther, back in human form, bare-naked and mouth open, standing in complete awe.

"A siren, a siren," he mutters while pointing at Rhana.

Hearing Luther's distinct human voice, I bound to my feet. Immediately, I sense the presence of another being. Without a sound, I slip my bare feet into my cold boots.

"Mikiel, there is someone here," I tell him telepathically.

Sensing the presence of the unusual energy, I creep over to where I heard Luther's voice. First, I see Luther's naked and quite hairy backside! That is not a sight anyone wants to wake up to. Mikiel, now standing behind me, is too close, as usual. I hear him draw his sword as he also senses the presence.

"What is it?" I ask him quietly, but my voice carries.

"It's a siren, a siren," I hear Luther mumble again.

Moving past me, Mikiel gives a humorous glance at Luther's bare ass. Then I observe his demeanor relax when the figure comes into his view. Sliding his sword back into its sheath I hear him say, "Rhana, you're looking well."

"As are you, Mikiel," I hear a soft female voice retort.

I do my best to avoid Luther's portly naked form, but there it is! Navigating around him, I see this Rhana. I also see Kriyo. With his back to me, he appears to be under some kind of trance.

"Meelah, I am Rhana," she says to me.

"You know who I am. May I ask, what is your purpose here?"

"Don't trust her, she's a siren," I hear Luther grumble again.

"Luther, snap out of it!" I yell. "In those boxes you'll find some of my father's clothing. Get dressed!"

"I'm naked and I'm human again," I hear him ramble. "I seem to have lost my clothes."

Trying again to focus on the form before me, I become acutely aware that Mikiel has also fallen to her charm. He, too, is awkwardly standing quite close to her. Rhana moves her hands as if parting the Red Sea and both Mikiel and Kriyo move to the side as she struts my way.

"A siren," I again hear Luther murmur before he slips back into her trance.

I take a closer look at Rhana. Her white gown outlines her female curves, while her abundant golden locks cover her plentiful bosoms. She exudes femininity with an overpowering sensuality. I become aware that her power seems to affect everyone but me.

"I can't help my affect on males," she says as she passes Luther, grazing the side of his face. Luther looks at her with great wonder.

"I will ask you one more time, what is your purpose, Rhana?"

"I assumed you would already know," she answers.

"No games! I simply wish to hear what it is you want."

"But games are fun," she says, while strolling around me. "You are quite beautiful, Meelah. You simply need a little polishing," she whispers into my ear before she loosens my bun. "Look, already we have an improvement."

Grabbing her hand midair, I see who she is and why she has come. The small chest housing the amulet comes into sight. I release her wrist, and watch as she rubs it as if I've injured her

"Did I hurt you?" I ask, insincere.

"You will end all life if you don't locate the amulet in time. Kriyo has been chosen to assist you," she responds. But quickly her demeanor changes and, with this shift, she arrogantly adds, "Just between us girls, I have given him the location of the chest, but it will come at a cost. How ironic."

"What is?" I ask in defiance.

"You see, if you don't locate the amulet before the Dark Force does, all will be lost, but if you do…it will cost you the life of Kriyo. Either way, your heart will break," she says as she circles both Kriyo and Mikiel. Unaware of our conversation, they continue to fawn over her.

Unfortunately, her words are truthful, I can sense it. Mulling them over, I feel sick to my stomach. The sorrow of my father's death floats again to the surface and I experience it anew.

"Who makes these unfathomable rules?" I ask her, barely containing my contempt.

"Meelah, Meelah," she answers as she glides around the room. "You have foolishly attached yourself to these beings. And it was you who didn't follow 'the rules' your last lifetime. Now you are paying for that action. Karma's a bitch! I love that human expression, don't you?"

Anger mounts within me and begins to overflow like a flooding, raging river. In a flash of fury I stand before Rhana. Vehemently, I press her up against the wall by her throat. As I glare into her unaffected blue eyes, she has the nerve to laugh in my face.

"Tell your council to send someone else if they want me to save their world," I say, heartless.

She stares into my eyes and sees another side to me. The side connected to *him*. Fear alters the expression on her face, and her spell over Kriyo, Mikiel and Luther lifts.

"What are you doing, Meelah?" Mikiel asks, as he approaches me. "Rhana poses no threat here."

"I'm naked and I'm human again," I hear Luther sputter yet again from somewhere behind me.

"Mikiel, she means to kill me. Look at her eyes," Rhana cries.

"Rhana, you're not worth it," I say coldly. "Make sure your council sends another representative. I owe you and your kind nothing!"

Releasing my grip, I hear her fall to the floor. I don't even look at her. I am done with rules that I had no hand in setting. Storming off, desperate for space, I close my eyes and leave.

"Where did she go?" Kriyo asks. Getting into Mikiel's face, he demands again, "Where did Meelah go?"

Meditating for a brief moment, Mikiel views where I've gone. "She is in the rooftop garden," he answers.

Mikiel observes Kriyo as he runs after Meelah, but Rhana's persistent muttering in the background captures his attention. "She's dark, we have no hope. We have no hope! I should not have taunted her. I should not have done that," Rhana repeats over and over again.

Rummaging naked through boxes of clothing, Luther adds his two cents. "Mikiel, she will prevail. I know Meelah! Don't listen to that siren. She'll just cast a spell on you." Then bending over, exposing his hairy backside, he continues. "You also know Meelah. Why are you paying that siren any mind? Hey, do you want to get something to eat? I am so hungry," Luther prattles while stepping into a pair of Samuel's jogging pants and pulling on a puke-green sweater. "Looks nice, don't you think? Samuel always had great taste," Luther affirms while modeling his random ensemble.

Mikiel turns back to where Rhana was standing and sees that she has gone. He wonders what she saw that terrified her. Never having seen a siren panic as she did, he remains intrigued; but this he knows. "Meelah is not dark," he states out loud.

"You got that right," Luther states as he comes to a stand. "Are you ready for some grub?" he asks, realizing that he is completely alone. "Where did everyone go? At least that good-for-nothing siren has left," he mutters to himself.

Promptly, Mikiel travels to the greenhouse desperate to find Meelah. Concentrating, he feels her presence toward the rear of the room. He also senses that Kriyo has not arrived yet, affording him a brief moment alone with her.

"No, Mikiel," I say as he approaches me.

"No to what, Meelah?" he asks in his calm voice.

"No to everything, especially to more pain," I answer, consumed by emotion.

"Meelah, what happened? What did Rhana say to you?"

"The truth! Please leave, Mikiel. I don't want you or anyone to see me like this."

"Like what, Meelah? I do not understand."

After a reflective pause with my back still to him, I ask, "Are you certain that the Dark Force can't come to earth?"

"After your eighteenth year on earth, he can and will; you know this. Now what has happened?"

Turning around, I lift my head then open my eyes. Mikiel stares at me with a stunned expression. Within the reflection of his eyes, I see mine. They are consumed with darkness. The distress that I feel ushers me away from the horrified expression Mikiel wears. I spy a greenhouse window. Swiftly I leave by climbing through it then onto the roof.

Greeted by winter's blustery wind, I continue onward as if I have a plan though I don't. All I know is that the Dark Force has risen within me. The anger that I felt brought him to me. Rhana was right, I have formed attachments and these bonds are my weakness. Tears overcome me and, as I wipe them away, I see that they, too, are tainted black. Dropping to my knees, I watch my black tears drip onto the concrete. I honor their need to fall, my need to release. Lost in this space for a spell, I study the murky puddle my tears have created. There is a message within them. I hear, no, feel something. Their essence asks me to have faith and to look up, now! In the grey clouded sky, a unique ray of light appears. This brilliant beam streams downward, first connecting with the top of my head then my shoulders. Soon it completely overcomes me. Again I look down into the black pool of tears. The light consumes the shadowy puddle, altering it into pure white light.

"Darkness cannot exist within my light," I hear a voice say.

In the luminescent brilliance, I see what I must do if I hope to spare my heart from this loss. Honoring my free will, the choice is mine alone to make. Step by step, I understand who I must meet and what I must obtain if I am to spare Kriyo's life.

Still kneeling, I experience a sense of inner peace filling my being again. For a brief moment, I'd lost the divine connection that resonates within me. But, if all of life is comprised of choices, I now know what I choose. I will resolutely stand against the Dark Force. He will never again try to slip to earth through me. I will never be his puppet!

Though I inexplicably dislike Rhana, I am indebted to her. Her crass, but truthful words and repulsive, seductive demeanor brought me to where I now kneel. Rhana, exactly as she is, has opened me to this epiphany and, most important, to my solution.

I know what I risk by taking this detour, but this I must do.

"I will do it!" I proclaim to the Light Force. "And thank you," I voice from my heart.

Once inside the garden, Kriyo sees Mikiel. "Where is she?" he shouts. "What's the matter with you? Where has Meelah gone?"

Trapped in thought, Mikiel raises his arm and points to the opened window. Hastily, Kriyo makes his way to it then crawls through the window. Instantly he is affected by the ensuing bitter and turbulent gusts of air. Crossing his arms against his chest, he begins his search.

On the opposite side of the rooftop, an unusual being appears and I rise to meet him. With his arrival, I recognize that the plan has commenced. This creature, adorned in a gown that looks like it's made from the bark of a tree and branches woven together in the form of a crown atop his head, is imitable. Reverent, I lower my head. This being's energy is powerful. Nevertheless, what brings him to where he now stands is the same reason that I stand where I am. It is love.

As I stand before him, we are both silent. In this pause, I continue observing this remarkable being. His body is quite burly and his long, thick brown mane frames his bearded face. One arm resembles that of a human while the other is a thick brown branch. He raises both of his arms and it begins to rain, but not everywhere, just on me. The gentle yet warm water rinses away the residual black streaks from my tears. Then, as he lowers his arms, the shower ceases. The ensuing brisk air chills me. Wiping my face as I try to dry myself, I can't help but shake while my teeth chatter.

"Are you Kune?" I ask while my body shudders.

His answer comes in the form of a gentle smile. Entranced by the manner in which his stoic demeanor softens with this acknowledgment, for a few moments I am no longer over-wrought by the unbearable cold. But like all moments, this one ends and again the frigid air wraps tightly around me. Sending me a message in a thought, he illustrates how he wishes to dry my dampened clothing and hair. Though his method seems peculiar to me, I eagerly give my consent. I loathe being cold!

Anxiously I wait. Rubbing my arms, I see him close his eyes. Serene and with soft breaths, I observe his shoulders subtly rise and fall. He appears so peaceful whereas I am nearly freezing! Veering away from the thought of the nagging, nearly painful elements, I allow my mind to race. My mind focuses on one specific point. *Now, this being asks for my permission, but what about earlier? Why didn't he advise me that he was going to rinse away my black smudges before saturating me in these blustery conditions?*

Curious of what his answer may be, since I am quite certain that he heard me, I fix my eyes on him. My piercing stare seems to get his attention since his eyes are connected with mine.

"A higher source of divinity advised me to rinse away *His* likeness, Meelah," he says with a pensive pause. "You are not a reflection of *His* darkness. The light within you is your source of power. Standing before you now, I affirm this truth."

Touched by his observation, I bow forward to him, shuddering. As I rise, he blows at me with steady force, and I find relief in this pleasant stream of air. Without fear, I lean into the warm breeze. In no time, my clothing dries as does my hair and skin. This restoration is beyond wonderful.

When he closes his mouth, I balance myself. As the warm air ceases, even though I am dry, I again feel the effects of the brisk, chilly temperature. Stepping nearer to me, he looks upward and an opening within the cloudy sky brings with it a ray of sunlight that spotlights me. As the sun thaws me, I gratefully lower my head to him. His patient demeanor becomes observant, as if he's in search of something deep within me. With the sun's warmth restoring my confidence, I wait for him to speak. I know what he wishes for me attain. I also know who it will liberate. This action will also spare Kriyo.

"Do we have an agreement, Meelah?" I hear him ask. "I wish to hear the answer directly from you. I have waited endlessly for this. My kingdom has waited timelessly for you."

Though I am unsure of what he means about his kingdom and the connection I have to it, I have faith that time will provide me clarity. For now, I provide him with my answer. "Kune, you have my word. I am certain of what I must do. Are you sure that Kriyo will not locate the chest?"

"The chest is already in safe hands."

"How will I find it?"

"If you follow the plan, I promise that it will find you. But Meelah, this you must understand, while it will not be at the expense of Kriyo's life, a life nonetheless must be taken. A life for a life."

Suddenly, he pulls back and looks over my shoulder. I, too, hear someone running toward us. Raising his humanlike hand, he faces his palm forward and the sound of footsteps stops. Turning, I see Kriyo in the distance frozen in place, mid-stride.

I race over to him. His hair flailing behind him is ice-covered and stationary along with the rest of him. I touch his cold face and I sense Kune watching me. Though I know this state is temporary, I wish that Kriyo did not have to experience this. Gazing into Kriyo's startled eyes, I hear, "We haven't much time, Meelah. Your Light Warrior will soon be here, as well. Do you have any questions?"

"No," is my succinct answer. Still watching Kriyo, I mutter, "A life for a life. Though you will be spared, who will fall? " Looking at Kune, I ask, "A life for a life? This does not make sense. I will receive the chest at the expense of a life? How does this equate to a life for a life? "

"You will have your answer," is his reply.

And that is that. Soon I will understand but now, there is one truth I wish to convey. "Kune, please thank Rhana for me. If she wasn't the being who initially came, circumstances might be quite different."

"Indeed. I will make sure that she hears your words. Though all is occurring precisely as it was fated," he says as he takes hold of my right hand, turning it palm-side up. "Do you know what you must do?" he asks keenly.

"Yes," I reply, hoping to assure him.

"You have been entrusted with a grand task, but you needn't be alone. You have the undivided support of the Realm of the Mystics," he says as he lowers his head.

"Thank you. I will not fail you."

Kune outlines the X mark on the palm of my hand. His energy is grounding. He's the spirit connection to earth. His smell is similar to fresh pine needles and sweet flowers. I gaze up and into his eyes and see that he has begun to fade. The wind carries him away. Though he has disappeared from sight, he is still very much present, around me. He observes my next move.

At full speed, I run across the top of the building and then stop, balancing at the edge. Looking downward, I see the alleyway far below. My hair lifts and whirls in every direction as the forceful wind gusts twirl around me. Closing my eyes, I focus within. It is now that I am certain that my heart and mind are in sync. With this synchronicity, I know what I must do.

I set the plan in motion by yelling, "Here I am!" I lure the remaining Shadows. I beckon to them. I wait for them. I feel their inherent desire to locate me. Their unsatisfied hunger for me lingers in the frigid air. As I feel them approach, throbbing consumes the right palm of my hand. The X mark on my hand has been lanced open by a small winged being. The diminutive creature remains with the dagger in its grasp. By me allowing my wound to drip blood onto the rooftop, the Shadows have been effectively baited. Bringing my attention to the small form, I see it struggle to keep afloat within the gusty winds. Extending my other hand I make a platform for the miniscule essence to land. With this intention she does just that. I sense the truth of this being. Its pure heart speaks to my heart. Adorned in a vibrant, shimmering-green gown this tiny brunette lowers her sweet head to me.

"Meelah, they are coming," she spouts into the wind. "I hope I didn't pain you. I will see you again," she adds before playfully joining the blustery current.

"What are you doing, Meelah?" I hear Kriyo ask from behind me.

Surprised to hear his voice already, I glance over my shoulder and see that it is indeed him. Not answering him yet, I also sense Mikiel approaching. Together they must witness my actions. This is what I've been shown to do. My actions will bring forth a sequence of events that must occur if I am to succeed. I do this for them. I do this to selfishly avert my heartache.

"Why are you bleeding?" Kriyo asks, acting as though he feels my pain. Inching closer to me, he then says, "Come down from there. You can't fly."

I feel Mikiel as he stands alongside Kriyo. He delves into my thoughts, curious about what I am doing, but I block him. He again moves toward me. His concern is palpable.

I face them both. I take a step backwards, closer to my fate. I don't want them to come any further. The overwhelming presence of Dark Shadows gives my arms goose bumps. It's time.

"Meelah, I will catch you!" Mikiel shouts.

And I know he'll try, but he won't be successful. This is my path, not his. Fixing my stare on them both, I state, "You must trust me."

Spreading my arms, making a T with my body, I fall backwards off Religards' rooftop. Mikiel runs past Kriyo, takes flight and dives toward me. I see his desperate eyes on me. I cannot tell him that my action will satisfy a grand plan, so I look away from him. Gravity quickly draws me downward, but this time I know it's not my destiny to impact the surface below. Sensing the two remaining Shadows as they drool at the whiff of my fresh blood, I hear Mikiel. "Meelah, the Shadows!" he shouts incessantly.

Bracing myself, I allow the Shadows to snatch me. The plan has commenced....

Chapter Fourteen

Relentless, Mikiel scours the entire city. As darkness coats the night sky, another meeting is called to order at Religards. Kriyo paces back and forth, overwhelmed by a feeling of helplessness.

"Dudley, Tamilia, Cal, what have you learned? I need news," Pasha demands, her shattered nerves coming through in her voice.

"I have spread the word regarding Meelah across the city and down the northeast coast. My sources have heard nothing thus far," Dudley replies.

"Pasha, I cannot sense Meelah anywhere," Tamilia adds.

"Nor I, Sherlock," Roger states as he and Rose take their seats.

"Kriyo, sit down! Your persistent pacing is grating on my nerves!" Pasha shouts.

"Okay, this is what we heard," Roger explains to the group. "Mikiel hasn't stopped searching; actually, he's mixed it up. That dude has quite the thing for Meelah," he says, capturing Kriyo's attention. "He travelled all the way to the Realm of the Mystics to have words with Rhana! You know Rhana, she's that fine siren. Sorry babe, but you know I'm right," Roger says to Rose. Rose acknowledges his statement with a casual nod of agreement before Roger continues. "Okay now, we were told by an accurate source that furies, trolls, gnomes, and fairies, you name it, were involved. They kicked that Light Warrior's ass out of their realm, warning him to never come back. Even I know that there's a protocol to initiate in order to step into that place. But Mikiel just busted in and roughed Rhana up in the process. But here's where it gets interesting, right? A fairy or some other mystical presence told my source that they are all preparing for a battle that will soon take place there."

"Rhana told me that we had their support," Kriyo states. "I hope that Mikiel's uninvited intrusion didn't destroy that."

Roger claps his hands together, creating a resounding boom, and he smacks his jean-clad knee as he begins to chuckle. "Are you telling me that you also have a thing for Meelah? Damn, you two sure know how to pick 'em."

"Enough, all of you, we must be productive," Pasha commands over the noise. "What do we know? Dudley, take notes for me so I can attempt to make sense of all this," she orders. "Son, you saw Rhana?"

"Yes. She appeared to me downstairs. Luther was also there," Kriyo answers with a hint of defensiveness.

"Yup, I saw that siren. A piece of work she is," Luther says while gnawing on a piece of chicken.

"Can either of you tell me, in detail, an account of her visit?" Pasha asks them.

"Well, first I turned back into human form and I was naked...it's cold downstairs. I don't remember where I left my clothes," Luther continues, rambling.

"Luther, Luther," Pasha exclaims, to capture his attention. "Thank you for your rather detailed account, but I would like to hear about Rhana."

"Oh, that siren, I can tell you about her. Mikiel and Kriyo were entranced by her, but not me. I like a woman with a little substance and hair. You know what I mean by hair, right? I mean hair all over."

"Sick, dude, sick!" Roger spouts.

Dudley wears a peculiar grin and nods as if he knows precisely what Luther means. Next to him, Tamilia rocks tensely back and forth in her chair while Rose, seeming to be the only one unaffected by Meelah's disappearance, loudly chews a large wad of gum. As the small room fills with useless and unneeded banter, she blows a huge bubble.

"ENOUGH!" Cal screams as he slams his fist on the conference table.

"Thank you, Cal," Pasha says.

"No need to thank me," he returns. "I didn't protect her. The Dark Force's Shadows still got her. I'm sorry," Cal mutters.

"No one is blaming you, Cal."

Then, like someone flicking on a light switch, Pasha has an epiphany. Her eyes brighten and she begins to process possibilities. Turning away from the unproductive group, Kriyo and Mr. Giblet pick up on her body language.

"What is it, Mother?" Kriyo asks with newfound hope.

"Mr. Giblet, bring me the book of the mystics. Go now! That clever girl," Pasha murmurs.

"Kriyo, call to Mikiel. I need to speak with him."

"How do I call to him?"

"Son, really? Figure this out on your own, and find him now," she states as she leaves for her office.

"Here it is," Mr. Giblet states as he carries a bulky tome in front of him into her office. Wobbling as he walks, he struggles to see around the dense, heavy book. Placing it on her desk, he takes a moment to catch his breath. But as soon as he does, he adds, "Do you wish to remain here or should I take the book into the conference room?"

"This will be quite fine. Thank you, Mr. Giblet."

"You are welcome, Pasha. Now what are you thinking?" he asks, anxious.

"It is only a theory, but I believe Meelah has been in contact with Kune."

"The leader of the Mystics?" Mr. Giblet inquires.

"The same," she answers as she flips through the thick pages. "I recall a dowsing incantation," she mumbles as she scours through the countless instructions.

"Pasha, stand back, I'll locate that for you," Mr. Giblet states.

Stepping back, she observes Mr. Giblet preparing himself. One by one, everyone from the conference room locates them. Spotting them, Pasha raises her hand, signaling the need for immediate silence, and they all wait for Mr. Giblet. With his eyes firmly closed, he raises his wee little arms and remains in this pose for a moment or two. Gradually, the pages of the book begin to flip forward, eventually gaining speed as they turn. The sides of his blazer flap in the breeze the pages emit.

"I didn't know that little dude was magical," Roger exclaims.

"Shh," Pasha says, halting any other interruptions. "They're like handling human children," she complains.

Then the incessant flipping sound ceases and more than three-quarters of the tome later, the page has been located. The smile of certainty upon Mr. Giblet's face is all the proof Pasha requires as she heads back to her desk.

"Thank you, thank you," she says as she begins to decipher the ancient language.

"Mr. Giblet, have you seen the sisters? Maya is quite fluent in this early language."

"Come to think of it, I haven't seen them all day," he answers.

"Has anyone seen the sisters today?" Pasha asks the group.

"Yeah, I have," Rose answers, while persistently chewing her gum. "Me and Roger saw Riya downtown. She was hanging out with that creeper. What's that creep's name, Roger? You know, the dude that sliced up Sammy last week—"

"Dixley," Roger answers. "Yeah, that dude is messed up from all the powder he pushes. He's always off the charts. I wondered what Riya was doing with him. Let Rose and me check it out, it's a little pub downtown, not too far away."

"Oh, can I come?" Luther yells. "I haven't gone to a pub since Samuel and I lived in Ireland."

"Down, down, whatever you are. I can't babysit you," Roger snaps.

"Too bad," Rose says, while touching Luther's face, his features registering his disappointment.

Passing the couple as they depart, Kriyo goes over to his mother and reports, "Mikiel is here."

"Good, he may know how to read this, as well. Where is he?" she asks.

"He's in the conference room. He would like to meet alone with you, Mother."

"Please excuse me then," she adds, while slipping a bookmark into the book. Picking up the tome, she brings it with her.

Dudley begins to walk behind her and Cal halts his steps. "Mikiel and Pasha want to be alone."

"Kriyo, please join us!" Pasha shouts.

Again, Dudley begins to proceed behind Kriyo. "No, you haven't been invited," Cal again states. Like impenetrable wall, he remains obstinately in place.

"Fine, fine," Dudley acquiesces. "We're all on the same team here," he adds.

The persistent ringing chime of "I Like Big Butts" by Sir Mix-A-Lot fires off Dudley's cell phone. Hastily, he silences it by answering the call. He talks in hushed tones as he walks away from the group. Cal watches him with a keen eye.

"Classy ring tone, Dudley," Tamilia mumbles under her breath.

"I like big butts and I cannot lie," Luther sings as he sways back and forth. But he's easily distracted, as a flame emitting from Tamilia's hand diverts his attention.

"What a pretty light," Luther declares, ambling over to her.

"I must bounce," Dudley announces. "Tell Pasha that I'll return in about an hour. Okay, chump?" he spouts at Cal.

Standing his ground, while also creating a barrier to Dudley's progression, Cal remains still. Though he may appear simple-minded, he and all of his kind have an infallible inner guidance. He watches every step Dudley makes and he's pleased to see that it's in the direction away from Pasha and her private conference.

"Sorry, Cal," Mr. Giblet says, with compassion. "That Dudley...I have nothing to say about him that is acceptable in present company," he affirms. "I suppose you could always lock him out of Religards."

Cal chuckles and relaxes his demeanor. "Lock Dudley out?" Cal expresses with amusement.

Mr. Giblet and Cal share a brief moment of levity. But the energy within the conference room is nothing close to light. Specifically the energy encompassing Mikiel. It is dense and quite heavy.

With his back facing Pasha and Kriyo, he seems to search for the right words to explain what he has most recently learned. Patient, Pasha and Kriyo wait as they observe the pensive Light Warrior. His once-pristine white-and-grey wings are tattered and splattered in mud. A few pulled feathers hang loose, threatening to fall out. The exposed skin on the back of his legs has superficial scratches all over it. With his head still down, he faces his audience. The front side of him is also riddled with battle marks. All of his uncovered skin has been properly marked by tiny scores, leaving behind bloody lines. As he raises his head, they see that the surface of his face has also been grazed with small lacerations.

"Oh, Mikiel," Pasha says as she assesses his superficial injuries."Why did you go to the Realm of the Mystics? You know that one must summon Kune," she mumurs. "You of all beings, especially having been in form as long as you have, know the edict of other realms and worlds. You know better than what your actions have demonstrated," she asserts. "That being said, what have you to share?"

First spreading his soiled and tattered wings as he affords them a much-needed stretch, he addresses his select group and utters one word, "Meelah."

"Yes, what about Meelah?" Kriyo demands.

"Give him time, Kriyo," Pasha orders, waiting out Mikiel's delay.

"In the garden, she turned toward me," Mikiel says in a quiet voice as if he doesn't desire anyone else to hear. "Her eyes were consumed by darkness. Devoid of light, they were completely black, and I hesitated. Kriyo ran past me while I felt frozen by what I had seen. As soon as I sensed Kune, I went to her, but I was too late. I scoured the city after the Shadows enfolded her. It was then that I breeched the Realm of Mystics. I know that Rhana did or said something. She was of no help to me and—"

"You were given the boot," Pasha interrupts him. "We must commence the incantation. Atleast you have confirmed my theory that Meelah met with Kune. Time is of the essence."

"No, Mother," Kriyo states, ardently. "There is more. Allow him to finish."

Mikiel lowers his head to Kriyo then continues. "Galdi—"

"You spoke with Galdi, the right hand to Kune? Did he mention what Meelah might be up to?" Pasha asks.

"Mother, please allow Mikiel to continue." Kriyo insists.

After a glare at her son, Pasha adopts a more conciliative tone and says, "Please continue, Mikiel."

"Unfortunately, he didn't speak of Meelah. Galdi told me that a member of this team has turned. They have contacted the Dark Force through the two existing Shadows. He also advised me that Kriyo is the being from which the amulet will surface."

"Rhana already showed me where it is," Kriyo says to them both.

"And that chest has a curse upon it," Mikiel announces. "If you retrieve it, it will be your life that is taken. You have been set up," Mikiel reveals, with a touch of acrimony. "A member of this team has had a hand in this."

"Why would Rhana come here and mislead us?" Pasha asks.

"It was not Rhana who misled us," Mikiel says. "The amulet was indeed in that precise location. But someone close to you, Pasha, had the power to travel deep beneath the surface and obtain the true chest then replace it with the cursed one," Mikiel adds.

"Is Meelah still the only one who can open the chest?" Pasha asks.

"Yes, for now. But when the vortexes resume, the Dark Force and all of his warriors will descend upon earth, tear it apart and he will find a means to open the chest."

"Why doesn't the Light Force intervene? Where is he when his brother is on the cusp of blanketing this planet with his darkness?" Kriyo asks, furious.

"My creator abides faithfully by the universal laws," Mikiel explains. "Meelah, our leader, was a gift to him for unfailingly honoring the universal laws. Then, with ardor, he created every Light Warrior in existence. He fashioned us using Meelah as a paradigm. It is our passion—our purpose—to instill and preserve light within all. As time evolved, we became active warriors against the enormity of the Dark Force. Again and again he would overstep the boundaries of the universal laws," Mikiel says with deep-rooted frustration. "This predicament is the reason why Meelah is now a Churrian. Her purpose is to balance the power between both forces," he adds with divine reverence. "And this, she will do!" he proclaims with conviction.

"Indeed, she will," Pasha agrees. "Meelah is clever. I know she has a plan. I will request a meeting with Kune and confirm my thoughts," she says. After a brief pause, she instructs, "As for the members on our team, for now we will keep our findings only within this group. Kriyo, be aware of your thoughts and seal them."

"What do you wish for me to do?" Mikiel asks, desperation in his voice. "Give me a task."

After reading the intricate incantation, Pasha takes paper and jots down several ingredients.

"Bring me these, Mikiel. And be prompt about it. All of these herbs are in my garden. I will need them fresh. Hurry!"

No sooner does Mikiel have the torn yellow paper in his grasp, than he disappears from their sight.

"Mother, what do you wish for me to do?"

"Kriyo, I wish for you to return to Churria with me as soon as everything is resolved here on earth. I could not bear to lose you."

"I will do what I must for the greater good."

"Indeed, you will, but you have a future, son. I have seen it. Don't allow your youthful zeal to waylay it.

"What have you seen, Mother?"

"Every drawing that Father has created...it is all right here," she answers while patting her skirt pocket.

"May I see?" he asks.

"I was under the impression that you didn't like to see your father's creations?"

"Before I left our Churria, Father's paintings humbled me. How could I have been so blind to his gift?" he asks in earnest. "Right beside me was my father whose gifts could have smoothed out so much in my life."

"Son, you are precisely where you must be. No one can write a future with certainty. Do you recall the two branches upon the wall signifying the outcomes, but not your decision?"

"Yes, it was I who determined which path I walked. Mother, have you seen any recent illustrations?"

"Indeed I have, and if you listen to your heart, you will experience the path that will include Meelah."

"Mother, is it wrong to love someone that I have only just met?"

"Listening to your heart is never wrong. Now, shifting gears, my son, there is something that you must find for me."

***

On the other side of town, Roger and Rose arrive at Fullgary's Pub. The small bar has poor lighting and reeks of liquor as if the timbered floor has been drenched by it. A few of the regulars, already beyond their limits, fill four of the six barstools.

"Baby, I'm gonna use the ladies room," Rose shouts over the clamor of the drunken regulars.

"Damn, girl, I'm not deaf!" Roger retorts.

"I'm so tired of your attitude, Roger. I've had it," Rose barks while storming off.

"Rose, you know we don't have a ladies room here. There's only one for the gents," the paranoid bartender by the name of Michael hollers.

"Whatever, Michael," Rose shrieks.

"Women, can't live with them and sure as hell don't want to spend a night without them," Roger states coldly to his drunken comrades. "Michael, have ya been busy tonight or what?"

"What's with the questions, Roger," Michael asks while pouring him a shot of scotch into a questionable 'clean' glass.

"Simply making small talk, man. Thanks," he adds as Michael slides him the glass.

Roger listens to the repartee between the other guys in the bars. Hoping that Rose is able to sneak into the rear room, he signals for another shot. Michael begins to relax a bit when Roger downs his second drink. Seeing Roger raise his index finger for another, Michael brings the bottle over with him.

"Rose really has you shook up," Michael states.

Roger, continuing to play the game, nods his head. He then takes the bottle and pours another drink. Slamming a hundred dollar bill on the counter, Roger picks up the bottle again and begins to drink directly from it.

"That's what I'm talkin' about," an inebriated patron spouts. "Too bad Sammy was snooping around," he adds, slurring his speech. "Hey Michael, you were friends with Sammy. Why in the hell would you let that crazy bastard, Dixley, back into your bar?"

Roger watches Michael's face. It's consumed by fear at the mere mention of Dixley. Fumbling around, he attempts to conceal his apparent connection. Using the same rag used to dry the cleaned glasses, he wipes his sweaty forehead.

"You all right, man?" Roger asks.

"I'm fine! Where's Rose? She's been in the gents' room for a long time now."

"You know women and their make-up," Roger states, attempting to buy her a few more minutes of snooping.

"Why are you so sober, Roger? Your kind doesn't get affected by alcohol? I'm tired of all you...things hanging out in my bar! I didn't ask for this. I didn't set up Sammy, either! I know what you think! He and that Riya thing got what they deserved. Anyway, Dixley's leaving town; some urgent matter. He'll be out of my hair and my bar!"

Roger gives a covert glance to the back of the bar hoping that Rose will soon emerge. Michael has given him all that he needs.

"What is Rose doing?" Michael asks suspiciously as he begins to walk in her direction.

"Hey Michael, what's the rush," Rose says, sauntering past him. "By the way, your bathroom is filthy! Ready, babe?" she asks Roger.

"Yeah, let's hit the pavement. It's been real, Michael," Roger exclaims as he and Rose stroll out the door.

Well beyond the entrance of the pub, Rose, in a low voice, begins to explain her findings. The brisk night air surrounds them both as they swiftly head back to Religards. Snuggling up to Roger, she whispers in his ear, "We have a traitor amongst us. A member on our team is working with those Shadows."

"Are you sure?" Roger asks.

"Yes," she answers.

"Where are the sisters? Michael sounded like Dixley did her in, like Sammy."

"My source said that Sammy retrieved the chest that was supposed to contain the amulet. Dixley paid him big money for it, but the chest had some kind of curse on it. Dixley destroyed Sammy when he learned of the curse." Pausing as a group walks by them, she continues in a whisper, "My source said that a member of the Northeast Team has the chest and is negotiating with the Shadows."

"Damn!" Roger shouts. "What about the sisters? I know them and I know the betrayer isn't among them."

"No, it's not. My source was certain of that. It was Riya who divulged the leak within our organization. My source gave me this," Rose affirms solemnly. "Riya told her that if we came looking for her, then she must give this to us. What do you think it is?" Rose asks, slipping him the intricately folded and sealed paper.

"I don't know, but I'm certain that we can trust that crazy Light Warrior. No snitch would breach the Realm of The Mystics and get thrown out. We'll bring this to him. You did well tonight. I almost believed you when you trounced off all mad at me," Roger says, only getting a smirk from her.

***

Back at Religards, Pasha awaits the last ingredients. The one task she assigned Kriyo is what she now needs. Down in the bowels of the school, Kriyo hunts for it.

"Over here," a tiny voice speaks.

Kriyo sees the small pale-skinned creature as it signals for him to follow. Faithfully, Kriyo trails him deeper into the damp moist basement. This slight-framed being stands no taller than a two feet in height. Thankfully, its white long-sleeved shirt with contrasting dark suspenders makes this little creature stand out from the surrounding dimness. Dipping under low piping and rafters, Kriyo begins to question why his mother asked for him to do such a revolting task.

"They're over here," the small creature says in tune with his thoughts.

"Why do you wish to remain here on earth?" Kriyo asks. "There are numerous other planets that would appreciate your gifts."

"We are connected to the life-force here on earth and we are selflessly committed to it," the diminutive being sincerely answers. "Why are you dedicated to the chosen one?"

"Meelah?" Kriyo asks.

"You needn't name her. You only need to honor your instinct, which is pure dedication to her. You feel it and this commitment satisfies you. This is how we feel about earth. More than a home to us, earth is our legacy. Now look down and be careful not to step on any of them. The mother has given us two of her offspring willingly. Even mammals are connected."

Down in the wet, damp corner, he sees a nest of newborn rats, hairless and vulnerable. The mother clutches two of them in her mouth and waits for Kriyo. Bending down he extends his hand and the mother lowers her two progeny gently. Seeing the sacrifice that this mother, even if the mother is only a rat, is willing to make, touches his heart.

"Thank you," Kriyo says to the mother, still standing on her hind legs.

"Your honor and compassion for all life is why you have been chosen, Kriyo," the being says while closing his hand.

"Chosen for what?" Kriyo inquires.

"Only you will connect the true chest that houses the amulet with Meelah. This is what we know."

"And what is your name, fine sir?" Kriyo requests.

"I am Dilly," the being states with a bow.

"Thank you, Dilly, and thank you, too," Kriyo adds, addressing the mother. "Dilly, what's the quickest way out of here?"

"Follow me," Dilly answers.

***

Roger and Rose wait for Cal to open the rear door to Religards. Cal inspects them, making certain that they are who they appear to be. Once he's certain, the rear doors unlock. Roger eagerly pushes them open and he and Rose proceed back to the main office.

They meet Kriyo in the hall. He is also going back to the main office. Roger gets a good look at his tux and chortles.

"I don't understand why you're laughing," Kriyo states.

"It's your getup, man! Where's the wedding or the bar mitzvah?" he retorts as he and Rose have a laugh. "Hey, what's in your hand?" Roger asks.

"Nothing, Roger."

"No, man, seriously, what's in your hand?" Roger asks in a somber tone. With a betrayer amongst them, one cannot be too careful. "Rose, he's the new guy. I want to know," Roger declares, adamant.

Kriyo pauses, reluctant to respond, but knowing what Roger is implying, he opens the palm of his hand, revealing the pink-skinned newborn rats.

"Damn! What're you doing with little critters like that?" Roger hollers as he shakes with disgust. "What's the matter with that Churrian? That's just not right," he continues. "Rose, if he eats them things, I'm throwing up. Seriously, I cannot handle weird stuff like that. You know I have a sensitive stomach."

"Aren'tyoutwocleaners?"Kriyoaskswitharesoundinglaugh.

"What you mean by that? Rose, is he putting me down?" is Roger's emotional response.

"He gets this way when he ingests human alcohol. He has a quick metabolism. He'll be right as rain in no time," Rose explains to Kriyo.

"What are you whispering about, baby?" Roger asks in a paranoid manner.

"Nothing, baby, we're almost there."

After rounding one more bend, all three of them come into the office. Kriyo walks past Cal and into the rear conference room. Roger and Rose head back, but Cal blocks their way.

"What're you doing, man?" Roger asks. "We need to speak with Mikiel. Where's he at? Mikiel! Where you at, you crazy Light Warrior?"

When Kriyo enters the conference room, Roger's garrulous voice follows behind him.

"Mikiel, tend to them, please," Pasha commands.

With that, Mikiel leaves the room, to address the demands of Roger. He taps Cal on the shoulder and Roger and Rose proceed past the pale protector. Mikiel stands before them, unimpressed by their peculiar zeal.

"We have news," Rose whispers, instantly capturing Mikiel's interest. "We must go somewhere private," she adds obstinately.

Mikiel dives into their weak minds and sees their findings. He also learns of the sealed message from Riya. Shaking his head, he wonders who else knows of their findings. Their news was naive, far too simple to be of use. Mikiel remains before the couple for a few more moments, making certain that they are completely detached from the betrayer amongst them. Once satisfied, he turns and strides back to the conference room. Roger and Rose are slow to follow, but in time they do.

"What was that all about?" Pasha asks, while grinding fresh-cut herbs.

"Roger and Rose are exonerated," Mikiel states. "They have also obtained a message from Riya."

"And where is this message?" Pasha asks as she wipes her hands on a rag.

"It's right here," Rose says as she begins to hand it to Pasha. But then, she hesitates. "Roger, how do we know that we can trust them?"

Mikiel draws his sword and points it directly at the two of them. "Give the letter to Pasha. We have no time for this. Everyone in this room is a telepath. We all know everything except the contents of Riya's letter and if any of us were connected to the Shadows, you wouldn't have made it back to Religards in one piece."

Rose willingly gives Pasha the message. Instantly, Pasha is transfixed. Outlining the wax seal with her index finger, she shows it to Mikiel. Sliding his sword back into its sheath, he, too, becomes fascinated.

"That is the seal of Kune, The Ruler of The Mystics," Mikiel states.

"Indeed it is. Perhaps we may not need to request Kune's presence, after all."

Kriyo, still cradling the newborn rats, feels relief that they may not be used. Aware of Dilly's presence, he senses that Dilly, too, feels respite, but he also heeds a grave warning.

"Dilly, what is it?" Kriyo asks, sensing his overwhelming panic. "Mother, don't open it," he states ardently.

"What is it, Dilly? You're talking far too quickly for me to understand."

"The rat-carrying Churrian has finally lost it," Roger exclaims. "Look at him talkin' to himself."

"Can't you see him?" Kriyo pleads. "Mother, Dilly wants you to put the message down." Kriyo adds as he speaks to the diminutive creature that only he can see.

"It's what?" Kriyo asks Dilly. And then he repeats what he's told. "It is Kune's seal, but that seal was not executed with Kune's royal blood and it has been poisoned! When the seal is broken, toxic fumes will be released into the air. Mother, please put it down!"

Pasha drops the message and it slowly floats to the floor. Mikiel again draws his sword and presses it into Roger's chest.

"Stop him," Rose pleads. "We didn't do anything wrong. Pasha, please stop him," Rose shrieks again.

"Mikiel, we both hear their thoughts. They have not betrayed anyone," she affirms, watching Mikiel hesitantly withdraw his sword. "There are only two among us whom we haven't read yet. After reading the two of them, you can decide if their punishment will be your sword. Mikiel, please bring in Dudley and Tamilia."

Roger falls in a crumpled, spent heap on the floor and Rose attempts to soothe his jumbled psyche. Pasha gazes at the fatal, venomous message supposedly from Riya. Then she directs her focus at her son who is very much engaged in conversation with Dilly, though no one else can see this creature. She walks over to them and looks in the direction of where Kriyo is speaking and says, "Thank you. Though I cannot see you, I discern your presence. I am indebted to you."

"No, Mother, he says that it is they who are indebted to us."

"I hope that earth and all beings who call this planet home do not fall to peril."

Mikiel bursts back into the room with Cal, Mr. Giblet and Luther in tow. "They both have left; Dudley, over an hour ago, and Tamilia, only moments ago," Mikiel states. "Do you wish for me to find them?"

After a solemn, yet reflective moment as she realizes that the betrayer is, indeed, real, she answers, "First, Mr. Giblet, please analyze that tainted seal, then—"

A resounding, crashing reverberation from above them draws their attention. Nearer and nearer it comes. All eight beings in the conference room brace themselves, as something smashes through their ceiling, then slams onto the conference table, shattering it into pieces. Once the dust and debris slowly settle, Meelah's unconscious body comes into view. Mikiel instantly looks from where she fell. Above them, above Religards, and most importantly, here on earth, is the Dark Force himself.

Chapter Fifteen

"My dear," Pasha exclaims, rushing over to Meelah. "Kriyo, are you hurt? Kriyo!" she yells again as she coughs out unsettled dust. "Mr. Giblet, are you out there?" she adds.

"Yes, but I'm pinned down," he answers from underneath a pile of rubble.

"I will help him," Luther says, tossing chunks of concrete. "Is Meelah okay?" Luther asks, nearing panic. "I don't know if my heart could take another loss," he mutters.

Mikiel takes to flight through the opening to the night sky. Though he was certain that he saw the Dark Force, he can no longer sense him or visualize him. While he encircles Religards, he notices humans are encompassing the building en masse. Meelah's reverberating return was heard by many.

"What the hell happened?" Dudley yells. "Are you all all right?"

"I'm not sure. I fear that time is of the essence. Dudley, make your calls and buy us as much time as you can," Pasha answers.

"I'm on it," he states, dialing his cell.

"Mother, how is she?" Kriyo asks as he slides Meelah into his arms.

"Son, I thought I had lost you for a moment. I called to you and when you didn't answer, I feared the worst," Pasha says, her attention on her unscathed son. There's no dust in his hair or debris of any kind on him.

"It was Dilly. He pulled me somewhere else right before the impact."

"I am here," Mr. Giblet states, breathless.

"As am I," mutters Luther, as he wipes a stream of tears from his face.

"Thank you both. Please find Roger and Rose," she says as she strives to maintain her composure. "Son, I don't know where to take her. Religards had Cal's protective shield and he was the only one of his kind here on earth. His shield was quite effective against the Shadows."

"What do you mean, had?" Kriyo asks solemnly.

"I can no longer sense Cal. The intense breech to Religards, I feel, has fatally injured him."

Mr. Giblet returns and his poignant expression confirms Pasha's instinctual supposition. From behind him, both Rose and Roger emerge covered in dust and small debris. Pasha scours her mind for a safe shelter for all of them. With Religards exposed, Meelah is no longer protected, especially with a betrayer amongst them.

Mikiel slowly hovers down from the vast opening above them. The consequent wind from his massive wings lifts the fine dust back into the air. No sooner do his feet land on the large chunks of debris, than he dashes over to Meelah. Cradled in Kriyo's arms, she lies unconscious. Kriyo observes Mikiel's grief. He senses the deep-rooted love that Mikiel possesses for her. Closing his eyes, Mikiel places his hands over Meelah's forehead and incrementally moves it down to her abdomen.

"Though she is wounded, her body is actively healing the damage. We must move her carefully, if we wish not to further injure her spine."

"Mikiel, where do we go?" Pasha says, quite distressed.

"Fire, EMS and police are all on their way," Dudley proclaims.

"Roger, Rose, commence your cleaning. Find Cal," Pasha instructs. "Do what the two of you do. We will reverently hold a ceremony for him anon. Mr. Giblet, please conceal all of the tomes, we'll come back for them at a later date. Hurry, all of you, and return to my office. If my office is still intact," she states, a question in her voice.

"Yes, it is," Dudley answers.

"Oh, Dudley, Mikiel must speak with you for a moment," Pasha adds, nudging Mikiel.

Reluctantly, Mikiel pulls himself away from Meelah. Spreading his wings, he lifts himself over the debris and lands before Dudley. Roger scoots past, apparently uncertain of what the outcome might be, but it's apparent what Mikiel will surely do to him if he has deceived them. Getting up into Dudley's face, Mikiel devours his plentiful thoughts. Then he sees a note from Riya floating within his inner reflections. Closing his eyes, while moving in nearer, he can sense Dudley's overwhelming fear. Mikiel can also feel Riya's energy. Like a bloodhound catching the alluring scent of prey, Mikiel sniffs Riya's aroma all over Dudley.

"What are you doing, Light Warrior?" he asks with a quiver to his voice.

Dudley begins to pull away and Mikiel throws both of his arms up against the wall. Though Mikiel has already sensed the location of a note from Riya, he is still intrigued.

"Let me go!" Dudley exclaims, nearing panic.

Getting as close as he can to Dudley's neck, Mikiel inhales. The usual mix of fragrances is quite curious. Mikiel feels the imminent onset of humans, tempering his interest for now. Again Mikiel pokes around his abundant thoughts determining that the betrayer is not he.

"What are you doing, you sick Light Warrior?" Dudley clamors, while thrashing about like a fish out of water.

Holding both of Dudley's wrists together in one of his hands, Mikiel reaches into Dudley's inner pocket and recovers Riya's letter.

"Wait in the office. I will retrieve the others," Mikiel orders.

"Give that back to me, Light Warrior," Dudley demands.

"You better shut your mouth," Roger tells him. "That dude is crazy. Where did you get that letter, anyway?" Roger inquires.

"Riya gave it to me yesterday," Dudley answers frankly. "She's always giving me notes."

A clear and powerful spray emits from Roger and Rose's mouths, instantly removing Cal's remains. Roger tosses the larger chunks of debris while Rose emits her caustic mist on every piece that Cal's remains have affected.

Once done, Rose wipes her mouth and asks, "Hey Dudley, you never thought about opening that letter since Riya's gone missing?"

"I haven't had the time," he quickly replies.

Back in the conference room, Mikiel lands beside Meelah. She's still unconscious, and he again scans her form. Mikiel is intent, his eyes on her chest. "Dudley is clear, but I did find a letter from Riya on him," Mikiel says, while still fixedly staring at Meelah's torso.

"What is it?" Luther asks Mikiel.

"I'm not sure," he answers.

"Is there something else wrong with her?" Kriyo asks.

"I see something, but I can't analyze it now. The humans are here. We must leave."

"Luther, get the others. We will follow Kriyo," Pasha says.

Luther scampers off and quickly alerts the others. The voices of firemen ring out down the hallway. A small Mr. Giblet wearing his favorite hat hurriedly rounds the bend, joining the group. They all climb back into the conference room.

"But I have been forbidden to return there," Mikiel says, while passionately staring at Meelah still in Kriyo's arms.

"I told them that if Meelah is to save their planet, then we must remain united," Kriyo affirms, his eyes on Mikiel.

"And why did you do that for me?"

"Because I know you can help her," Kriyo answers as he comes to a stand with Meelah in his arms. "Dilly, we are ready."

A diminutive Dilly nods his head and begins to open an invisible veil separating the dimensional levels. Each reality uses the other to maintain balance. They are threaded delicately together. After Dilly opens the channel, he communicates to members of his family up in the conservatory. He asks them to camouflage all evidence of their presence.

Flashlights come into view along with the sound of several human voices. The firefighters search for any signs of causalities while simultaneously checking the stability of Religards. They crowd into the main office, and the faint sounds coming from the back room filter in.

"Over here!" one of them calls out. "I hear something back here!"

"Would you look at that?" the first firefighter on the scene proclaims.

"What the hell?" another fireman spouts.

As other firefighters join him, they too are amazed by what they see. All raise their flashlights illuminating quite a sight.

The massive hole above them spans through several floors and one of them holds Pasha's conservatory. Petals from the abundance of roses, orchids and other flowers from the extraordinary rooftop garden are raining down on them. Each petal floats aimlessly down, creating a miraculous shower that covers the debris-laden floor.

"Well, I have never," the chief states. "The room is all clear!" he shouts as he continues to take in the unusual sight before him. "After thirty-two years, you think that you've seen it all and then there's a moment like this," he adds, shaking his head.

***

After walking through an invisible veil, the group arrives at the Realm of the Mystics with Dilly as their guide. Flowers thrive in abundance. This natural world is thick with greenery and is teeming with life.

Glancing at her group to make sure that all are accounted for, Pasha observes them all lost in wonderment—everyone but Mikiel, who walks swiftly over to Kriyo and homes in on Meelah's chest again.

"What is it? Are you sure that you see something?" Kriyo asks him, curious.

Mikiel scrutinizes Kriyo for a moment before returning his energy back to Meelah. Mikiel can sense the ruler Kune's approach. Immediately, Mikiel reverently drops to one knee and begins to apologize for his rude intrusion earlier in the day.

Kune, silent and still, stands as stoic as a mature oak tree. His brown garb, resembling a robe, resists the soft surrounding breeze. The hem of his bulky garment lies on the earthlike soil as steady as he. His face rests expressionless and his gaze remains fixed on Mikiel. Kune signals for Mikiel to rise, then quietly and only amongst the two of them, there begins a conversation. Galdi, Kune's, assistant, stands aside. Kriyo intently watches the exchange as does the rest of the group. The succinct dialogue ends with Mikiel again reverently bowing to Kune. Then he makes his way back to Meelah.

"I must take her now," Mikiel states to Kriyo.

"I will take her to wherever she must go," Kriyo answers.

"Kriyo, there isn't time for you to make the journey. You must trust me."

Galdi walks over to Pasha and, at length, introduces Kune. This gnome-like creature is adorned in a green vest with matching pants. Beyond him, Mikiel flys off, carrying Meelah in his arms. Pasha can sense that something is very wrong.

"I beg your pardon, Galdi," she says as she bows to Kune. "Thank you for providing us with temporary shelter, but where has Mikiel taken Meelah?"

Kriyo stands alongside his mother and also lowers his head to the inimitable ruler before them. He senses Dilly nearby watching the exchange. Even though he is deeply concerned for Meelah, he recalls the newborn rat babies and wonders what happened to them. In the midst of the chaos, he is unsure where they have gone and if they survived.

Kune attunes to Kriyo's sincere concern and extends his human-like arm to him. Mindfully, Kune opens his hand, revealing two pink-skinned baby rats. Nestled together in his palm, they are unscathed in spite of the destruction, as Kune, watching Meelah's return, made certain of it. Galdi takes the miniscule critters and hands them gently to Dilly. Kriyo is relieved that Dilly will take care of them, as is illustrated by his genuine smile His heart still remains touched by the sacrifice the rat mother was willing to make. The idea of surrendering your offspring for a greater good is the ultimate act of altruism.

Now her babies will be returned unharmed. Observing Kriyo, Kune sees his true character and is impressed.

"Kune, may I again inquire as to the precise location of Meelah?" Pasha asks politely.

"Mikiel saw something in her chest, Mother. He took her to the resident surgeon. He will keep her safe, he promised me that he would, but I must go to her," Kriyo answers.

"I know what you feel," Kune intones to Kriyo.

Curious as to what he means, Kriyo gazes into Kune's powerful cavernous eyes. Instantly, he senses the pain that resides deep within. There is a story floating inside—a tale that he feels he will soon be an intimate part of. Suddenly, as if he is waking from a dream state, Kriyo adjusts his stance. Kune disconnects from Kriyo and, with no words, departs into the thick woods that surround them. Galdi quickly shuffles over to Pasha and addresses her and the group. He seems more than overjoyed that he, again, has the stage.

"You have stepped into our realm," he begins, while waving his petite hands in the air. "And you have been welcomed by Kune. This is essential, very essential! We can't have any being here that has not been either invited or welcomed," he continues, with a deliberate pointing of his crooked finger. "Now if you would all follow me," he orders, while hurriedly walking off.

A screeching sound rings out around the group; halting their steps. Again, they listen to a shriek, but this time, it's closer to where they stand.

"What the hell is that sound?" Roger asks.

"In this realm, there are many creatures. We should move quickly," Galdi tells them as he nervously scampers off.

"Hell no! I won't be any creature's meal!" Roger declares.

"Then we should all follow Galdi," Pasha says as she gathers the group together like a mother hen.

Dudley, Luther and Rose remain silent as if fear has stolen their voices. Following Pasha, they take long strides to keep up with Galdi. But Mr. Giblet intently studies everything in this new environment. Unafraid of the howling sound, he lags behind as he pauses with every other step, quickly accounting for his new findings. He's enchanted by the rich wooded landscape. His undersized legs work twice as hard to keep up ordinarily and now, with his own prescribed delay, he finds himself alone. Moving as swiftly as his little legs can carry him, he sees Kriyo ahead in the distance; he, too, is lagging behind the others. Out of breath, Mr. Giblet struggles to keep up. Kriyo, sensing his distress, turns and walks toward him. He doesn't want Mr. Giblet to become a meal to whatever might be lurking in the dark thickets.

"I...I am exhausted," Mr. Giblet murmurs.

Kriyo can't help but chuckle at the little man. An out-of-breath Mr. Giblet drops his hat, then his book while bending over to effectively seize his breath. The book opens to a sketch. The drawing illustrates the meeting between Kune and Kriyo. A curious Kriyo bends down to get a closer look.

"Who is that female?" Kriyo asks him.

"To whom are you referring?" Mr. Giblet responds.

"The female behind Kune and myself, I did not recall her there?"

Picking up his sketch, Mr. Giblet scrutinizes the illustration. His hands flip though the many pages that he has doodled on since their arrival and each page has an illustration of a powerful female standing in the background. Shaking his head in astonishment, he attempts to understand how this manifestation has come to be.

"It is her," an alluring voice speaks.

Walking around them like a predator encircling its prey is Rhana. Her golden shimmering hair flows behind her with every undulation of her hips. Stopping before Mr. Giblet, she gently lifts his book from his tiny hands. Immediately under her spell, smitten, he smiles at her with longing ardor. Kriyo, wiser this time, turns his back toward her while covering his ears and closing his eyes.

"Oh, Kriyo, I thought that we were beyond these games," she purrs coyly.

"I felt something prowling about! I'm not surprised that it would turn out to be you, Rhana! Leave us. We want nothing to do with you," he states adamantly after hearing her muffled voice from behind him.

Her ruthless cackle vibrates the air behind him while her foreboding presence sends chills running up and down his spine. Though his eyes remain closed, he senses her energy now standing before him. Her warm moist breath lingers over the surface of his face. Her scent is as alluring as the precise aroma that draws him to Meelah. Then his heart connects again to Meelah. Every part of him feels that he must go to her, now.

Listening to his inner voice, he remains steadfast. With divine resolve, he manages to afford Rhana no attention. He can't see nor hear her and, like a petulant child, Rhana steps back. He knows that she is still near and doesn't dare fall prey to her games.

A rush of air begins to fan against his back, kicking up small pieces of earth with it. His shirt presses into him while his hair moves in rhythm with this peculiar draft. As abruptly as the wind began, it ceases, leaving behind a new energy that surrounds him. This all-encompassing presence is infused with profound wisdom and compassion. No longer sensing Rhana, Kriyo opens his eyes and gazes at the panoramic sight around them. Encircling both Mr. Giblet and Kriyo are un-usual female beings. They are slight-framed and all possess sleek hair extending down about three-quarters of their height. Their tan-and-brown speckled gowns reach only to their knees. Giggling joyously, they fill the air with tangible bliss. As these unusual beings move about in delight, so do the mature trees around them. Both Kriyo and Mr. Giblet become overwhelmed, witnessing the cheerful dance.

Then, without provocation, all but one of these magical beings run swiftly into the deep thicket, camouflaging them instantly. After following their seamless departure with their eyes, both Kriyo and Mr. Giblet gaze at the remaining stranger before them. Her simple, natural beauty is profound. Her skin is as fair as a cumulous cloud and her lengthy ginger hair nearly touches her knees. This being's intense brown eyes and regal demeanor as she stands silently before them entrances them. Then, without a sound, she moves closer to them. Her bare feet hardly graze the surface of the ground. Her movements are as fluid as a stream.

Stooping over, she picks up Mr. Giblet's book and hands it to him. Like a child on Christmas morning, Mr. Giblet seems overjoyed to be handed his book. As he holds it, she opens his book and points to the picture of the female image in the back-ground. She flips the page and again points to this female's picture and again looks steadily at him.

"I don't remember drawing this image," Mr. Giblets states.

"You didn't," she answers softly. "We did."

"Who are you?" Kriyo asks.

"We are Dryads and we sent Rhana away. She wanted to delay you from getting to Meelah. She sees the love you have for Meelah and wishes to destroy it."

"Thank you for ridding us of her," Kriyo replies.

"Dryads, of course," Mr. Giblets states. "And to what tree are you connected?" he asks.

"Our name is Reema and she is both the wisest and oldest tree in this realm." Then, addressing Kriyo, she continues, "Go to Meelah, this is your destiny. Her actions will soon free our monarch, the sovereign of everything you see. Go to her, Kriyo."

"So the images in my drawings are of Drana, Kune's beloved?" Mr. Giblet asks.

"Yes, Giblet." Then, focusing again on Kriyo, she repeats, "Now go to her! We will show you the way."

Her words consume the air around Kriyo and quickly sink into his being. Feeling a sense of urgency within his gut, Kriyo turns and scans the area in order to gain his sense of direction. Then ahead of him, he sees another Dryad signaling to him.

Before following his guide, Kriyo turns back to Reema, lowers his head and says, "Thank you."

Bowing her head in return, she only smiles.

A gentle breeze blows against him as the surrounding trees begin to sway around him. The breeze is soft, at first, but it becomes increasingly harsh until Kriyo turns and moves in flow with it. As he pauses and looks back at Mr. Giblet—concerned about his welfare—the airstream again picks up, lifting dirt and leaves into the air. The surrounding trees move about fiercely as well.

"Go, I will be fine. I would like to remain with Reema for a few moments, anyway. She has a great deal for me to document," Mr. Giblet cries out into the ensuing currents.

Unable to resist the torrents of wind, again Kriyo turns and allows it to take him on his way. His feet don't even feel as if they touch the ground, as they swiftly carry him to Meelah.

While he travels through this unfamiliar place, he can't help but notice that the purity of nature in this realm is unaffected by humans and their caustic damage. The clean air is organically infused with rich oxygen. Harmony and a sense of peace reside in this ubiquitous life. Every bit of greenery and tree has a being tending to it. He thinks to himself that if humans were aware of the pristine life that exists within all of nature, perhaps they wouldn't be so reckless. As he travels by foot, he becomes aware of the many unique life forms in this realm. Small winged beings peer around mushroom caps and through low-growing vegetation as he passes. Sensing his benign presence, more and more miniscule figures appear as he quickly moves past them.

He senses that something has happened to Meelah. Every fiber of his being swells with agitation. The sense of urgency he feels propels him forward even more rapidly. Dryad after Dryad direct him through the thick dense forest and, with each one he passes, he tries to lower his head. Finally, he comes to a clearing. On the other side of this grassy meadow he sees Kune's bastion. *They must have taken her there,* he thinks to himself. A narrow pathway emerges through the long grass and, as fast as he can, Kriyo journeys upon it. Turning around, he sees that the narrow pathway has closed behind him. Then again he is flooded by a sense of exigency. Now with only rock beneath his feet, he speeds onward.

Chapter Sixteen

Kriyo notices that the energy encompassing Kune's bastion is quite different than that of the woods. There are no flowers, trees, or green life; not even the sound of birds or other creatures. Everything around Kune's forbidding stone castle is devoid of life. The energy is suppressed and consumed by grief. This heaviness, this sadness lingers in the air.

Impatient with his timely journey, Kriyo wishes he could teleport. He feels Meelah's need for him. Travelling onward over the unsteady rocky terrain, the distance between the thriving woods and Kune's abode seems endless. Finally, with sweat streaming down the sides of his face, he reaches the vast entrance. Columns strewn with dead rotted thorny vines stand guard. The energy here is increasingly anxious and rather unpleasant. Oddly, no one is in sight. Also, he hears no audible noise other than his swift footsteps.

Pausing, Kriyo closes his eyes and tries to sense Meelah. Instantly, a connection is forged and he hurries onward through the desolate, seemingly abandoned castle. Sensing his arrival, Pasha is already running toward him. Her distraught expression swathes Kriyo with a sense of dread. Fearing the worst, he darts toward her.

"Quickly, Kriyo, they are waiting for you."

"What has happened to Meelah? Mikiel said that she would be safe. What is it?"

"There's no time, my son. Please, just come with me."

Without a further exchange of words or thoughts, Kriyo follows Pasha, who navigates promptly through the castle. The pathway is lit by candles set high above on its stone walls. The damp and musty air brings a chill to him. Going deep within the bowels of the fortress, Kriyo can't help but worry. His unsettled energy touches his mother. Pasha stops and turns toward him. Her countenance is consumed with emotion—a sentiment that he is unable to decipher.

"Son, a path has been laid out, but it is you who must decide whether or not to take it."

Kriyo is more confused than ever. He looks into his mother's eyes and begins to see what she is trying to convey. His presence here on earth is part of a greater plan and it, in every way, is connected to Meelah. But it ultimately is his decision to follow this path.

"I wish I could prepare you for what you will soon witness, my son."

Meelah's shriek in the distance immediately redirects him. Without another thought, he runs past his mother as swiftly as his body can carry him. Following the sound of her unsettling scream, he journeys to the end of the hallway. As he enters the richly lit room, the clamor of many voices falls silent. The encircling room has several doors leading to who knows where and it is filled with diminutive beings resembling Galdi. Breathless, Kriyo stands in the center of the room. He nears panic as he hears another pain-infused howl from Meelah. Galdi quickly comes out from one of the rooms and gestures for Kriyo to join him.

He enters the chamber and the sight before him takes his breath away. He feels his mother's hand on his shoulder as he grabs the wall, struggling to stand. On a table in the center of the room lies Meelah. Her clothing is soaked with her blood. A being who, in every way, resembles a human, is working on her. But it seems to no avail.

"What has happened here?" Kriyo exclaims.

"They cannot remove the key that is embedded in her chest," Pasha answers. "Mikiel has returned after speaking to the Light Force."

"Look at her, she's dying!" yells Kriyo.

"Yes, she is," Mikiel answers from behind him.

"You were supposed to keep her safe," Kriyo screams at him with loathing rage.

Kriyo then strikes out in anger at Mikiel, punching him in the face. Mikiel merely takes it. His eyes are also consumed with pain. Kriyo, seeing his mutual remorse, steps away from him. His heart brings him to Meelah.

"You can save her, Kriyo," Mikiel states.

"I will do anything," he answers, touching Meelah's face.

Kune enters the room. The expression he wears depicts that he too feels their anguish. In his hands is a book. Opening the ancient tome, he shows Kriyo an illustration. Writhing again in pain, Meelah releases an agonizing sigh.

Kriyo's eyes well up with tears. Nearly nauseated, he glances at the page while holding Meelah's cold hand. His hand grazes the crude strap holding her right arm down. Then, again, he brings his attention to the illustration in Kune's hands. The picture shows a male removing a key from the heart of a pure being. This key is destined to release Drana and reunite her with Kune.

"I must remove the key from Meelah's heart?" he asks in terror. "I am not qualified for such a procedure. She could die," Kriyo cries.

"You must," Mikiel demands. "I don't know why you have been chosen, Kriyo, but you have. You must do it. Her body is failing. She cannot heal with that key in her and she's bleeding out. Please, I can't lose her again," Mikiel pleads.

"She is losing more blood than she can regenerate," the surgeon states. "Soon, the choice will be made for us."

"What must I do? Just tell me!" Kriyo shouts.

"Go to the sink and scrub up; we'll prepare you," answers the surgeon. And then he raises his voice and adds, "Everyone with the exception of the surgical staff must leave." All depart and Kriyo is left to his fated task. Meelah is no longer making sounds. Slipping into a gown, he watches her and sees that her chest still rises from breath.

"She is dying. We must move quickly. Kriyo, I opened her chest but I could not remove the metal object. It simply would not release. I will reopen the area and you will have one chance to extract it," the surgeon warns.

"Will she live?"

"Not as she is; so let us begin. Are you ready?"

"Yes," he answers. "Please hurry. I can't lose her."

Meelah's chest is quickly exposed and her incision re-opened. A clamp is inserted and her rib cage cranked open. Kriyo cringes at the cracking sound of her ribs. Leaning over, he sees her heart as well as the key, which is piercing the side of the organ. With each weak beat, Kriyo sees blood leaking out and pooling into the cavity of her chest.

"Kriyo," the surgeon urges, while handing him an instrument, "you can save her."

Chaos surrounds him, yet everything seems to slip into slow motion. Medical staff members seem to lumber all around him.

Looking up, he takes the instrument in hand and, with a skill he didn't know he possessed, he reaches into Meelah's chest cavity and touches the metal object embedded there. Once his energy connects to the foreign object, a light fills her chest, then the room, blinding all within it. When the light dissipates, the surgeon sees the key within Kriyo's grasp. One of the surgical assistants takes the instrument holding the key from him, and Kriyo steps back. The wall halts his step and becomes a support for him. He leans against it and allows his tears to overflow his eyes and run down his face. The surgeon and all the other medical staff continue to work on Meelah.

Kriyo pulls off his gloves and rakes his hands through his hair. He stands helpless as the life force seems to be leaving Meelah's body. In his mind, he witnesses her smile and her passionate eyes. His heart is filled with sorrow at the thought of losing her. Time passes as the medical staff continues to sew and mend the damage to her chest.

"Meelah will survive. She must," he chants over and over again in his mind.

Then he wonders, what happened to her? How was she impaled by the key—the very same key that will free Drana, Kune's wife? Who did this to her? Questions flood his mind, but his heart tethers him to where he stands. He knows that Mikiel will have answers, but he can't leave her. Silent—fearful—he watches.

The surgeon's metal tool hits the tray with a resounding clang. The sound sends fear racing up Kriyo's spine. Coming to attention, he waits for the surgeon to say something. But no words are needed; the smile as he looks at Kriyo says it all. He affirms, "Her body is healing."

"She will be weak for a short time, but as it appears now, she'll pull through," one of the assistants adds as he removes his gloves.

"May I go to her?" Kriyo asks.

After receiving an acknowledging nod from the assistant, Kriyo approaches Meelah's bedside. He notices how cool her skin is when he takes her hand in his. As he rubs his thumb along the surface of her hand, some of the beings begin removing her blood-soaked and soiled clothing. With respect, he turns away. One of the benevolent beings gently taps his hand and he temporarily releases his grasp. Once she is adorned in a fresh garment, his hand is returned to hers. When their skin touches, a deep connection to her awakens within him. He knows now that his heart has found its true counterpart.

"Kriyo, you may open your eyes," a soft voice whispers.

Before him now stands a female dressed in a richly decorated, multi-hued robe. This being possesses an innate power that is quite dissimilar to all others in the room. Softly the outline of her form emits a golden radiance. He wonders where she came from. With her hood raised, in part blocking the female's face, she studies Kriyo then Meelah. Her powerful essence is transmitted through her eyes. She extends her arms, and her hands reach out to Meelah's healing body. With palms face down, she holds her hands just inches above Meelah's head. She moves them slowly over Meelah's body, pausing at her chest. Then, with an expression of contentment, she follows the full length of Meelah's body. When she reaches her feet, the being lifts her head and again, fixes her eyes on Kriyo.

"It has been done," she announces. "Soon we will meet again, Kriyo."

"Who are you?" Kriyo asks her.

The image, wearing an odd grin now, fades—vanishing from sight.

"Who was that?" Kriyo asks.

"To whom are you referring?" one of the gentle beings on the surgical team answers.

"The female who was just here, dressed in a hooded robe."

The two remaining surgical staff members stare at Kriyo.

"Perhaps you are fatigued, sir, for no one else has been in this room other than the doctor."

Behind him, a chair appears and he sits at Meelah's bedside. He knows that the robed figure wasn't a figment of his imagination. But, here before him is Meelah and she becomes his focus. So close to death, she now heals. Stroking her hand, he waits. He waits for her to open her eyes, to look at him. He waits to hear her spoken voice. He simply waits for her to emerge into life from the precipice of death.

Chapter Seventeen

Pasha, peeking into the room, sees that her son has fallen asleep. His head rests heavy atop the edge of the bed, while his hand remains entwined with Meelah's. The color of Meelah's face is improving with every passing moment. Sending loving thoughts to them both, she closes the door, leaving them to recover.

"Mikiel has...left," Luther stammers.

"Do you know where he went?"

"I don't know. Do you think I should find out?" Luther starts to run off, then he halts his steps as he recalls Mikiel's message for Pasha. "Oh, he already left," he says, reminding himself.

"Indeed," Pasha says, wondering if Mikiel is running away or off doing something to help.

Pasha moves off, lost in contemplation of what Mikiel might be up to. Luther follows, moving as slowly as she. In a grand hallway she takes a seat on a dusty velvet-covered bench. Again she brings her gaze to Meelah's chamber.

"Can I see Meelah yet?" Luther asks, bright-eyed, following her lead.

"She is resting, Luther. But soon she'll be up to seeing visitors."

"I am also tired. I can't tell if it's night or day in this dark place. Should I rest, too?"

"Yes, Luther, that is a good idea."

No sooner had she released those words, than the castle began to vibrate underfoot. As the castle stone walls shake, dust fills the air. Pasha brushes off the fine debris that has found its way onto her lap, shoulders and head. Luther shakes as if he was a wet dog, sending particles back into the musky air.

"She soon will be free; come look," a small winged being sings cheerfully as it whips past.

"Mother, what is happening?" Kriyo asks, peering out of Meelah's chamber.

"Meelah did it, son. I believe that her actions will soon free Drana."

"What the hell was that?" Roger bellows with Rose by his side.

"Shhh," Luther states. "Meelah is resting."

"If she can sleep through that, then my voice ain't gonna bother her. Now, what is happening, an earthquake or something?"

"More like a long-awaited liberation, Roger," Pasha answers. "Where is Dudley?"

"He scampered off with a water nymph. I haven't seen him for some time. Can't blame him, that water nymph was foxy."

"Roger, will you please have some reverence? When Dudley comes back, tell him to stay near. We must devise a strategy for our return."

"I heard that Mikiel left," Rose says with a timid voice.

"Yes, regrettably, he did," Pasha answers.

"I'm glad he left. That Light Warrior is mad crazy," Roger states. "I didn't know what he was going to do to Dudley. What was Dudley doing with that note from Riya anyway?"

"The note—I forgot all about it," Pasha mumbles while rifling through her pockets.

Deep within her pocket, her hand makes contact with the folded piece of paper. Upon opening it she quickly gathers that this note is a personal exchange between Riya and Dudley. Perhaps Riya's note intended for her was destroyed. The context of the next sentence brings with it a blush of her cheeks. Quietly she folds the love note and respectfully slides it back into her pocket.

Closing her eyes, Pasha attunes herself to the greatly anticipated reunion. It is proceded by an unexpected pause—a pause to which all in this realm have become acutely connected. Kune's longing adoration for his wife, Drana, wells upward from deep beneath the castle and overflows like a brimming cup of tea. All space is affected by the imminent and long-awaited reunion. The castle falls silent. All life within the confines of the Realm of the Mystics waits with immense expectation and bated breath.

Within the bowels of the castle, Kune travels with key in hand—the key that nearly ended Meelah's life. His mind regresses and he revisits the events that now draw him into the darkness of his bastion. He recalls a time more than five hundred earth years ago when Drana and he reigned in harmony with the indigenous people of earth. There was synchronization and balance, affording the continuation of earth's pristine health. Veneration and respect were present in all. But one day the sun did not rise. Darkness fell and fear consumed all.

Kune and Drana knew that they had to move their kind if they were to survive. They ascended to a higher dimension.

Painfully, they acknowledged they didn't possess the ability to include the people of earth nor were the peoples of earth ready for such a shift. A new reality was created and The Realm of the Mystics was birthed. This ascension separated them eternally from the indigenous people of earth.

The beings within The Realm of the Mystics were able to manifest illumination, nourishing the flora, while in opposite effect, mankind suffered. The lack of sunlight on earth yielded the demise of green life and this long-lasting reality was devastating. Drana became overwrought by the plight of the people. She heard their cries and felt their pain as if it was her own. Thousands began to starve to death in the ensuing gloom. Sacrifices, both human and animal, were made by the indigenous tribes in an attempt to lift the everlasting darkness, but even these extreme measures were to no avail.

Drana's tears affected the earthly rivers, which made them run unbridled. The heartache she felt spread throughout the Realm of the Mystics, affecting all within it. Kune remained devoted by Drana's side. He hoped that his love for her would lift her from her own all-consuming darkness.

One predestined day, having fallen to the ground in utter despair, Drana lay in her garden. Her assistant ran into the castle to get Kune. Quickly, he dashed to her. But, when he located Drana, he saw that she was not alone. An insidious murkiness welled up around her. Wisps of darkness floated about her, swirling even in her hair. Drawing his weapon, Kune made a run to her aid. But before he made contact, the shadowy outline of the Dark Force lifted from around Drana and, simultaneously, so did the looming shadow blanketing earth.

The warmth of sunlight immediately touched earth again. The rebirth of hope spread as fast as the sun's light travelled. Sensing Kune behind her, Drana turned to face him with joy deep within her essence. Kune insisted that she tell him what had transpired but she would only respond with, "We have this moment, my love."

Their love was celebrated by all. The Realm of the Mystics thrived, as did earth. Lush green trees and flora spread over earth's surface again, bringing with it abundant life.

On the year anniversary of the return of light, it was time for Drana to make good on her unspoken deal with the Dark Force. Drana's soft-spoken words still floated in Kune's memories as if she has just uttered them. Looking lovingly into his eyes, she began, "If all we have are moments, know my heart is filled with the ones we have shared. I must leave you now." She touched the side of his face. "But I am not saying good-bye, my love, for I have faith that one day we will hold each other again."

At those last words, a shadow overtaking the sun's light darkened The Realm of the Mystics. Drana again reached up to touch Kune's face, knowing what was fated to occur. Kune grabbed her arm to pull her into the castle, but she remained fixed in place. Bringing his panicked face to meet hers, she took hold of his hand while passing him a letter rolled and tied with a lock of her hair. Kune glanced down at it, then back into her eyes. At that moment, a dark swirling mass lugged her by the waist. Kune squeezed her hand with all of his might, but could no longer hold it. Drana, before his eyes, was pulled away. The malevolent force dragged her into the castle. Kune, running as fast as he could, followed them down into the bowels of their home. Once at the deepest level, the Dark Force waited for Kune to join them. Breathless, he rushed over to Drana, but an invisible field stood between them. Both raised the palms of their hands toward one another while fixed on each other.

"Why is this happening?" Kune agonized.

Drana looked tenderly into his eyes then said, "For I have love in my heart."

No sooner had she spoken these words, than an opening in the wall behind her appeared and she disappeared into it. Kune kept striking and pummeling the invisible force that separated them. He did everything in his power to follow but the wall closed and he was left alone. Endless battering rams were used and magical spells cast. Nothing affected the impenetrable wall. Every day since, Drana's letter has remained in his close possession, even today, as he travels alone with key in hand.

After the massive reverberation shuddering through the castle, there is a profound sense of stillness. A vibrant wave of golden radiance floods The Realm of the Mystics, temporarily blinding all. As it recedes, all is restored to its true magnificence. All is aglow and the doleful gloom of the bastion is washed away. Pasha holding Luther, who is again in Galidrome form, Rose and Roger all journey outside in awe of this magical transformation. As soon as the fresh air grazes their faces, they witness the immediate rebirth of life. Green vines slither over the stone walls and trellises, giving birth to vibrant multi-colored flowers as they come full into blossom. Grass pushes up from the seeming lifeless ground, spreading as far as the eye can see. Birds chirp and insects soar. Life in The Realm of the Mystics has been restored.

"Kriyo," Meelah whispers.

"Yes, I am right here," he answers, while squeezing her hand.

"Where is Mikiel? It is important that I speak with him."

Rolling my head to the side, I gaze at Kriyo. His striking face looks downward. His pain at hearing my inquiry is as plain as day. Squeezing his hand, I press into my elbows and attempt to sit upright. Quicker than I knew he could move, he bounds to his feet and lays me back down. Dropping down again, he rests his forehead gently against mine. His warm breath swirls around my lips. Time as I know it pauses and all of my concerns fall by the wayside.

"I thought I was going to lose you," he murmurs through his hot breath.

The sound of someone clearing their throat floats in the background. Kriyo already senses who it is. With a heavy sigh, he pulls himself upward while his eyes remain connected to mine. I see Mikiel's silhouette in the background.

"Meelah, I will be right outside," Kriyo says as he lets go of my hand.

"Thank you," I answer him.

I watch Kriyo walk from the room while I sense Mikiel keenly gaze at me. Softly, the door is pulled shut and Mikiel and I are alone. He paces the room, not exchanging a word or thought. He has much to say, but chooses silence instead.

"Will you stop encircling me as if I were prey?"

The moment I release my words, he halts his grating walk. The conflict within him is all but tangible. Then I feel it, his rage and love waft around me in their confusing polarity. He rushes over to me, the air from his wings around me causes my gown to undulate like a wave. His eyes remain fixed upon mine, and within them I see his passion and his anger.

"Drink this," he says, pressing a vial into my hand.

"And what might this be?"

His glare causes me to gather that he is not going to answer me, so, taking its top off, I sniff it. Its bitter yet sweet aroma seems familiar to me, but still, I am unable to identify it.

"Do you not trust me?" he asks.

"I trust you, Mikiel."

As soon as my words soak into his essence, he sits alongside me. Taking the vial from my hand, he brings it to my lips.

His soft blue eyes cut through me and, at this moment, I feel absolute conflict. I reach for the thin glass tube. As I do, our hands meet. Deep within me, I know that we have a connection; perhaps we always will. The extensive past we share is undeniable, but I cannot afford any of these distractions of the heart even though they are becoming increasingly more difficult to ignore. I allow my lips to fall open and he pours the liquid into my mouth.

"Why, Meelah? Why? You knew I would find out."

"What have you learned, Mikiel?"

"I know that you made a deal with Kune, a trade for his alliance in exchange for the key that would free his beloved Drana. You waited for the Shadows when you were on that rooftop and you knew where they would take you. You went to the Dark Force, himself. What were you thinking? The life of one is not more valuable than all life!" he barks, then struggles to remain composed.

"What did the Dark Force gain from you, Meelah, before he pierced your heart with the key and threw you through Religards? What did he take from you?" he shouts.

Before I can answer, Kriyo bursts into the room. He has fire in his eyes. Mikiel rises with the disruption then again paces the room. I watch as he rudely chooses not to acknowledge Kriyo's presence.

"I am fine, Kriyo. Thank you, but please, leave us."

Surprised by my tone, he silently steps out and closes the door. Feeling immediate improvement from the tincture, I push myself upward to a sitting position. Taking a few deep breaths, I continue to regain my strength. I sense Mikiel watching me.

"It is you who doesn't trust me," I say to him.

"No, Meelah. It is I who cannot lose you again," he states adamantly.

                    S.M. Huggins

"Mikiel, I will not exist in fear of my eventual end. I know that I am mortal. I know that time is fleeting. I must obtain my amulet and leave earth. I know earth's fate if I fail!"

"Then include me. I can help you. I want to help you," he pleads, taking hold of my hand.

"Did you find Riya?" I ask, with apprehension.

"Yes," he answers.

"Alive?"

"I found her with little life in her body."

"Is she alive?"

"Yes. I brought her here. I returned to you as soon as I could. How did you know where she was?"

"I heard her call to me when I was on the rooftop. I demanded that Kune tell you where I thought she was. Who would do that to her? Who would bury her alive and why was she unable to teleport out?"

"She was heavily sedated and drugged, rendering her unable to teleport. The amount of drugs that she was given should had killed her. I am surprised that she was still alive. As to whom," he says, while studying my hand. "I believe she learned that Tamilia was working with the Shadows. I also believe that she knows the location of the amulet."

"Tamilia, why would she choose an alliance with the Dark Force?"

"Power, riches...the possibilities are infinite."

"I must communicate with Riya. Even if she's unconscious, I can listen to her mind. I must go."

"Meelah, your body needs more time to heal."

"No, it doesn't. Look into my chest and you will see what I feel."

"Are you inviting me to look at your chest, Meelah?" he asks with a grin.

"You know what I mean, Mikiel."

"Meelah," he entreats me, while lifting his eyes to meet mine. "I will always love you."

He caresses the side of my face. My eyes close as I search for words. I feel him lean in, bringing his face closer to mine. I open my eyes, and we connect.

"I can't, Mikiel. Though love exists between us, I can't share that with you."

As if he doesn't hear me, he leans in and presses his warm sweet lips against mine. Lost in brief fervor, against my better judgment, I melt into his kiss.

Then, prying his lips from mine, I whisper, "No. This can't be." At that time, I look up and see Kriyo standing in the background. His astonished expression causes my heart to sink. Seeing Kriyo's reflection swirling in my regret-filled eyes, Mikiel straightens up and comes to a stand. As he is still holding my hand, I promptly withdraw it from his grasp. He remains before me, hoping that I'll look at him, while his back is still to Kriyo.

"Kune and Drana wish to thank you, Meelah," Kriyo states. "I knocked, but apparently neither of you heard me. I apologize for intruding," he adds, despondent.

"Kriyo," I say, unable to muster the words I want to convey.

"What do you wish for me to say to Galdi? He hopes to arrange the meeting as soon as you feel well enough," Kriyo says, his voice cold.

"I am so sorry, Kriyo. Please give me moment to explain."

Unable to look at me, he waits for my answer. With his lips tightly pursed, he holds his head high. The tangible tension between Mikiel and Kriyo surrounds us.

"Kriyo, will you not look at me?"

"I will check on Riya," Mikiel states, as he lowers his head.

Keeping my eyes fixed on Kriyo, I slightly lower my head in acknowledgment of Mikiel's statement. I observe Kriyo rigidly hold himself as Mikiel passes him to leave the room. I wish I could rewind time. Deep despair washes over me and my heart is flooded with an ill feeling. I suffer the pain that I have inflicted on Kriyo. Words should be spoken, yet none are exchanged.

A jarring and persistent knock lifts the heaviness in the room. I watch Kriyo unexpectedly bow forward. From beyond the threshold enters Drana, wearing a shimmering gown and an authentic smile. She pauses briefly as she passes Kriyo before proceeding over to me. She seems to tune in to his emotional state. Kriyo glances at me expressively then steps out of the room.

I attempt to rise to a stand. This bed has been my support for far too long. My bare feet lower to the cool surface beneath me and I push myself off the bed and rise. Feeling strong enough, I bow to Drana.

"No, Meelah. It is I who should be bowing to you," her commanding voice instructs.

Then stepping forward, Drana lowers her head to me. Her scent is that of a rose in full bloom, sweet and alluring. Adorned in an emerald colored gown that is fitted at the bodice with intricate silver beading, she remains in this reverent pose. Her golden tresses are pulled up into a bun festooned with tiny white flowers. Her essence is overflowing with a sense of hope and joy and I can't help but smile in her presence. I watch as she gradually rises and I notice the beauty of her face, even a twinkle in both of her green eyes.

As I continue to gaze at the queen before me, she expresses, "Meelah, words cannot convey my gratitude for your selflessness. Your actions have restored my guardianship over earth and you have reunited me with Kune. Again, words seem insufficient, so we would like to host a ball in your honor; though even this gesture does not nearly equate to what you have restored."

"Drana, you are most welcome, and a ball will not be necessary. I must check on my friend Riya and prepare to leave."

"The ball is tonight, Meelah. This is a statement, not a request. You must be able to receive after you most honorably give. This is the basic foundation of karma. This duality balances all life as we know it. Even the Dark Force must abide by this basic concept. With every action, there will be an equal reaction."

Her words all but wound my heart with their astonishing relevance. The vision of Kriyo and his wounded expression float into my thoughts as if drawn on canvas. His deep brown eyes sear into my mind, and I close my eyes in an attempt to escape the pain.

"Meelah, matters of the heart always come at a price. Your heart has already made its choice."

"I cannot afford the distraction of love."

"Nor can you deny it. A life without love is not worth living. Honor your heart and stop resisting your destiny." Then, with a gleeful grin she continues, "Tonight we shall celebrate. When night pushes up the light of a new day, you will depart. Tomorrow is the anniversary of your eighteenth year, Meelah."

My heart fails with her words. I have lost all sense of time. I have to obtain the amulet by midnight tomorrow!

"Drana, I must be going. With all due respect, I don't have time for a celebration."

"Meelah, all we have is now and now we really must begin to prepare my guest of honor. Ladies, please enter."

Drana's authoritative voice signals to what seems like an endless stream of whimsically pastel-adorned females. One after another, they enter the room and encircle me. Drana again bows to me then departs. A brown-haired being wearing a flowing yellow-flowered gown enters the room. While humming a merry tune, she pushes in with her a large basin. Others promptly fill it to its brim with steamy water. One after another more striking ladies enter my chambers with buckets in hand. I watch as fresh-cut stalks of lavender are submerged in the hot water, releasing its pure and relaxing essence into the air. Blissfully two elegant females pull my gown over my head. I'm offered no time to be bashful. Taking both of my hands, the attendants escort me to the tub and I slip into its cleansing water. Warm water cascades down the back of my head and my hair is massaged clean.

My mind races as it becomes consumed with all I must do and what I risk if I fail. Overcome by the warmth of towels, I struggle to breathe. Breathlessness befalls me as an overwhelming sense of exigency floods every cell of my being. Then I see him…. In the corner of my room, amongst the chaos all around me, I see him. He tethers my ungrounded sense like a string restrains a balloon from the heavens. Samuel, my dad, gives me his reassuring smile. I miss him. Though I wish to run to him, I dare not move. I fear that if I do he will leave. I intently remain fixed upon him as the females continue to prepare me for the gala.

As the ladies brush my hair and apply makeup to my face, I see my father beaming at me. I wish to selfishly freeze time, and I hope that he does not leave though I know he will. Gradually… slowly…he disappears from my sight. I do not blink. I do not breathe. I do not move. I will not miss a moment that has him in it. But this moment ends. He has left. I no longer sense him, and I already miss him.

The persistent pulling at my hair as it is brushed deepens my breath. Then the tugging at my hair as it is lifted atop my head has become quite tiresome. Finally, their contented smiles indicate that they have indeed finished their polishing. Asked to rise, I feel my robe slip away and I step into a form-fitting black-and-white elegant gown. They push a full-length mirror before me and I hardly recognize the image within it.

My hair is pulled back in a bun, twisted like a vine atop my head. One red rose in full bloom nestles against my sheer black hair. My makeup is like that of a princess and my black-and-white gown shimmers like the twinkling of stars on the night of a new moon. This evening dress prefectly conforms to my body. It looks like it has been painted on. Slipping my feet into black heels I feel a little bit like Cinderella, minus the pumpkins, prince and mice.

"May I come in?" I hear Pasha ask.

"Please do," I answer.

Adorned in a white evening gown decorated with beads that sparkle when they catch the light, she glides across the room and over to me. I appreciate the small pink flowers that decorate the bun atop her head, this flora brings out the pink in her lips. As the distance between us narrows, I feel my agonized emotions regarding her son begin to resurface.

"You are a vision to behold," Pasha says. "Don't allow tears to ruin the masterpiece before me, especially before my son gets to see you."

"Pasha, I ruined things," I say with shame. "I kissed Mikiel, though my heart wished me not to."

"Dear, we all make errors. That is why we must learn to forgive and never forget that we all can falter. My son will listen to his heart."

"I have to locate the amulet by tomorrow."

"Meelah, be reminded of the now. We must leave to attend the celebration for all are waiting to see you. All is precisely as it should be, my dear, this I feel and I ask you to have faith only in that divine truth."

❧⬥❧

Chapter Eighteen

As I head down the pathway leading to the honorable Kune and Drana, I hear a voice from deep inside say, "Don't be afraid to be weak and don't be too proud to be strong. Connect to your heart and return to self. Believe in your path. Believe in your destiny."

Attuning to my heart, I feel an unsought awakening spilling over me, like abundant water surges over a weir. My step halts and the lids of my eyes close as if they are weighted by an unseen force. Memories—my memories of all my soul's time—nourish me. My essence feels cultivated by my recollections—my growth. My mind attempts to process what I am seeing, feeling and hearing then...I awaken.

The return to self; the return to me; the return to destiny, my destiny. I remember my purpose. This is my destiny. I not only remember the leader I once was, I recall with clarity why I am here and what I must do.

I open my eyes and everything before me seems changed. My panoramic view is brighter and clearer. My essence is strong and a renewed self-confidence consumes me. The throng of mystical beings, all adorned in their best attire, have fallen silent by my stillness. I have no idea how long I have stood here nor does it matter. I have been reunited with purpose.

Ahead of me sit Kune and Drana on their royal throne. Kune has altered greatly in appearance from the first time I met him. Once as stoic and as aged as a mature oak tree, he is now youthful both physically and energetically. Perhaps Drana's presence melted away his brusque exterior revealing his true self. I feel great honor as I approach them.

Onward I continue forward with Kune and Drana as my focal point. My heels striking the pristine, golden-flecked stone path is the only audible sound. I'm aware of the eyes set upon me as I pass with my head held high. I feel my inner confidence shine through to illuminate my exterior appearance.

Then ahead of me stands Mikiel. He's mixed amongst the mystical beings of all shapes, sizes and appearances, and I feel him wait for me to connect with him. But I don't. I can't. I sense his longing as I pass by him. I also sense his disapproval of my revealing, form-fitting dress from Drana. I even hear his feathers ruffle. I can feel his eyes sear my skin where it is revealed through the open back of the dress. I remember everything from my past incarnation. I remember his care for me, his ardor and now, in my sultry dress, I feel his aching desire, and the heat that radiates from his eyes. I also recall with clarity that I had a true love that satisfied everything in me and this love was not for Mikiel.

Kriyo...It has always been him. In my mind, I visualize his perfect face. Where is he, I wonder? I yearn to see his face, as I ached to be with him after he was killed in our past-life. Scanning the brightly dressed mass of encircling mystical light beings, I do not find him. Yet I know that he is near. This challenge stimulates me.

I needn't search for him with my longing anymore...I see him and he sees me. Adorned in a fresh black suit with the white shirt and black tie, he's perfection. Kriyo watches me as though my awakening—the rebirthing of our past, our love—is somehow contagious. His eyes lock on me and I wish to stop time, but not yet.

A profound and uncontainable smile overtakes my face as I fill with bliss. I pass him and revel in his close presence. I feel his forgiveness. I feel his love for me.

At the end of my walk, I stand before Kune and Drana and bow. As I rise, I appreciate this journey that has brought me to where I now stand. I also realize that a great deal lies ahead of me, beginning with the amulet that I must locate. But in the presence of Drana, I will embrace the now. As soon as my mind conceptualizes that thought, I see Drana grin at me.

Both Kune and Drana rise. Kune's branch-like arm is now the arm of a man. His face, at close proximity, is now that of a youthful human. All deep wrinkles have been ironed out and his eyes are renewed. His energy is as light as a butterfly and his heart as warm as a summer day. Drana radiates compassion from deep within her. Both speak in length of their gratitude for what I have done and for their shared plans to restore the health of earth.

Then, from the corner of my eye, I see two unexpected guests, a wearied Riya nearly standing and Shelly. Astounded by her presence, I focus on Shelly, wondering why and how she's here in The Realm of The Mystics. I recall the first time I came upon her in the ladies room in Religards after Tali gave me an abrupt introduction. She was accompanied by the self-absorbed Sharon and Sally. I was able to read the useless banter from Sharon and Sally, but Shelly remained silent, an intriguing mystery. Again her mind seems blocked as I attempt to delve into it. Frustrated at being unsuccessful, I glance next to Shelly and see Riya. I feel her gratitude as our eyes connect. She gives me an authentic smile and I return one to her. "Meelah," Drana's kind voice says, breaking my reverie. "We would like for you to choose a partner."

"A partner?" I ask, confused.

"Yes, a partner for the opening dance, unless you wish to dance alone," Drana states.

I turn around and am met by many eager persons, but there is only one with whom I yearn to be. Looking over the masses to where Kriyo was standing, I don't see him. Feeling closed in by the gathering of hopefuls, I find myself needing space. Then a tap upon my shoulder redirects my attention. It is Kriyo. Our eyes meet with unbridled passion. He takes my hand and pulls me through the chaotic mass. He brings me to the center of the gala. Wrapping his warm arm around my lower back, he draws me near. I connect with his dark brown eyes. His sweet, delicate natural scent empassions my senses. Lowering his head, he rests his forehead against mine and in natural cadence with the music, we move like the soft lull of the ocean tide.

"I have never seen anything as beautiful as you, Meelah," he whispers.

"Kriyo, I am sorry for offending you."

"Meelah, let us begin again now. I will not look back if you are able to do the same," he murmurs, in rhythm to the melodic tune.

"My heart has chosen you. It always chose you," I whisper into his ear as I take in a breath of his sweet aroma.

"I know," is his sotly spoken response.

Though I feel the presence of many others around us, in Kriyo's arms nothing else seems to matter. All the weight on my shoulders melts away. The now—the present—is a wonderful place to rest. I linger in it.

"As do I," Kriyo replies sensing my thought.

Pulling back, I observe him studying me. His eyes scan my gown and lead up to my face. I stand proud of who and what I am. My pride shines through me and, again, our eyes meet.

"Meelah, you are amazing. Not just your physical body, but the energy propelling you is..." he mutters, seeming unable to finish his intimate assessment.

"May I have this dance?" a frolicking Luther sputters.

His simple face brings a chuckle to us both.

"Yes, Luther. But please allow me a moment with Kriyo, first."

Bringing my attention back to Kriyo, I study his brown, cavernous eyes. I realize that I am seeing into the soul that truly knows me. Moving upward, I bring my lips to his. Readily, his soft lips touch mine. With an infusion of love, his mouth, tender yet passionate, kisses me. My eyes close as his hands gather at my lower back. The warmth of his hand grazes my exposed skin, as he reaches around to hold me closer. I hear him inhale then I feel him detach from our intense moment.

"That was not easy."

"What wasn't easy?"

"Pulling away from you," he answers. "You should go to Luther. He looks dejected over there. Meelah, I will be right here waiting for you."

I turn around and see Luther awkwardly moving by himself to his own sense of tempo. It is as though he works to be out of time with the harmonic composition of the song. His hair is as wild as a windstorm and his clothing as peculiar as always. But regardless of his eccentricities, he is a most dedicated member of my family. I cannot restrain my happiness as I observe my sweet friend. Still in my blissful state, I turn back to Kriyo and he strokes the side of my face as gentle as a feather.

"Go to him, so you can return back to me."

Reluctantly, I walk over to Luther, moving away from Kriyo. Each step I take creates distance between us and I miss him. I feel him long for me, as well.

Then again I see Shelly ahead of me. I feel her journey past me. Her energy is unlike any other. Luther takes me into his arms and swirls me around with skill I didn't know he possessed. As I twirl in his arms, I search for Shelly amidst the bevy of mystical beings celebrating Drana's freedom and their renewed kingdom. Luther, oblivious to my plight, is interrupted and his step halted by Mikiel.

With wings slightly spread, indicative of agitation, his expression is quite solemn. He is here because he has something to say—something that I may not wish to hear. Awkwardly, Luther lingers close by, prohibiting whatever it is that Mikiel must convey.

"Luther, would you excuse us please?" I ask politely.

"Of course, of course, I would very much like to see what food they just brought out. It smells like warm butter. I cannot wait to taste it," he says as his stomach emits a loud and comical grumble.

"Go, then, my friend, and enjoy yourself."

As Luther scuttles off, I turn around and search for Kriyo. Whatever it is that Mikiel must tell me, I want Kriyo to be here when he does. I look over to where he said that he would remain and there is only an empty space.

"What have you done, Mikiel? Did you do something to Kriyo? Now that I have made a decision, you still cannot accept it!"

Mikiel's stunned and wounded expression answers my question for me.

"I am sorry, Mikiel. I shouldn't have said that."

"But is it true? Have you made your decision?" he asks, his focus intent on me.

"Yes, I have, I love Kriyo," I answer in a resolute tone. "Mikiel, where is he? I do not sense him near."

"Meelah," I hear Mikiel say in a subtle tone over the sound of the music. But I continue to examine the crowd for either Shelly or Kriyo. Both seem to have disappeared.

"Meelah!" he demands. "The sisters have died. It happened just moments ago. Pasha was with her. She was just too weak."

"How can that be? I saw Riya not long ago over there. She was with Shelly, a student from Religards."

"Who did you say you saw with her?"

"I saw her with a female about my age from Religards. Are you sure, Mikiel?"

"Yes," is his somber answer. "But Meelah, if Riya appeared to you with this Shelly, I am sure it was no coincidence."

"I must go to her. I must say goodbye," I say with a heavy heart.

"I will take you," Mikiel affirms.

I follow him through the gathering of fantastical life forms. Unaware of the passing of our friend, they remain joyful in their celebration. Beings of all sorts intermingle and exchange their exhilarating and blissful energy. Mikiel's wings are still slightly spread, creating a convenient opening as I walk close behind him. My mind begins to ramble, frantic with my concern for Kriyo, curiosity regarding Shelly and pain from the sisters' passing. Riya had a lead to the whereabouts of my amulet, the amulet that I still must obtain within the next twenty or so hours. The reality of what could happen if I do not locate it is overwhelming.

Finally, we are beyond the mass and just in time. The smiles and gaiety were becoming far too much. All should rightfully celebrate. But as for me, I can't afford more distractions. Down the hall, I follow Mikiel. He doesn't look back at me, though I know he senses me. The clickety-clack of my heels has worn thin, so pausing a brief moment I slip them off, liberating my sore feet. As I look up, I see Mikiel standing outside a massive door. Though he now faces me, he does not make eye contact. As I approach, he opens the doors and stands aside. I have injured his heart. Bringing him pain was never my intention but that's what my indecision has done. Pausing a moment at the threshold, I place my hand on his shoulder. He turns and faces me and I see the emotional wounding floating within his eyes. His sadness isn't only from the sister's death; it's also from my choice to be with Kriyo. With my heart, I inform him that I never wished to hurt him. Lowering his gaze, the moment ends. Redirecting my focus, I remove my hand from his shoulder and proceed into the room.

Entering the bright and airy chamber, I see Riya's form lying on a bed covered in a white sheer panel. I almost expect to see the panel lift with her breath as I approach, but it lies as still as she does. Their life-force has left, leaving behind the sisters' physical shell. Alone, I stand by my friends.

"I am sorry that I couldn't save you," I murmur.

"You did save us," a familiar voice answers.

Turning around, I see Riya, Tali and Maya—the three of them all together. They bow and rise in unison with a contented smile gracing their faces. I look at their perished form and it's still there. Looking back to my friends, I see all three come toward me in unity.

"It's about time someone put a dress on you," Riya jests. "You look elegant dressed as a lady."

"Riya, was it you there earlier at the celebration?"

"Yes. Did you think that near-death would keep me away from a party?" she answers with a laugh.

"How is this possible?" I ask.

"Anything is possible," Maya answers.

"I am sorry that I couldn't have saved you," I say again.

"You did, Meelah, when you were fated to do so. We did what we were supposed to do and now we will rest with our family," they avow in unison.

"But the amulet, do you know where it is?"

"Ask the one you call Shelly," Tali answers. "After our first meeting in the ladies restroom, I had Shelly make her presence known to you. She is not what she seems but you already know that Meelah. Do you remember when you first met her?"

"I remember tasting my blood for the first time," I say with a rueful smile. "I also remember Shelly."

All three ladies lower their heads in reverence to me. I see the background come through them as they fade seamlessly into it. I wait to blink, not wishing to miss a microsecond of their exodus. A subsequent gentle breeze wafts by and through me from within the closed-off chamber. The wisps of air are as sweet as Riya, as wise as Maya and as skilled as Tali. I appreciate their final gift and now, a sense of peace mends my heart—they're home.

Leaving the chamber, I see both Drana and Kune standing near Mikiel. My presence breaks their conversation. Based on their grave expressions, again I feel that I am to receive unpleasant news.

"Reema wishes to speak with you," Kune states.

"And who is Reema?" I ask, curious.

"Reema is the energy that embodies the oldest oak tree on earth. She is the eldest of the Dryads," Drana answers. "But, Meelah, there is more," she adds in a somber tone. "It has begun."

"The vortexes are opening. Soon they will resume and every Shadow and dark energy will descend upon earth. They will seek the amulet, then you," Mikiel exclaims. "It is no longer safe here. We must leave."

"Have Pasha and the others been warned?"

"Yes," Drana answers. "Pasha went in search of her son."

"Kriyo, has anyone seen him?"

"Not to my knowledge," Drana answers.

"We have transportation waiting for you that will take you to Reema. She has answers for you," Kune adds.

"I believe I know why the vortexes are opening," I say, mulling over my thoughts. "There has been a rift that has accelerated time. It is whatever 'Shelly' is. Her presence in this realm has altered time. Prepare all in this dominion, keep them safe. Though you offered your support, I wish for no more blood to be lost on my pursuit."

"Go then, Meelah. And know that you always have allies here."

"Thank you," I return with sincerity in my heart.

I move as swift as the wind. I hear Mikiel's footsteps close behind. His presence to aid me with whatever lies ahead is comforting. With all that I've put him through, his devotion is humbling. Upon our exit from the bastion, I feel Mikiel take hold of my arm, halting my step.

"I brought this for you," he informs me.

"What is it, Mikiel?"

"I gave this to Tali for you, but she was unable to pass it on to you. These are yours. You once wore them as my leader. I retrieved them, certain that you will need them."

From behind the pillar, Mikiel hands me a heavy tied bundle. Quickly, I unravel it and to my disbelief, I hold the apparel that I wore when I was the leader of the Light Warriors, even the boots—most importantly the boots. I'm barefoot.

"I will turn around so you can change," he tells me.

"You did not think it wiser to give this to me when I was inside?" I ask him with a raised brow.

"The night sky is still blanketed by darkness. I did not think it would matter," he answers while turning around.

In response to his incredible gift, I say, "Thank you, Mikiel. I appreciate this."

I slip out of the elegant dress from Drana and allow it to drop to the ground. I look over my shoulder to make sure that Mikiel doesn't sneak a peek. Satisfied, I put on each piece as I recall doing numerous times before. It occurs to me that my garb looks like the uniform of a Roman soldier. I suppose they stole the design from the best. I pull on a short white skirt with fitted undergarments, extending down to my upper thigh, and a sleeveless white shirt outfitted with lightweight golden armor. And to finish, I pull on boots also fitted with golden armor in the shape of leaves.

"Mikiel, you may turn around."

Without hesitation, he turns and looks at me like a hungry child seeing a chocolate bar. "You look almost as I remember."

"And what am I missing?"

"Beside wings, these," he answers, moving off into the low-growing greenery.

In his hands now are my helmet and sword. "I would inquire as to how you knew to get all of my things, but I know better than to ask. Thank you not only for what I'm wearing but for being with me right now."

"I would be nowhere else, Meelah. I would die trying to defend you."

And he would. I see this truth within his eyes. From my core I tell him, "And I would do the same for you."

As the delightful music that danced in the air falls silent, replaced by an eerie stillness, I shift my focus. Slipping on my helmet, I hear Mikiel as he does the same. While I keep my sword drawn, we advance forward. The utter darkness makes me rely on my other senses. The only sound is that of our footsteps. The ride waiting to take me to Reema is nowhere in sight. The outside of the castle is as still and as quiet as the woods before us. I stop listening with my ears and, instead, I open my mind. As soon as I make this subtle adjustment I hear a soft female voice. It is as though Reema was waiting for us to intuitively hear her.

"Come to the woods and come quickly, Meelah! My children will guide you."

Before she finishes the thought, I slip my sword into its sheath. I see that Mikiel also heard her message. Hurriedly, we head out and into the woods. The thick, dense woodland is vibrant and alive though inexplicably silent. Standing near the tree to which they are intimately connected are the Dryads. They are all closely linked and perhaps related. Without the use of audible words, they navigate us through the opaque, seemingly impenetrable omnipresent growth. We attune our minds to their unique vibration and swiftly move on foot under the cloak of darkness. My eyes close as I rely on this new awareness that seems to pull Mikiel and myself deeper into the coppice. Our state becomes hypnotic while our pace is hurried and as silent as cat feet. Maintaining both our breath and gait in unison, we bound onward with ease. The energy from the thriving and abundant encircling life nourishes me. This realm is quite dissimilar to earth where I spent almost eighteen years. The energy here is raw, pure and natural.

I feel Mikiel at my side. Like numerous times before, he remains beside me. Together, we will face whatever awaits us. He's dedicated and devoted. I'm honored to have him with me. As my thoughts reach him, I am assured Mikiel appreciates my sentiment.

As we near Reema, the spell drawing us to her lifts. Our pace slows and our eyes open. Breathless, Mikiel walks ahead of me. In a small clearing, Reema waits, standing beside the magnificent oak that is an extension of her. I am unsure which of the two is more amazing in the subdued lighting of a new day. The magnanimous oak is massive and its canopy, substantial.

As the slight illumination of dawn brings with it clarity, Reema's pristine beauty also comes into focus. Her alabaster skin contrasts with her long ginger locks and her energy is as wise as the oak to which she's linked. Dropping down to one knee, both Mikiel and I bow with reverence.

"It is my honor to meet the destined one," she states in a whispery voice. "But Meelah, we have little time for formalities. Before the vortex beneath my roots resumes, they must meet with you."

"Who must meet with me, Reema?"

"The Timeera. Soon they will depart, taking Kriyo with them."

"Kriyo? Where is he?"

"Meelah, this is Kriyo's destiny. You mustn't interfere."

"Reema, where is he?"

"Meelah, Reema is right. You mustn't obstruct the Timeera, they are both powerful and mysterious," Mikiel admonishes me.

"But what do they want with Kriyo and where are they taking him?"

"I do not know," he answers.

Then like the shifting wind, Mikiel directs his attention to Reema and asks, "What do the Timeera want with Meelah?"

"Ask them yourself," she answers while taking a few steps back.

From the silhouette of her canopy walks Shelly. As I draw my sword she halts her step and cocks her head, curious as she regards me.

"Don't, Meelah, the Timeera are immortals. They are not our enemy," Mikiel assures me.

"Anyone or anything that stands between Kriyo and me is not my ally," I readily answer.

Shelly oddly brings her chin in toward her chest. Her physical form begins to shudder and her head thrashes upward. Blinding golden light emits from her. Instinctually, I shield my face. The radiant light warms the air around us. It feels as though it's threaded with veneration for something greater than I understand. As the brightness subsides, Shelly or the Timeera transform into something quite unexpected. Standing before us is a being of light; golden light, to be precise. Enshrouded in luminescent mist the Timeera approaches us.

Mikiel drops to one knee as I stand in utter awe of the presence before us. I slip my sword back into its resting place and near the peculiar, yet profound sight before me. The haze around this being settles, bringing with it lucidity. Cloaked in a hooded robe is a skeletal form. As I peer into its unique, yet kind eyes, a connection is forged between us. Then, extending its hands, it presents to me the most unexpected object—the chest. It shimmers within the apparition's boney palms like a pearl resting within an oyster shell.

"Is this the chest containing the amulet?"

The Timeera representative lowers its head in acknowledgment. I remain mesmerized by the small chest. Its embellished, yet tarnished form is here before me. With that thought, my right hand aches. I look at my palm. It throbs then my scar opens, revealing a fresh-cut X mark. My hand is drawn to the chest. Upon its very top is a mark matching the scores upon the palm of my hand. Once they meet, an explosion of light overtakes us all. When my eyes refocus, the chest is gone. Shocked, I look at the Timeera who lowers his head to me.

"But the amulet, where has it gone?"

With those words, I feel isolated heat upon the skin of my chest. Looking down I see it. I am wearing the amulet. It hangs by a thin gold chain and rests at my sternum atop my armor. The amulet connects with my heart, my arms move out to my sides, and power surges around me then through me, filling every cell of my body. All the hair on my body stands on end for a moment while I assimilate the increased energy. I bring my attention again to the Timeera.

"The amulet's power has not been fully actuated," the Timeera intones. "Your physical form needs time to adjust to this increase. We will contact you again."

"I am uncertain how the chest ended up in your hands, but I am grateful to you for keeping it safe. Thank you," I say humbly while lowering my head. Returning my gaze to the Timeera's eyes, I add, "May I ask a question?" After the Timeera nods in agreement I ask, "Why must you take Kriyo?"

"For this is his destiny and the amulet and all of its power is yours," it answers, again in a monotone.

"May I see Kriyo before you take him?"

The Timeera bows his head and I see Kriyo already running my way. We fall into each other's arms and hold tight. Not wishing to let him go, I feel him pull away. With each step back our hearts are flooded with more grief.

"We will be together, Meelah. I promise this. I have seen it," Kriyo proclaims.

Pain steels my voice and I struggle to stand with composure as I honor the journey he must make.

"Though providence has separated you, even this is temporary," Reema states, standing beside me. "The two of you are destined to be together."

I hear her soft-spoken words, but my focus remains on Kriyo. Golden light radiates from the Timeera's hands and engulfs the two of them.

"Watch out!" Mikiel exclaims, pushing me to the ground.

The weight of Mikiel's wings as they spread over me, press me into the soil. Then I feel it. The vortexes have resumed spinning. The energy beneath my body swirls like a whirlpool, creating a tunnel that bridges inter-dimensional travel to unseen worlds. As the weight from Mikiel lifts, I spring to my feet. The light of a new day reveals the encircling Shadows from the Dark Force. They sense the power of the amulet as it hangs around my neck. They taste its energy and they grow ravenous.

I see Reema covered in dirt lying lifeless beneath the canopy of her tree. As Mikiel prepares for battle, I run to her. Kneeling beside her I see dark blood oozes from her mouth, staining her fair skin. Her eyes are open and they stare at me. She's dying right before me. I can sense her life-force grow weak. I can feel her peacefully submit to her path. The sound of Mikiel thrashing his sword pulls my attention and in the near distance I see flames and black smoke filling the air. This realm is being destroyed. The sound of Reema's cough redirects me back to her. Her eyes lock upon mine and sadness consumes me.

"A life must be taken after you wear the amulet. Nothing is forever; this is my fate as the amulet and its power is a part of yours," she assures me in her now weak voice. "Meelah, bring the Shadows to water," she whispers.

Then the little life remaining within her lifts. The leaves from the oldest tree on earth fall. They rain down upon me, covering everything. They encase Reema's body.

I stand, tuck my amulet beneath my chest armor, and turn to face the ubiquitous Shadows. Mikiel, struggling to maintain his hold over them, yells at me, "Leave, you must leave! Use the vortex."

I have never run away and will not commence that tactic now. I spread my arms and close my eyes. I call to them and quickly their attention is directed to me like bees to honey. I emit a small shield around me as I feel them surround me en masse. Swirling around me, the wind generated from their movement lifts my hair and whips it in every direction. Their malevolent and repugnant energy encircles me. I feel more of them join in the frenzy.

"Meelah, NO!" Mikiel cries.

Pure darkness surrounds me, yet I wait. I linger to allow every last Shadow to join the dark swarm. I continue to bait them with the presence of not only myself, but that of my amulet. The power of the amulet throbs against my chest. It, too, senses the looming presence and it grows warm. It begins to blister the skin of my chest. When the searing becomes over-whelming, I open my eyes and face the malevolent energy.

Mikiel throws himself into the impenetrable wall, trying to free me. Each attempt tosses him backward. I feel his panic as his energy, which is speckled with terror, becomes entangled in the weave of encircling darkness.

"You must trust me, Mikiel," I state telepathically. Then for his ears only, I send him my plan.

It takes several moments for him to hear my message. Then, I feel his harmony—his accord as it blends seamlessly into the agitation of the circling Shadows. Mikiel spreads his magnanimous wings in an attempt to gather in the Shadows. Digging the balls of his feet into the soil beneath him, he pushes the malicious mass forward and I take a few steps back.

Nearing the vortex, I lower my protective shelter and the Shadows attack. Like in a feeding frenzy, they thrash through my skin as they attempt to seize my fiery amulet. But to my surprise, they are unable to grasp it. It remains protected by an unseen force. Their wispy darkness grazes my skin, but somehow they cannot touch the amulet.

The inside of Mikiel's wings splatter with my blood. My vital essence centrifuges into the rotating mass of darkness. Sensing Mikiel's fear as he wears my essential life force, I raise my shield again. I trap the Shadows within the shield. Excluding Mikiel, I protect him from the frenzy.

With all the Shadows in close proximity and distracted, like famished lions ravishing their prey, I use the vortex beneath us and we depart from earth. Traveling swiftly to Churria, I direct our arrival to a specific place. Falling through the atmosphere, we plunge into Calla. Her torrent engulfs me and the Shadows. The inundation of darkness struggles to free itself from her violent surge. My body beats against her rocky base as my shield dissipates. I keep the Shadows submerged for as long as I must. This is where they will die. My body, already ravaged, continues to be ripped. My blood fills the torrents of water and I grow increasingly weak. Using what's left of my diminishing energy, I continue to hold the mass beneath the water until at last I sense them weaken. Moments pass and I feel the Shadows perish.

Releasing my hold on them, I struggle to return to Calla's surface. Weak now, I kick my legs. I see my freedom; I know where I must go. My life is above the water and I try with all my might to get there but my lack of oxygen, coupled with my substantial blood loss, pulls me somewhere else. In an unconscious state, stillness overcomes me. Remaining in this lull—in this condition between consciousnesses—I feel at peace as I disconnect from my wounded body. Is this death?

"No, Meelah. This is not your ending, not yet, anyway," a powerful voice speaks from the silence. "You must stop my brother and return the Dark Force to his domicile."

"I will live my destiny, this I promise you," I return.

"He grows stronger with every moment. Though Churria will be a safe hold for you, this is temporary. He will attack and attempt to destroy everything you cherish."

"He will attempt," I repeat in answer.

With a grand inhalation, my senses become inundated with agony. Upon opening my eyes, I see Mikiel holding me in his arms. I observe his face relax when he sees life within me. Taking stock of my surroundings, I notice that we're on the shore.

"You did it, Meelah," he says. "You eradicated the Shadows from earth and destroyed them. How did you know that Calla was the key to their demise?"

"Reema," I reply. "You pulled me from Calla?"

"The Light Force directed me to you but if he hadn't, I still would have saved you."

I witness Mikiel's loving countenance, even though I told him that my heart now belongs to Kriyo. By the tender expression on his face, he did not or, perhaps, cannot hear my thoughts and I'm grateful. I do not want to hurt him anymore than I have.

My hand reaches up to feel the amulet resting on my chest. It remains unscathed by the Shadows. This amulet holds so many answers but, at this moment, my only wish is to speed my body's healing process.

My eyes close as pain surges through every part of me. I want my body to repair itself. I pray that it does so quickly. Then I sense Ruzi and Nala approaching as if they have been waiting for our return. As I open my eyes, the two of them come into view. One by one their feet touch the surface and their wings retract. Mikiel rises with me still in his arms. I still feel so weak but many of the lacerations on my arms are healing and already closing.

"My liege, it's good to have you back. How badly are you injured?" the female voice of Nala asks.

"I am weak but I will heal, thank you, Nala. We have some catching up to do."

"Indeed, we do."

"Ruzi, how is Shria?"

"She is right behind you and, by the looks of her, she wishes to answer you herself." Then he adds, "My liege, you've returned to us. Though you still lack wings, you have been restored to the leader that I remember and devotedly followed."

As Ruzi words reach my ears and affect my heart, I smile at him. It touches me that he has noted my restoration, my awakening. As Mikiel turns around with me in his arms, Shria, Trall, a Churrian whom I believe to be Faro, and Pasha appear with Luther in hand. Luther wiggles in her arms.

"Meelah, you did it, my dear," Shria states with pride.

"My son and I are proud of you, Meelah," Trall adds.

"Can you stand? How wounded are you?" Pasha asks me.

"I feel weak, but thankfully the throbbing is subsiding. Mikiel, perhaps you should let me down."

"No. I will not leave you this time. I will bring you home."

"Home, where is that?" I ask.

"It is in Bursa with me," Shria answers. "Mikiel, please bring her home. A chamber there awaits her. I will restore her health."

"Thank you," I say, touched by her kind gesture. "Shria, there is still so much to do."

"Yes, but I will be here to help you."

Luther leaps into my lap and begins to lick the slashes on my arms. He returns the smile to my face. He, too, is finally home.

The man standing beside Pasha makes his way toward me and says, "It is an honor to meet you, Meelah. My son will return to you," he says loudly as if to make sure that Mikiel is listening. "Kriyo made the choice that affords us all hope. His love for you and your love for him are destined," Faro adds, winded.

"Thank you. I cannot wait to get to know you as I have had the privilege of knowing Pasha. Without her I would not be where I am. Pasha, what happened to the members of the Northeast Team?"

"I left Dudley in charge of the team. Roger and Rose will recruit new members with talents such as theirs. Mr. Giblet was invited to remain in The Realm of the Mystics so he can properly document his findings. As for Tamilia, let's just say that she has been dealt with."

"Dealt with?" I ask, curious.

"I took care of her," Mikiel informs me with reassurance, as if his actions were in some way to protect me.

Then in my mind I see it. I witness Tamilia's ending. Cornered by Mikiel, she was violently destroyed. His actions were not only for me, it was also for the sisters, and for the team she betrayed.

Aware of the banter around me, my mind returns to the present. It feels wonderful to be surrounded by such support. Whatever the future holds, I know I am encircled by family. I am honored by their unified alliance.

"Let us all allow Meelah to rest and heal. Mikiel, please bring her home," Shria states.

Gazing at the family that I already adore, I feel Pasha retrieve Luther from my lap. The sound of Mikiel's wings spreading behind us makes me yearn to fly. Lifting from the ground, we soar over the dense omnipresent greenery. Blissful, I am reminded of flight. Warm air caresses the surface of my face. This breeze is curative in every sense.

Enjoying the breeze that seems to carry my father's spirit within it, I hear Mikiel say, "Meelah, you've returned to us wearing your amulet. Your Light Warriors have waited for this day." Then after a short pause, he adds, "I have waited for this day."

I reply, "Mikiel...my return comes with a fated war. You and I both know the reality of warfare." Silence follows my truthful words. Despite my fearsome statement, I take in the wonders of this world. Amid this beauty, I add, "But there will be no war today. I dedicate this day to healing. Tomorrow...I will dedicate my life to our cause. My destiny has just begun."

He holds me tight. He doesn't utter another word. Overwhelmed by what I will soon face, I rest my head against his shoulder. His strong arms draw me toward him. He has become my support. He has become an important part of my life. No matter what lies ahead, I can rely on him. To myself, I repeat my newfound truth, "My destiny has just begun."

Glossary

Ameira – Located on Churria, its glass-like reflective surface is the strongest teleporting station.

Amulet – A powerful talisman consisting of four stones. Each stone is from a quadrant of Churria. This charm was created by the Ultimate Force for Meelah. It holds unique powers as a result.

Ascend – Churrians at the age of roughly 750 to 800 years of age move on to a higher dimensional state of consciousness, taking their physical form with them.

Brandon Higgly – A shrewd teenage male who attends Religards.

Bursa – This is the greenest quadrant of Churria. Home to the majority of the Elders and to the Head Elder, this quadrant is known for its omnipresent flora.

Cal – This Caltrimidon being possesses the ability to energetically shield Religards from the shadows.

Calla – A river on Churria. She is very much alive and a part of the eco-system on Churria.

Churria – A star located in the Pleiades. It is home to the Churrians and Ameira.

Churrians – Beings from Churria. Most beings are similar in appearance to humans. They stand at a minimum of six feet and a maximum of eight feet, although a height of fifteen feet is possible.

Dilly – A gnome that travels to earth but lives in the Realm of The Mystics.

Dimension – A level of consciousness, existence or reality.

Drana – The current Queen of the Realm of the Mystics.

Drista – This is the arid and driest quadrant of Churria, with sandy terrain and clay-like homes encircled by the Dristan wall.

Dristans – Churrians who live in the quadrant of Drista.

Dryads – The spiritual beings eternally connected to one tree.

Dudley Kane – The media consultant for the Northeast Team.

Elders – Churrians who have been appointed by the Head Elder to teach and/or oversee their quadrant. They make up the political bodies of Churria.

Faro – A humble yet prophetic Dristan. He is the father of Kriyo and the partner of Pasha.

Galdi – A gnome who is the assistant to King Kune.

Head Elder – This is the leader of Churria. This position is nominated solely by the Elders and it must be won by a majority vote. The Head Elder remains as the leader until ascending.

Joseph Holmez – A kindhearted teenage male who is a student at Religards.

Kriyo – A handsome young adult Dristan. He's the son of Pasha and Faro and the student of Trall.

Kune – The current King of the Realm of the Mystics.

Light Warriors – Winged warriors created by the Light Force. They protect the innocent throughout the universes. Their mission is to enforce the universal laws.

Luther Rutherford – A disheveled male being who shapeshifts into a Galidrome.

Maya - She is one of the "sisters." The "sisters" are three beings that use the same physical form. This female being teaches historical lore and theoretical studies. She is a member of the Northeast Team.

Meelah Neegry – Young adult female being that appears to be human. She has sleek black hair, olive skin and a grand destiny.

Miguel Holmez – The father of Joseph Holmez. He tends to the conservatory garden and to Religards as a custodian.

Mikiel – A strapping blond Light Warrior selected to protect Meelah when she is on earth. He is second in command of the Light Warriors

Mikshe – A female Bursan who is the assistant to Head Elder Shria.

Mr. Giblet – A minute being who works at Religards specializing in incantations. He is a member of the Northeast Team.

Ms. Lucy – See Pasha.

Nala – A female Light Warrior with speckled brown-and-white wings. Bold and precocious, she proves to be a great ally to Meelah.

Pasha – Middle-aged female who oversees Religards, AKA Ms. Lucy. She is the leader of the Northeast Team, mother to Kriyo and wife to Faro.

Plai – This quadrant of Churria is supported and surrounded by water. Plaian live in castle-like structures and are deeply connected to the energy within their encircling waters.

Plaians – Churrians that live in the quadrant of Plai.

Preema –A wise, sage dryad connected to the oldest tree on earth.

Ralta – This quadrant of Churria is composed of enormous pieces of quartz, crystals and other minerals.

Raltans – Churrian that live in Ralta.

Riya – She is one of the "sisters." The "sisters" are three beings that use the same physical form. This female being teaches the art of social camouflage at Religards. She is a member of the Northeast Team.

Religards – A private school in New York City.

Rhana – A siren with golden hair and sensual charm.

Roger Hedley – One of the two "cleaners," who removes organic material with noxious vapors that he emits orally. He is a member of the Northeast Team.

Rose Cummings – One of the two "cleaners," who removes organic material with noxious vapors that she emits orally. She is a member of the Northeast Team.

Ruzi – A highly trained male Light Warrior with dark wings and a dark complexion.

Samuel Neegry – He is the pure-hearted and kind Churrian who raised Meelah.

Shadows – These energies were members of the army of the Dark Force, but their physical forms were destroyed by the Light Warriors and only their vigor remains. The Dark Force uses these energies to possess beings.

Shelly Ranoe - Teenage brunette female with silent thoughts. She is more than she appears to be.

Silvera – Churrian herb that releases emotion from the heart chakra.

Tali – She is one of the "sisters." The "sisters" are three beings that use the same physical form. This female being teaches tactical maneuvers at Religards. She is a member of the Northeast Team.

Tamilia – Mind sweeper that works for the Northeast Team.

The Dark Force – His energy personifies malevolence. He is the son of the Ultimate Force and brother of the Light Force.

The Light Force – His energy embodies purity, judiciousness. He is the son of the Ultimate Force and the brother of the Dark Force.

The Ultimate Force – They are the creators of both the Light Force and the Dark Force, as well as creators of all life.

Tincture – A liquid herbal drink made by Churrians.

Trall – A wise Elder of Ralta and the Father of Samuel.

Universal Laws – Laws created by the Ultimate Force to maintain balance.

Yall – Churrian room similar to the kitchen.

Acknowledgements

First, I would like to thank my incredible husband for believing in me and in this dream. I love you! I would also like to mention my children for their unwavering patience and faith in their mother. With appreciation, I express my gratitude to my dear friend, Heni. Her love for this story fueled me to keep writing.

Further, a special and profound thank you goes out to Patricia Fry, editor and author, and to Kathleen for editing my vision. Your polishing helped to make this book shine. I would also like to acknowledge Laura Gordon, the creative genius who designed the cover.

Finally, I would like to mention George Lucas, J.R.R. Tolkien, J.K. Rowling for opening the minds of millions of readers to unknown universes, worlds within worlds and magical realities. These highly regarded authors have forged the path to the unlimited joy we can find in reading their science fiction and fantasy works. Their belief in the imagination has given rise to the success of the subsequent writers who also reflect life outside the ordinary. I acknowledge the brilliance of these and the many other authors who keep dreams alive.

About the Author

S.M. Huggins lives in a quiet town of Connecticut with her exuberant husband, six entertaining children, four crazy dogs, two elderly horses, and an inane barn cat that has surpassed its ninth life. Amidst life's frenetic pace she has thoroughly enjoyed writing this page-turning series. Inspired by a dream, *Green The Awakening*, opened her imagination. It is her wish that you enjoy the journey as much as she has.

You can visit S.M. at her website: www.SMHuggins.com